S0-ADB-013

Spider Webs

Books by Margaret Millar

NOVELS

THE INVISIBLE WORM
THE WEAK-EYED BAT
THE DEVIL LOVES ME
WALL OF EYES
FIRE WILL FREEZE
THE IRON GATES
EXPERIMENT IN SPRINGTIME
IT'S ALL IN THE FAMILY
THE CANNIBAL HEART
DO EVIL IN RETURN
VANISH IN AN INSTANT
ROSE'S LAST SUMMER
WIVES AND LOVERS
BEAST IN VIEW
AN AIR THAT KILLS
THE LISTENING WALLS
A STRANGER IN MY GRAVE
HOW LIKE AN ANGEL
THE FIEND
BEYOND THIS POINT ARE MONSTERS
ASK FOR ME TOMORROW
THE MURDER OF MIRANDA
MERMAID
BANSHEE

OTHER

THE BIRDS AND THE
BEASTS WERE THERE (AUTOBIOGRAPHY)

Spider Webs

Margaret Millar

William Morrow and Company, Inc.
New York

Copyright © 1986 The Margaret Millar Survivor's Trust u/a 4/12/82

All rights reserved. No part of this book may be reproduced or utilized in any form or by any means, electronic or mechanical, including photocopying, recording or by any information storage and retrieval system, without permission in writing from the Publisher. Inquiries should be addressed to Permissions Department, William Morrow and Company, Inc., 105 Madison Ave., New York, N.Y. 10016.

Library of Congress Cataloging-in-Publication Data

Millar, Margaret.
Spider webs.

I. Title.
PS3563.I3725S6   1986   813'.54   86-5425
ISBN 0-688-06593-7

Printed in the United States of America

First Edition

1 2 3 4 5 6 7 8 9 10

BOOK DESIGN BY PATRICE FODERO

To Sally Ogle Davis and Ivar Davis

Laws are spider webs through which the big flies pass and the little ones get caught.

—HONORÉ DE BALZAC

Spider Webs

I

The
JUDGE

"*A*ll rise.

"Superior Court of the state of California, in and for the county of Santa Felicia, is now in session, Judge George Hazeltine presiding."

Hazeltine, a tall, spare man in his sixties, moved arthritically toward the bench, trailing his black robe and a strong smell of garlic.

Each morning after breakfast he chewed a clove of garlic, partly for health reasons, partly to help safeguard his privacy. People were not as keen on bothering him with their twaddle if they had to endure a certain amount of nasal discomfort. Attorneys kept their distance, and lesser personnel either spoke from the doorway or didn't appear at all.

In a rather obvious counterattack his secretary wore a great deal of perfume, most of which, ironically, had been given to her by the judge himself at Christmas, on her birthday and during National Secretaries' Week. She kept little balls of cotton saturated with perfume tucked into pockets and bras and pinned to the undersides of collars and hems of skirts. Sometimes one of these cotton balls would fall out, and the judge would pick it up and smell it and think: *That's very nice. I have excellent taste in scent.*

The judge sat down, cleared his throat and consulted the typewritten page on the lectern in front of him.

"Let the record show that the defendant is present along with his counsel, Mr. Donnelly, and the counsel for the people is present, Mr. Owen, the District Attorney. Let the record also show that the twelve members of the jury are present as well as the six alternates.

"Bailiff, would you kindly pass out the jurors' badges? These badges will be worn throughout this trial in order to identify the members of the jury and to warn other people to stay away from them and not to converse with them at any time on any topic."

The badges marked JUROR were handed out by the bailiff and the jurors pinned them to their left shoulders. With the badges in place they looked like oddly assorted delegates to a very solemn convention, environmental activists, perhaps, or anti-abortionists hell-bent on saving the world.

The youngest juror, a carpenter's apprentice barely twenty-one, brought his motorcycle helmet into court and kept it under his seat. The oldest was a seventy-year-old housewife with a reconstructed face and hair dyed black but turning obstinately orange.

"Ladies and gentlemen, you have heard the clerk read the information, the charges against the defendant, Cully Paul King, being murder and murder for profit to which charges the defendant has pleaded not guilty. It is now time for counsel to make opening statements. I must caution you that anything said in these opening statements is not to be regarded as evidence. Counsel may give you a synopsis of his case and tell you what he expects to prove. Before reaching any conclusions, you must wait until he actually proves it."

The judge paused. He disapproved of the business of

opening statements and the mandatory speech he had to make preceding them. It amounted to telling the jurors they were about to hear a lot of bullshit which they were then obliged to ignore. If the jury was to disregard opening statements as evidence, why bother with them at all?

The system did no credit to the lawyers themselves or to the law, and it was apt to befuddle the jurors and cause them to distrust any statement made by anyone during the course of the trial. It was a poor way to begin a case, forcing the jurors to listen to a whole day or more of oratory which they must then forget they heard.

Utter nonsense. No wonder the judicial system was bogged down.

"The opening statement belongs to the people," he said. "Are you ready, Mr. Owen?"

"Yes, Your Honor."

"Proceed."

The district attorney, Oliver Owen, rose and took his place at the lectern, facing the judge with the jury box on his right. He tested the speaker, which squawked in protest, adjusted it to his height, glanced at his notes and then fixed his eyes on the jury.

He was a good-looking blond man in his forties, and he spoke in a loud, almost belligerent voice as if he were already in the middle of an argument before the case even began.

"Ladies and gentlemen of the court, ladies and gentlemen of the jury, I bid you good morning.

"This is a simple case. I'm sure every attempt will be made to give it twists and turns, to confuse the issue by setting up detours. But the fact is, the road ahead is straight and direct, and it leads to one man and one man only, Cully Paul King.

"We, representing the state of California, county of

Santa Felicia, intend to prove that Madeline Ruth Pherson, a married woman, met her death at the hands of Cully Paul King.

"Mrs. Pherson, wife of Tyler Pherson, resided in Bakersfield, California. She was forty years of age and in reasonably good health. A recent death in the family left her somewhat depressed, so her husband advised her to spend a week or two on the coast.

"On the morning of May the first she arrived at San Diego's Playa Airport and took a taxi to Casa Mañana. She was carrying with her two pieces of luggage, consisting of a large suitcase equipped with wheels and a matching one half the size known as a weekender. She also carried a smaller case made of embossed green leather measuring approximately eight by twelve by three inches. She checked into a hotel at Marina del Playa, occupying the suite previously reserved for her by her husband.

"The two larger pieces of luggage were taken up to her suite, but the green leather one was placed in the hotel vault by the assistant manager, Mr. Elfinstone, at Mrs. Pherson's request. The case had a double lock and weighed about four to five pounds. Because of the double lock and Mrs. Pherson's request for vault space, Mr. Elfinstone, assistant manager of the hotel, assumed the case contained something of considerable value.

"From her room Mrs. Pherson telephoned her husband to tell him she had arrived safely and was going down to the lobby to people-watch. She seemed in good spirits and said she might even go into the bar and order a drink. The evidence will show that's exactly what she did.

"It was a fateful decision.

"She was seen at the bar talking to a black man in a navy blue blazer and skipper's cap; the evidence will show that the man was Cully Paul King, the defendant.

"They talked for some time. Then both parties got up and left the bar, King going into the lobby and Mrs. Pherson to the desk, where she asked for the green case, offering no explanation for her change of mind.

"Carrying the case and a handbag, she went up to her suite and returned shortly afterward to join King in the lobby. Then the two went out together. She was wearing a blue and white striped coat. She did not check out of the hotel, and her clothes were later found carefully hung up in the closet of her suite, her shoes in plastic bags and purses wrapped in tissue paper. She was a meticulous woman. When she put a garment on a hanger, she was careful to button or zip it to keep its shape.

"She was next seen boarding the yacht *Bewitched* in the company of Mr. King. The crew, Harry Arnold and his teenaged son, Richie, saw her come aboard, carrying the case and wearing the blue and white coat described by Mr. Elfinstone.

"Her gait was unsteady, and Mr. Arnold assumed she'd been drinking. She retired to the captain's quarters with Mr. King.

"During the day the boat had been cleared by customs and taken on fuel and provisions. It cast off before dawn en route to Santa Felicia. After reaching the open sea, the boat was put on automatic pilot and Harry Arnold went below to sleep. He was scheduled to take the night watch, a necessary precaution in busy shipping lanes where there is often night fog.

"While Harry slept, Cully King and Richie Arnold did the necessary work around the *Bewitched*, including the cooking. Mrs. Pherson did not appear in the galley although she was ostensibly taken on as cook.

"The evidence will show that Harry Arnold came on night watch as scheduled. During the course of it he heard a loud quarrel taking place in Cully King's quarters. He was not unduly alarmed since he assumed Mrs. Pherson's presence on board was for other than culinary purposes.

"Early the next morning Cully directed the berthing of the boat in its usual place in Marina Five. When he appeared on deck, he was not wearing work clothes but was dressed for going ashore in his navy blue blazer and gray slacks. Holding a folded handkerchief against his left cheek, he told Harry that he had a toothache and needed to see a dentist right away.

"When a yacht like the *Bewitched* returns to its home port, it is customary for the skipper to pay a courtesy call on the harbormaster and exchange information. This was not done. Cully began walking quickly toward State Street.

"Harry Arnold made breakfast for Richie and himself and Mrs. Pherson. When she didn't appear, he assumed she was still sleeping after an active night.

"When the galley was cleaned up, Harry and his son began going over the rest of the boat, beginning with the cabin occupied by Cully King and Mrs. Pherson. Mrs. Pherson was not sleeping, as Harry had assumed, sleeping off an active night. She was not there. Moreover, there was no sign that she had ever been there, no lipstick stains on the pillowcases, no damp towels, no hair combings in the bristles of the silver brush engraved 'Bewitched,' no used tissues in the wastebasket. Although the bed was freshly made, the laundry hamper was empty.

"Harry Arnold began to doubt his own senses. Had he really seen a woman come aboard the *Bewitched* the previous afternoon? Yes, and one thing stuck in his mind to prove it: The blue and white striped coat she'd been wearing matched one of the spinnakers belonging to the *Bewitched*. He could never forget that. And it brought to mind other items that reinforced the memory: a green case the woman had been carrying and the diamond stud earrings she wore. Now there was no trace of anything.

"Mrs. Pherson, with her spinnaker coat and green case, had vanished.

"Meanwhile, where was Cully King and what was he doing? The evidence will show that he was in a pawnshop on lower State Street, attempting to make a deal with the owner on a pair of diamond stud earrings. These earrings belonged to Mrs. Pherson, as her husband will testify, and she was wearing them when she went on board the *Bewitched*.

"Mr. King initially asked seven hundred dollars for the earrings but settled for five hundred. His story was that being a stranger in town, he was unable to get credit, and he needed the cash to pay a dentist. He appeared to be in pain, grimacing and holding a handkerchief against his left cheek, indicating that a molar was the source of trouble. Evidence that this was all playacting will be provided by the dentist who services the prisoners at the county jail. All of Cully King's teeth are in excellent condition.

"We don't know where Mr. King spent the next four days. A lot can happen in four days. A woman's body can be fished out of the water, and minor scratches on human skin can heal to the point where they are hardly noticeable. Now, I'm sure that counsel for the defense will bring to your attention my use of the adjective 'minor.' "

Donnelly stood up, a tall, brittle man with granite gray hair. He had none of the nervous mannerisms of most of the other people in the courtroom. He didn't scratch, twitch, frown, cross his arms, shift his weight from one foot to another. Something seemed to have frozen the moving parts of his body.

He sounded bored. "I didn't realize it was incumbent

upon the district attorney to read minds."

"Are you objecting, Mr. Donnelly?"

"Yes, Your Honor."

"Then say so for the record."

"I object to Mr. Owen's attempt to read my mind, on the following grounds—"

"Oh, don't take it so seriously, Mr. Donnelly. The jury has been warned in advance that what you gentlemen say in your opening statements may be nothing more than rhetorical claptrap. . . . Please continue, Mr. Owen."

"It's very difficult to recall the exact place where I was so rudely interrupted."

"Scratches," the judge said. "Scratches on the defendant's face that would heal fast because they were minor."

"Thank you, Your Honor. . . . Now, why were they minor? Because they were inflicted by a woman who was weakened in a struggle for her life, trying to loosen the vicious hold those hands held on her throat. A deadly hold indeed. Does Your Honor consider this just so much rhetorical claptrap?"

Ho hum & lordy, lordy. The judge sat in silence, his chin resting on his locked hands, his eyes fixed on the ceiling as if they were expecting the arrival of something interesting, a bit of weather, an earthquake, a skyquake.

The silent treatment was a new ploy on the part of the judge, and it enraged the district attorney. To regain his composure, he went over to the cooler and poured himself a paper cup of water. It was hardly more than a mouthful and it didn't help much. *The old bastard's trying to make a fool of me, and Donnelly's gloating over it, eating it up.*

The three men were now so intent on each other that the other people in the room seemed to be forgotten, the jury, the court reporter, clerk and bailiff, even the defendant, Cully King. He seemed irrelevant, like a spectator at a boxing match which needed only two contestants and a referee.

Cully Paul King. Nobody knew him; nobody cared about him. He was a black man from the other side of the continent.

The judge stirred inside his black robe, which was turning green with age. He was anxious to retire, rid himself of this robe like an old crow molting its worn-out feathers.

"Whose turn is it?" he said suddenly.

"I had asked a question," Owen said testily, "and was waiting for a reply."

"Who was supposed to reply?"

"You were."

"And I shall. Yes, indeed, I shall."

Eva Foster, the court clerk, leaned toward the bailiff, who was sitting at the same table. "He's been tippling again. Lock up the booze."

"Waste of time," the bailiff said. "He's got keys hidden all over the place."

"You're supposed to be a cop. *Find* them."

"I shall answer," the judge repeated. "Now, what was the question, Mr. Owen?"

"It has lost its relevancy by this time."

"Too bad, yes, indeed, a pity." The judge sounded like a man ready to face even more dire adversities with good cheer. "Let's go on to something else."

He took off his glasses, rubbed his eyes and looked down at the defendant as if he'd just been brought in to meet the jury. "Do *you* have anything to say?"

"I don't think so. Nobody's asked me anything yet."

"I'm sure someone will."

"Yes, sir."

"In fact, I'll start the ball rolling myself."

The court reporter, Mildred Noon, lifted her hands

from the stenotype machine and pushed her chair as close to the judge's bench as possible. "I don't think that's such a good idea, Your Honor. Why don't we allow the district attorney to finish his opening statement?"

"We, Mildred? *We*?"

"Us."

"Us. That's better. Very well." He glanced briefly at the district attorney. "You may proceed, Mr. Owen."

"It's almost impossible to proceed after this kind of interruption."

"Do your best, Mr. Owen. I'm sure words will occur to you. They always do."

The defendant sat quietly in his chair beside Donnelly. Only the pupils of his eyes seemed to move, brown and shiny like melting chocolate. His skin was as light as copper, a color rare and much admired in the islands he called his own.

In his thirty-seven years Cully had been in quite a few courtrooms around the Caribbean: in his own island of St. John, one in the Bahamas and another in Puerto Rico that was so small the entire courthouse and jail could have fitted into this one room. Its shoebox dimensions, the heat and humidity and the noise of everyone talking at once had a tendency to quicken the judicial process. A case rarely lasted more than a day or two. Somebody usually landed in jail. Whether it was the right one or not hardly mattered since jail was the back room of the warden's house and the warden's wife was a very good cook and had a liberal outlook on life. She liked to play Monopoly but was a sore loser. When she ended up after a week of play owing Cully $349, Cully found himself abruptly released and sent back to his ship with $1.29 and the final comment from the warden's wife that that was all he deserved because he probably cheated.

"You may proceed, Mr. Owen," the judge said.

"Yes, Your Honor. . . . Harry Arnold and his son, Richie, remained on board the *Bewitched*, partly to keep it ship-shape for the arrival of the owner, Mr. Belasco, who was in Palm Springs with his sick father, and partly because they didn't know what else to do. They were not in the habit of issuing orders but of obeying them. In the absence of any order to obey, they stayed put.

"Richie body-surfed off the sandspit, and Harry spent considerable time talking to the fishermen on the commercial wharf. But he was getting more and more anxious about the continued absence of Cully King and Mrs. Pherson. Then, on the night of May fifth, Harry learned from the local radio news that the nude body of a woman had been found caught in a kelp bed. The body was extricated and brought to shore by one of the boats servicing the oil drilling platforms. We can assume that Cully King heard the same local news, for he appeared at the *Bewitched* about the same time as the police. Later in the evening Mr. Belasco also arrived from Palm Springs, and it was he who suggested examining the ship's log for any record of a woman being taken aboard the *Bewitched* at San Diego. There was none.

"When Cully King was questioned by the police, his answers were terse and guarded. Because of statements made by the two Arnolds, he was forced to admit that Mrs. Pherson had come on board ship, but he claimed to know nothing about what happened to her, and he refused to say anything further until he was represented by a lawyer.

"Before Mr. King even had a chance to call a lawyer, one appeared as if by magic just after King was booked.

"This was no ordinary lawyer, this Charles Donnelly. He was widely known not only for his defense of criminals but also for the rather substantial fees he charged for his services. No one can figure out why he is taking on this case since King has no money."

Donnelly rose to face the judge. "My fees, Your Honor, are beyond the scope of this trial and beyond the scope of Mr. Owen's knowledge. I must therefore object."

Before ruling on the matter, Judge Hazeltine leaned back in his chair and studied the ceiling again for some time. He rather enjoyed making both counsel wait. It reminded them that though this was a small kingdom, it was his and his alone, and they were but peasants toiling in the fields.

"Objection sustained," he said finally. "There is no need, Mr. Owen, to refer to Mr. Donnelly's fees since he is not on trial here for overcharging. Kindly confine your remarks to more relevant matters."

The district attorney protested. "I consider this matter relevant, Your Honor, in view of the fact that the defendant is not in a financial position to pay the kind of fee Mr. Donnelly charges."

"Do you want to be found in contempt, Mr. Owen?"

"No, Your Honor."

"Then proceed with more caution, as directed."

The district attorney shook his head and continued. "A court order was issued for the *Bewitched* to remain in port and the crew to stay aboard. Several searches of the entire vessel were conducted by deputies, but no trace of Mrs. Pherson's presence was found.

"A week later one of Mrs. Pherson's garments was recovered from the sea, caught in a commercial fisherman's net. It was the blue and white striped coat she had been wearing when she left the hotel. It will be offered in evidence, and you will see it for yourselves and observe the most significant thing about it. It is completely buttoned. And why is this significant? It shows that Mrs. Pherson was not wearing that coat when she went overboard. It wasn't torn off her body by the action of waves or sea creatures. That coat, as it was taken out of the fisherman's net, was buttoned. Mrs. Pherson, a fastidious woman, had a habit of buttoning or zipping a garment when she put it on a hanger in order to keep its shape. That coat was taken off a hanger and thrown into the sea. It is a reasonable assumption that her other possessions were also thrown overboard but have not been recovered. It is, I submit, more than a reasonable assumption. The man sitting in the defendant's chair was seen doing just that."

Lordy, lordy, the judge thought. *Owen dearly loves the sound of his own voice. If tape recorders weren't prohibited in court, he'd probably make a cassette of all this and play it for the family at dinner.*

The judge had met Virginia Owen several times, a sharp-eyed little bore like Oliver Owen. But even the most sensible woman will do something stupid now and then, and Virginia had not only married Owen but had presented him with three sons. The judge didn't much like children, so he avoided them, especially those related to Owen. They were stuck with some pretty rotten genes.

Owen's speech went on, sounding more like a closing argument than an opening statement, an oratorical performance rather than a synopsis of evidence to be presented later.

Charles Donnelly began to doodle on the blank yellow page in front of him, a barn with a crisscross wooden door drawn very quickly and without lifting the pencil from the paper. Then another barn and another, until there were three rows of them, as identical as tracings.

27

He had been doodling like this (the trick was not to lift the pencil) for so many years that he couldn't remember who'd taught him the trick when he was a child. The matter was too trivial to think about, let alone worry, but he'd finally asked a psychiatrist about it. The psychiatrist suggested that Donnelly give up doodling by not carrying any paper or pencils.

Though Donnelly seemed to be intent on his next row of barns, he was in fact listening carefully to what Owen was saying. During the course of his speech he had gratuitously mentioned the word "black," each time in a derogatory manner. Black man, white woman; evil, good; voodoo and black magic as opposed to common sense.

The trial had barely started when Owen's bigotry became apparent. He seemed boxed in by his prejudices, and the box was getting more and more crowded with Mexicans, Jews, blacks, gays, Orientals, until there was hardly room for Owen to do his job properly. In at least one instance he had neglected his homework. Juror No. 7, a computer technician named Hudson, had a sister who'd been happily married to a black for years.

"Greed," Owen said. "Mrs. Pherson came to a violent end because of a man's greed. Greed is one of the seven deadly sins, and in Mrs. Pherson's case it was deadly indeed. Yes, and in Cully King's case it may be deadly also. The profit motive makes this a murder with special circumstances. If the charge against a person is murder with special circumstances, that person is not entitled to bail and, if found guilty, must die in the gas chamber or spend the rest of his life in prison without possibility of parole. This indicates the gravity with which the state of California regards murder for profit. You, ladies and gentlemen of the jury, must do no less.

"So far we have no evidence to show how much profit

was involved. The five hundred dollars the pawnbroker paid Cully King is only part of what King received or hoped to receive. More, probably much more is involved. According to Tyler Pherson, her husband, the green leather case contained heirloom jewelry bequeathed to his wife by her mother. The green case has not been found, perhaps never will be. Cully King might have thrown it overboard in a moment of panic after Mrs. Pherson's death at the same time as he threw her other possessions overboard.

"Rhetorical claptrap? No, indeed. This is evidence that will be presented to you from the stand by Harry Arnold, who witnessed the damning scene."

During the pause that followed this announcement, a long, loud sigh of disbelief crossed the room. It was impossible to tell where it came from, perhaps the counsel's table or the court clerk's or even the first row of spectators. But the judge strongly suspected it had come from Donnelly.

He turned his attention to Charles Donnelly. Here was a man who'd puzzled him from the time they first met. *A queer duck,* the judge thought, and glanced at the wall clock, then at his watch, and found a discrepancy of two minutes. He chose to believe the wall clock, which was two minutes later.

He said, "Have you almost finished, Mr. Owen?"

"I have finished, Your Honor."

"Good. Court will recess for fifteen minutes. Jurors are admonished not to discuss the case with anyone else or among themselves."

He leaned over and spoke to the court reporter in a whisper: "Did you hear me say the word 'good,' Mildred?"

"I wasn't sure, sir. I thought you might be just clearing your throat."

"Of course, I was just clearing my throat."

Before removing the paper from the stenotype machine, Mildred deleted the word 'good.' She and the judge had had a long and close working relationship. Although she sometimes referred to him privately as Georgy Porgy, she called him sir to his face and had a genuine respect for his ability and common sense.

He should have remarried years ago, she thought, folding the long ribbon of stenotype paper over and over into a figure eight.

Eva Foster, the court clerk, noted the time of recess in her book. She had witnessed the whispered conference between the judge and Mildred and Mildred's subsequent act of deletion.

After the jurors and spectators had left, she accosted Mildred at the door.

"You shouldn't have done that," she said.

Mildred widened her eyes in an attempt to look surprised. "Done what?"

"Erased."

"I was merely correcting a mistake."

"Oh, bull," Eva said. "The way you kowtow to that man disgusts me."

"You disgust much too easily, dear. It's hard on your arteries."

"My arteries?"

"Disgust constricts the arteries and leads to fibrosis of the cerebellum and other complications I can't think of at the moment."

"You can't think of them because they don't exist. You're making fun of me."

"Have to," Mildred said cheerfully. "I got sick of waiting for you to do it yourself."

Eva walked away, not angry so much as disappointed

that Mildred persisted in underestimating her own role as a woman, downgrading the importance of the female in today's society.

Eva Foster had a pair of full, perfectly formed breasts, defiantly unrestrained. Everything else about her was long and thin and straight, her hair, her legs, her neck, her nose, her mouth, even her thought processes. Her mind could go from A to Z without a moment's hesitation or the slightest acknowledgment that there was anything in between.

Nobody would have suspected what a wild fantasy life she led and what divergent figures appeared in it. There were clues, however: a certain expression on her face in unguarded moments; a moony smile now and then; a wardrobe that consumed most of her salary.

Halfway down the hall to the filing room she met Donnelly. He didn't speak as they passed, and there wasn't the slightest glint of recognition in his eyes. She wondered how he would react if she told him about the dream she'd had the previous night: They were in a railway station, and Donnelly was on the train as it began to move. She ran alongside it, and he reached down and swooped her up in his arms and whisked her away with him.

She woke up happy, and this, more than the dream itself, enraged her. She wasn't swoopable or whiskable, and Donnelly lived on another planet and was married to a wealthy socialite (though unhappily, of course: Court scuttlebutt always had the married men unhappy and on the brink of ditching their wives for the love of a steno or file clerk).

"Screw you," Eva said under her breath. "You're a nasty cold fish. Stay out of my railway station."

The judge retired to his chambers and, as his doctor had instructed him to do, lay down on the brown leather couch. They had grown old together, couch and man. Both bore the scars of time, mysterious sags and bulges. One cushion of the couch was covered with scratches made by the paws of the little dachshund he used to bring to the office every day after his wife died.

When the dachshund was no longer able to jump up on the couch by herself, the judge lifted her up, and she would lie there all day with a break at noon, not caring very much where she was as long as it was with him.

One morning court was abruptly adjourned without explanation. No one knew why until Mildred saw the judge carrying the little dead dog out to the parking lot, wrapped in one of his sweaters.

Neither his wife nor the dachshund was ever replaced.

The judge's doctor had given him dire warnings and explicit instructions. During every recess and at lunchtime he was to lie down and think of nothing at all. He was to imagine a blackboard with words written on it in chalk and an eraser moving back and forth and up and down until all the words had disappeared. But the judge had found that as soon as the words were gone they were replaced by pictures.

This morning it was the picture of a young woman who had flung her two children off the bridge and been successfully defended by a court-appointed lawyer. A year or so after the trial she gave birth to another unwanted child, which she tried to flush down the toilet. The subsequent flooding led to her quick arrest. Much to nobody's surprise, she was found guilty and sent to Corona, where, the judge hoped, part of her rehabilitation would include birth control information.

The eraser moved back and forth across the blackboard and the young woman's picture disappeared and the judge slept.

Recess stretched from fifteen to twenty-four minutes. Chronic tardiness on the part of a judge with an already overloaded court calendar was inexcusable, in Eva Foster's opinion, and would not happen if a woman were sitting on the bench.

After the bailiff had buzzed for the judge, and while the court was awaiting his reentry, Eva stopped at the stenotype machine to talk to Mildred Noon.

"You and I should be running this courtroom," she said. "And why aren't we?"

"For one thing, we're not lawyers."

"We could be. We could attend night classes right here in town."

"Not me. That's the only time I get to spend with my husband."

"Don't you want to make something of yourself?"

"I thought I was already something."

"I mean, a real something something."

"I'm afraid I'll just have to settle for an ordinary something."

"Are you content to let men rule the world?"

"Well, I don't have time to do it," Mildred said cheerfully. "Now, get off this kick and go back to your place. The judge's door is opening."

"The king cometh. We'll discuss this further at lunchtime."

The hell we will, Mildred thought, and sat poised at her machine, looking comfortable and relaxed. It took years of practice not to get jumpy, especially at the beginning of a murder trial. She had learned to prepare herself by going over in advance the names of witnesses and by familiarizing herself with medical terms likely to be used by psychiatrists and pathologists.

The court reporters always worked in pairs. For the

past six years Mildred's co-worker had been a small, silent man named Ortig.

Ortig could have been anywhere from thirty to fifty years old. He never volunteered his age or any other information about himself. Since Mildred was easily encouraged to talk, it was advantageous for her to have a partner who never asked or answered questions. She and Ortig relieved each other every ten or fifteen minutes since the job required such intense concentration and quick reflexes.

When Ortig came in to take over, he would sit at the machine next to her and with an almost imperceptible nod of his head indicate that he was ready to pick up on the next sentence. They were like a pair of circus jugglers taking over the flying pins from each other in midair.

The judge came in, flapping his worn black wings, and perched on the edge of his chair. He was angry, at himself for oversleeping, the court employees who didn't have sense enough to wake him up, and the doctor who advised him to lie down in the first place. He didn't need rest. He needed activity. He wanted to bounce up and down to music like the aerobic dancers he saw on TV. Juror No. 12 taught aerobic dancing, martial arts and aquadynamics, and she looked very fit. He had not, however, seen men his own age doing any of these things.

"Ladies and gentlemen," he said, "you have heard the opening statement of counsel for the people, Mr. Owen. And it is now time for the opening statement of counsel for the defense, Mr. Donnelly. Are you ready, Mr. Donnelly?"

"No, Your Honor."

"And why not?"

"In view of what has been said on the validity of opening statements I wish to forgo the opportunity afforded me at this time."

"You are not going to make an opening statement?"

"No, Your Honor."

"This is rather irregular, Mr. Donnelly. Have you discussed it with your client?"

"My client puts his faith in my ability."

The defendant, who'd been looking as surprised as the rest of the people in the courtroom, now smiled, first at Donnelly, then at the jury, then at the judge. It was a warm, confiding smile that moved some people and irritated others.

Donnelly didn't even notice. "My client has been sitting here forced to listen to all kinds of accusations against him, most of them spawned in the dark recesses of the district attorney's mind. For me to stand up here and merely contradict would be futile. I will therefore wait for evidence to prove the innocence of my client, evidence provided by witnesses under oath and subject to cross-examination."

"There is no further need for you to convince me," the judge said. "You are privileged to forgo making an opening statement. Without further ado, we will start the testimony. Mr. Owen, do you have your first witness within call?"

"No, Your Honor. Witness was led to understand that he wouldn't be taking the stand before this afternoon."

"Do you have any witnesses ready at all?"

"Not here and now. The morning was to have been taken up by opening statements." He stared coldly and reproachfully down the length of the table at Donnelly. "I was not forewarned by defense counsel of this new ploy of his."

"So the court is at a standstill."

"It would seem so, Your Honor."

"Very well. We will adjourn until one-thirty this afternoon. Spectators will please keep their seats until after the jury has departed. Jurors will leave their notebooks on their respective chairs to be collected by the bailiff. They are admonished not to discuss this case with anyone else or among themselves."

The jurors filed out in order, looking self-conscious and carefully avoiding the eyes of the spectators and of the defendant.

Donnelly had a personal file on all the jurors, compiled by his legman, Bill Gunther, and two assistants, and containing a variety of facts from a social security number to favorite food, magazines subscribed to, vehicle driven, church affiliation, if any, marital status and number of children. Did he possess a library card? A dog or cat? Perhaps none of these things would influence the outcome, but Donnelly knew as well as the judge did that one of them, seemingly unconnected and trivial, might directly affect the verdict. One vote, one solitary vote, would result in a hung jury, and that was what he was going for.

The vote that could hang the jury might be that of Miss Lisa Roy, who clerked in a women's apparel shop and raised Burmese cats as a hobby. She might be less inclined to vote against Cully because he had taken a cat on the *Bewitched*'s 4,000-mile journey. Or the solitary vote might belong to Mr. Hudson, whose black brother-in-law in Chicago gave him reason to resent the district attorney's obvious prejudice against blacks.

Though the district attorney's case against Cully King was circumstantial, it was strong, mainly because of the absence of other suspects and other motives. The most Donnelly could hope for at this point was a hung jury.

One vote was enough, and Donnelly was going for it.

In his chambers the judge removed his robe and put on a tweed jacket. He felt suddenly exhausted as if he had in fact, not merely in fantasy, been bouncing up and down to music. His heartbeat was rapid, and when he looked in the mirror to comb his hair, he saw that his face was flushed and moist.

His normal routine when court adjourned for the morning was to get in his car and drive to a seafood café on the waterfront. Here he would relax over a bottle of Molson's ale and a plate of ridgeback shrimp or freshly trapped lobster. But it was too early for lunch, and he knew he couldn't relax with the sights and sounds and smells of the waterfront reminding him of the case. The *Bewitched* itself would be visible at the very end of the marina since it was too large to fit into the inner slips.

Instead of going out to his car, he lay down again on the brown leather couch. He knew these were bad signs—the accelerated heartbeat and flushed face, the feeling of weakness and the sweating without exertion. He was not afraid of dying, but it would be damned annoying to have to bow out of this case before it was finished.

It seemed straightforward enough: a man, a woman, lust and anger and greed. He had presided over dozens of them, knifings in sordid little bars, shots from a Saturday night special, blows from a fist, a hammer, a baseball bat. This case didn't fit the pattern. The setting was wrong, a well-known racing yacht; the woman was wrong, married, respectable, devout. These elements could be reconciled, of course; things happened on racing yachts, and good women sometimes had bad luck. But the third element, the defendant, didn't seem to fit in anywhere. He was an unlikely skipper of a famous yacht, a black, only thirty-six or seven years old and looking and acting younger. Perhaps at the helm of the *Bewitched* he was much older than his years, but here in the courtroom he was almost childlike, following the proceedings with bright-eyed interest, smiling at the slightest provocation, seemingly unaware of or at least untroubled by the situation he was in. The judge had read a newspaper article which quoted the ship's owner, Mr. Belasco: "Cully King is the best skipper money can buy. He's cool, confident and afraid of nothing."

He still appeared unafraid, though he knew that if he were found guilty, this same jury would decide his fate during the penalty phase of the trial, death in the gas chamber or life in prison without possibility of parole.

Somewhere inside he must be afraid, the judge thought, *just as I am probably afraid somewhere inside, and I'm thirty years older with very little to lose and no one to mourn my losing it.*

Sweat streamed down the judge's face. He took a handkerchief out of his pocket to wipe it off, and a garlic capsule rolled out on the floor. He picked it up, popped it in his mouth and began to chew. "Garlic," the manager of the health food store told him, "regenerates the bile ducts, the blood, the bowels." The judge was aware that these same claims were made for a dozen other products on the shelves, but proving fraud would be difficult since it was impossible to tell whether one's bile ducts were regenerating or degenerating. No matter. The garlic served its real purpose, generating privacy.

He closed his eyes and imagined the blackboard again and the eraser wiping out the words and a picture beginning to appear. The picture this time was the face of Cully King smiling at him, friendly, almost benign, as though he didn't blame anyone for his predicament and he hoped no one would blame him.

Where did this man's confidence come from? Certainly not from his background, which could only have taught him to be wary and suspicious. Born in St. John, he had run away to sea at twelve and spent his adolescence in and out of the waterfront dives and rum shops of the Caribbean, doing nearly every kind of job on nearly every kind of vessel. The skin of a white man exposed for that many years to sun and wind would carry the scars of old cancers and the keratoids that signaled others to come. But Cully King's face was smooth and placid as a pond. There were no worry lines from storms at sea, no reminders of bordello brawls or arguments settled by knives or bull pistols. He had survived unmarked, as if he had wiped out bad memories just as the eraser had wiped out the words on the judge's blackboard.

The judge finished chewing the capsule, and the smell of garlic drifted under the door into his secretary's office, where it competed with the scent of Estée Lauder's Youth-Dew.

It was no contest. Estée was beaten by a nose.

Court resumed at one-forty in the afternoon. The time was duly noted by Eva Foster in her book; then she crossed the area between the judge and the counsel table, carrying a Bible.

"Please state your full name for the record and spell the last one."

"Peter Gray Belasco. B-E-L-A-S-C-O."

"Raise your right hand. Do you solemnly swear to tell the truth, the whole truth and nothing but the truth in the matter now pending before this court, so help you God?"

"I do."

"Please be seated."

Belasco took his place in the witness box. A tall, wiry man in his late fifties with a habitual sun squint.

Belasco's full beard stretched at the corners in a brief, friendly smile directed at Cully. Then he turned his attention back to the district attorney.

"Where do you reside. Mr. Belasco?"

"Santa Felicia, Sixty-eight Rosalita Lane."

"And what is your occupation?"

"Mining engineer, retired. More accurately, semiretired."

"How long have you been retired or semiretired?"

"Fourteen years."

"Have you found any special hobby to occupy your time?"

"I race my yacht, *Bewitched*."

"Will you describe this yacht for the benefit of the jury?"

"It is an aluminum ketch eighty-five feet long."

"Where do you race this yacht?"

"Wherever there's a race I can get to. All over the world, actually."

"Such as?"

"New York to Bermuda. Sydney to Hobart. Fastnet off the southwest coast of England. Transpac from here to Honolulu. That's the race I was preparing to enter before this misfortune occurred."

"Have you ever won any of these races?"

"No, never even came close. But at least I never sank her. We arrived first in the Transpac a couple of years ago but because of our handicap had to settle for fourth place."

"How is a handicap computed in a yacht race?"

"It's a time handicap based on the size of the ship and the amount of sail carried. A smaller ship might come in a day later than *Bewitched* and still be declared the winner."

"This yacht, the *Bewitched*, how would you describe it?"

"As I said, it's an aluminum ketch eighty-five feet from bow to stern."

"Did you, last spring, compete in a race from Nassau to St. Thomas in the Virgin Islands?"

"Yes."

"And what did you do after the race?"

"Commiserated with my crew—we came in last—and then flew home to California. I have too many pressing business interests here to allow me to spend all my time sailing."

"What arrangements did you make for your boat?"

"Cully King is my skipper, and I told him to bring her back here through the Panama Canal."

"Is King in the courtroom at this time?"

"Yes, sir. He's sitting over there. First-rate skipper, knows the boat well and is very competent."

"We need not dwell on the ability of Mr. King to do his job." The district attorney gave Belasco a cold sour look to remind him that he was a witness for the prosecution, not a press agent for the defense. "You had a contract with Mr. King to bring the boat back here?"

"Yes."

"And what were the financial arrangements of this agreement?"

"It is customary to pay a skipper by the mile, a dollar, a dollar-fifty, two dollars. I offered Cully top price, two-fifty, because I have a great deal of money invested in the *Bewitched*."

"Approximately how long is the journey by sea from St. Thomas to Santa Felicia?"

"It varies with weather conditions. Four thousand miles is a close estimate."

"So Mr. King earned approximately twelve thousand dollars."

"Yes, but out of that he will have to pay his crew. With only three men aboard, the *Bewitched* is tight-handed, and the men must work long, hard hours and be paid accordingly. There is some danger involved as well as hard work. Along the west coast of Central America, because of political unrest, passing vessels are sometimes chased, brought back to port and detained. In view of all this, I expect Harry Arnold and his son to get a sizable portion of the twelve thousand dollars. So far it's all just theoretical since I haven't had a chance to pay anybody anything."

Once more he smiled at Cully King, and Cully returned the smile. The exchange annoyed and aggravated the twitch at one corner of Owen's mouth. Right from the beginning he had disliked Belasco, whom he privately referred to as a rich bleeding-heart liberal like Donnelly, a socialist, a possible dope smuggler, even a spy. Why did he have to race all over the world? Why couldn't he race up and down the coast like a normal person?

When he spoke again, his voice was tight. "How long does the journey from St. Thomas in the Virgin Islands to Santa Felicia take?"

"Again, it depends on the weather. There are favorable winds, the trades, from St. Thomas to Colón, that's about a thousand miles, roughly one week. There are often delays at the Canal, where the ships pile up, waiting their turn like the planes at a large airport. Panama is the crossroads of international shipping. From Panama to Mazatlán there are areas of calm, but north from Mazatlán you often run into head winds. Time must be allowed for provision and fuel stops. Altogether I'd say the voyage takes a month. The duration of this particular one is documented in the log of the *Bewitched* right down to the last minute. But that log is not in my possession. You have it."

"Indeed I do. In fact, I'm about to use it." He approached the table where Eva Foster was sitting. "Would you bring in the blue book I gave you this morning?"

Eva went back to the exhibit room and returned carrying a blue vinyl book with the name *Bewitched* printed on it in gold letters. The district attorney took the book from her and offered it to Donnelly to examine. Donnelly did so briefly.

The judge said, "Are you offering this in evidence, Mr. Owen?"

"Yes, sir."

"Then let it be marked people's exhibit one. At this point I would like to explain to the jury that all people's exhibits will be marked by numbers, and those of the defense by letters of the alphabet."

The district attorney showed the book to the witness. "Do you recognize this, Mr. Belasco?"

"Yes, sir."

"What is it?"

"The log of the *Bewitched*."

"What is entered in such a log?"

"Everything that concerns a boat."

"Give us some examples, please."

"Well, the obvious thing is the weather, wind velocity and direction, water conditions such as size of swells, information on whether the vessel is proceeding under sail or power, how much fuel is added to the engine, et cetera."

"Is such information entered in the log on a regular basis?"

"Yes."

"How often?"

"Every hour or half hour, depending on the circumstances. . . . Since you've seen the log, you already know all this."

"The jury doesn't. For their benefit I am trying to set the stage, to show them the setting in which this tragedy occurred. Now go on, Mr. Belasco. What circumstances would increase the number of entries in the log?"

"If the weather is foul and the seas are heavy; if one of the crewmen is ill or has met with some kind of accident; if the jimmy is kicking up—"

"Jimmy?"

"The engine is a GMC diesel commonly referred to as jimmy."

"I am going to open this logbook," Owen said, "and show you the initial entry for the journey we've been discussing. Can you see the first entry?"

Belasco squinted down at the page a couple of times, then took a pair of reading glasses from his pocket and put them on. "Yes, I see it."

"What does it indicate?"

"The time and date and point of departure, St. Thomas. Seas calm, wind five knots. Proceeding under power. Two crewmen aboard, Harry Arnold, Richie Arnold."

"Stop there a moment. Is it standard procedure to record the names of the crew?"

"Yes."

"What about passengers?"

"I'm not sure what the question is."

"If there are passengers on board, is their presence duly noted in the log?"

"It depends on what kind of boat it is and the policy of whoever is in charge."

"The boat I'm referring to is the *Bewitched*. Does that clarify my question?"

"Yes."

"Then answer it, please."

"Usually the presence of passengers aboard the *Bewitched* is recorded, but it's *not* a hard-and-fast rule."

"Before you answer the next question, I would like to

advise you that I have been over this entire log. Can you, Mr. Belasco, recall any journey where the passengers were not listed in the logbook?"

Belasco tightened his mouth as if he were reefing a sail during a storm. "Evidently you know more about my journeys than I do, Mr. Owen."

"We are back to square one. Is it customary for the log of the *Bewitched* to show the arrival of a passenger on board?"

"Yes."

"We could have saved time if you'd answered that in the beginning."

Owen turned his attention to the judge. "Your Honor, I think at this point the jury should be advised that Mr. Belasco is a reluctant witness, if not a downright hostile one."

"I object," Donnelly said. "Witness has shown neither reluctance nor hostility, only a desire for the district attorney to be more precise in his questions."

"Sustained. The jury will disregard the last remarks of the district attorney."

Owen took the log from Belasco's hand and opened it to a later page, indicated by a bookmark. "Please note, and state for the record, the time of arrival in San Diego's Harbor Island."

"April thirtieth. The boat cleared customs, took on fuel and provisions and prepared to leave the following morning before dawn."

"And did it?"

"That's what the log says."

"Does the log indicate a passenger coming on board with Mr. King?"

"No."

"There is no record of a passenger coming on board?"

"No."

"Yet one did, isn't that right?"

"So I'm told."

Donnelly was about to get up to object, but the judge spoke first. "Take heed, Counselors. I have warned you before about the time element. This case promises—or shall I say threatens?—to become one of the longest in the county's history. We must try to keep within the budget allotted to us by the Board of Supervisors. We now know every square inch of the boat and just about every square inch of the people on it."

He gave each man in turn his sternest look, but it was a wasted effort. Donnelly was whispering to his client and Owen was consulting his notes.

I have lost my personal ascendancy in this courtroom, the judge thought. *In the old days attorneys quailed when I stared at them like that. Now they don't even notice. They know I won't be here next year. Maybe I'm not altogether here this year, judging by the way Mildred and Miss Foster look at me. In order to regain my prestige, I might have to do something quite drastic, make a very unusual ruling that will be quoted decades after I'm gone.*

"You previously testified, Mr. Belasco," Owen said, "that the *Bewitched* is eighty-five feet in length, is that correct?"

"Yes."

"That is long for a yacht. But it is quite small when you consider it as an area where people are confined. It is, in fact, something less than one-third the size of a football field. If you put four people in an area one-third the size of a football field, it would be difficult for them to remain unaware of each other, would it not?"

"I've never put four people on one-third of a football field."

"You are rather frivolously evading the question, Mr. Belasco."

"I don't mean to. The fact is, a yacht like the *Bewitched* is not simply a length; it is a structure like a house with a number of rooms, an upstairs, downstairs, cellar. One person could easily remain out of sight of the others."

Owen's throat was beginning to feel constricted, a warning that his voice would start to rise in pitch and to sound peevish.

He was a student of voices, especially his own. He could tell by listening to a tape whether he had had an argument with his wife, Virginia, or one of the boys had gotten into mischief at school. Trouble that could be hidden inside the eyes or behind a smile showed quite clearly in a voice.

Owen took three or four deep breaths to relax his throat muscles before he spoke again. "At several places in the log there are references to communications with P. B. Who is P. B.?"

"They're my initials."

"When the *Bewitched* is at sea not under your command, do you keep in touch with the skipper?"

"When possible or necessary we talk by radiophone."

"Do you give Mr. King, for instance, orders?"

"I may make suggestions, but usually Cully merely keeps me informed what's going on."

"Did you discuss with Mr. King the upcoming race to Honolulu, the Transpac?"

"Naturally."

"Did you ask him to try to pick up a cook for that race? A simple yes or no answer, please."

Belasco hesitated. "Well, I didn't exactly—"

"Did you ask Mr. King to pick up a cook? Yes or no."

"No."

"I have no further questions at this time."

"You may step down, Mr. Belasco," the judge said. "Before Mr. Donnelly begins his cross-examination, we will take the afternoon recess of fifteen minutes."

The jurors filed into the jury room, and most of the spectators into the corridor. The judge remained where he was, summoning the bailiff, Zeke di Santo, with a slight nod of his head.

The bailiff approached the bench, moving awkwardly for a young man, as though he were not yet used to the extra weight accumulated during a year of sitting in a courtroom.

"Yes, Your Honor?"

"What's the matter with the air-conditioning?"

"It isn't working, sir."

"I'm aware that it isn't working. Why isn't it working?"

"I don't know, sir."

"Can you find out and do something about it?"

"Probably not. These matters seem to be in the lap of the gods."

"Surely the gods have left us the capacity to open windows."

"Yes, Your Honor. But that will mean an increase in traffic noises, which might prevent Your Honor from hearing things."

"At the moment I'm not listening to anything except your fatuities. . . . Speaking of hearing things, every now and then I hear a kind of low, humming noise. Have you noticed it?"

"Yes, Your Honor."

"What is it?"

"It appears to be a low, humming sound."

"I *know* that. But where's it coming from and why?"

"I think it's coming from the defendant, sir. He hums."

"Why?"

"Maybe it's because he's happy."

"Happy? Nobody in a courtroom is supposed to be happy. Are *you* happy, Di Santo?"

"I'm betwixt and between."

"You look fairly happy. I observe you laughing at my jokes."

"Oh, yes, sir. The loudest."

"The loudest? Why?"

"I appreciate Your Honor's sense of humor." *Also, I got a wife and kid to support.*

The bailiff opened a window, and cool, noisy air pushed past him into the room as if it had been waiting all day to get in.

Di Santo felt the coolness with surprise. The morning had been crisp and clear, and at noon the weather had been like August. Now, in midafternoon, it was fall again with the fog drifting in from the sea, draping the tops of the tall Mexican palms so only the trunks were visible like haphazardly placed telephone poles.

He looked out and saw the courthouse pigeons taking shelter in the bell tower, and the solitary emerald green parrot, once somebody's pet, gliding across the busy street like a flying traffic light. The bird was quiet for a parrot, probably because it had nothing to squawk about. From the pigeons it had learned to freeload, and it lived well on the handouts from a nearby restaurant and the contents of the lunch boxes and the brown bags of the office workers who ate in the sunken gardens, bologna sandwiches and hard-boiled eggs and pickles and pieces of fruit. It drank from the courthouse fountain and picked figs and hawthorn berries and pyracantha in season.

Di Santo envied that parrot. Nobody nagged it for eating too much; in fact, nobody knew how to tell whether a parrot was fat or thin except by weighing it, and this parrot was not about to be weighed. It had successfully resisted all efforts to capture it and flew merrily, fat or thin, from tree to tree, lunch box to paper bag.

Di Santo was not so lucky. His wife kept a scale in the bathroom and had pasted on the refrigerator door the picture of a fat man, an actor who had died quite young of a heart attack. For his birthday Di Santo's wife had given him a membership in a health club, to which he paid a few halfhearted visits. He preferred bowling and beering with his friends. It seemed more sensible than lifting weights with his feet.

The courtroom was almost empty now. Donnelly and Cully King sat talking in whispers, and Eva Foster was still at the table she shared with Di Santo. She watched him cross the room with the same critical appraisal as his wife and the receptionist at the health club.

Di Santo knew what was coming, and to avoid it, or at least postpone it, he stopped at the water cooler.

Eva joined him there. "What did you have for lunch?"

"You know I never eat lunch."

"How could you after that breakfast?"

"What breakfast? All I had was an orange. And maybe a piece of dry toast. That's all my wife would give me."

"So you went into McDonald's and ate two eggs McMuffin. I saw you."

"A guy has to have protein," Zeke said. "I read in the *Reader's Digest* that without enough protein the brain shrivels."

"Your brain has already shriveled so you don't have to worry about it. Do you want my honest opinion?"

"No."

"Here it is anyway. When the judge retires, this courtroom will have a new presiding judge who'll want his—or hopefully her—own bailiff. That will give you a chance to ask the sheriff for a more active job. You're not burning off your calories. The only exercise you get is unlocking and locking doors and letting your belt out another notch. Wouldn't you rather be outside in the open air, investigating things and chasing criminals?"

"No."

"Why not?"

"They might chase me back."

In spite of the open windows, the room was still hot and smelled of people under stress.

Donnelly addressed his client without looking at him. There was something about Cully King's face, an innocence, even a sweetness, that was too disarming. It made him want to believe whatever came out of the soft, sensuous mouth or was expressed in the soft, sensuous eyes. Donnelly knew it was a mistake, this trusting. Clients lied, all of them, innocent or guilty. They tilted the truth, and it was his job to level it again.

"In our first conversation," Donnelly said, "and in subsequent ones you told me that Belasco asked you to hire a cook for the Transpac."

"He did. At least I had the impression he did. We talked about it."

"When?"

"When I called him from Mazatlán. It's in the log."

"That he asked you to hire a cook?"

"No. But the call itself is logged."

"Not the contents of it?"

"No."

"Repeat the conversation."

"There was the usual stuff, how are things going and all like that. Then he mentioned that he didn't have a cook yet for the race. He's a fussy eater, not the kind of guy who'd settle for beans and black pudding. Mr. Belasco has to have the best."

"You're veering away from the subject. Stick to what he actually said."

"I already told you. He said he didn't have a cook for the Transpac yet."

"Did he say he wanted one?"

"Well, sure he wanted one. The cook's very important in a race of any length. I got the impression that he wanted me to do something about it, try to get hold of one for him if the chance came."

"And the chance came in the form of Madeline Pherson?"

"I thought it did. I mean, I thought I would be doing Mr. Belasco a favor by taking her on."

"Come off it, Cully. You wanted a good screw."

Cully considered this for a moment, then shrugged his shoulders. "Maybe. It sounds kind of disrespectful now, but at the time it was just natural. She didn't look to me like the way Mr. Owen described her in his speech, all that church stuff and everything. And she didn't order any Perrier water either. She had a double martini. I should know. I paid for it."

"What was Mrs. Pherson wearing when she came into the bar?"

"I don't know. I told you that before. I don't know."

"Tell me again."

"I can't remember. The only thing I notice about women's clothes is whether they're on or off."

"Oh, great. Terrific." Donnelly pressed his pencil so hard into the notebook that the lead broke. "That will sound wonderful in front of a jury."

"I wouldn't say that in front of a jury, Mr. Donnelly."

"You're goddamn right you wouldn't. You're not going

to get in front of a jury until we straighten out a few misconceptions. For instance, you think jurors are people, don't you?"

"Sure they're people."

"Wrong. They started out as people, but once they were sworn in and took their seats in that jury box, they changed. They turned into defenders of the truth. And at the beginning of every trial one truth is evident: A crime has been committed and a person has been arrested for committing it. Why has this person been arrested? Because the police are convinced he is guilty, the police whom we are all brought up to trust and respect. So we start off with a pretty lopsided situation. If a vote was taken now, this afternoon, you would be convicted."

"You mean they all think I'm guilty?"

"Probably. It comes with the territory, the territory being the county jail."

Drops of fear had appeared on Cully's forehead. "Hey, man, you're just trying to scare me, aren't you?"

Donnelly didn't answer. A scared client was a lot easier to defend than a confident one. A dose of reality might help cleanse Cully's system like a spring tonic. "When the jury returns in a few minutes, look at them carefully. They're your enemies. It's up to you to make them your friends, to convince them that cops are not infallible; they make mistakes like anyone else, and one of their biggest mistakes was arresting you for murder."

"It was a mistake. I didn't do anything."

"Of course you did. Maybe not all you're accused of doing but some of it. I never had a completely innocent client. Don't go spoiling my record."

Cully wiped the sweat off his forehead. He didn't understand this man, who had no feelings, who never smiled, never frowned, a cruel man who seemed to hate his job and hate his clients but never stopped working. The jail grapevine had him married to a rich woman. Maybe it did funny things to a man, marrying a rich woman.

"I've studied this jury," Donnelly said. "And it's no different from any of the others. What they want is a defendant who's humble. Do you think you can manage the humble bit?"

"I didn't do anything. Why should I act humble?"

"Because you have a smart lawyer who tells you to. Are you smart enough to take his advice?"

"I guess so. But it's tough to act humble when I don't feel humble, when I don't have anything to feel humble about. I'm not sure how to start."

"Oh, Christ, forget it. Just don't act like a smartass. Think you can manage that?"

Cully thought about it a minute. Then: "You're a pretty big guy, aren't you?"

"Six-three."

"I'm five-nine. But if I met you on a street in St. John and you called me a smartass, I'd cut you, man, I'd cut you like a piece of fruit."

"A piece of fruit," Donnelly repeated, looking somewhat amused. "I'm almost sorry you won't get a chance to try. It might be interesting. Right now, however, it seems doubtful that you'll meet me on a street in St. John or meet anyone on any street at any time in the future. That is, unless you start listening to your attorney. So are you listening?"

"I'm listening."

"Good . . . Time's nearly up. Do you have to go to the can?"

"No."

"I do. See you soon."

* * *

It was three-twenty when the judge reentered the courtroom and the witness took his place on the stand again. Donnelly approached the lectern. In the small well of the court he looked massive, and his slow, careful adjusting of the speaker to his height emphasized the shortfall of the district attorney. "Mr. Belasco, is it mandatory for a skipper to record in the log the names of passengers who come aboard?"

"No."

"It is up to the individual skipper?"

"Yes."

"Do you yourself list passengers?"

"Usually. In a race, of course, everything is recorded down to the slightest detail. But in casual sailing I may omit quite a few things, accidentally or on purpose."

"According to the log, Mr. King called you by radiophone from Mazatlán. Is that correct?"

"Yes."

"At that time did you tell him you were still lacking a cook for the Transpac race?"

"Yes."

"Can you recall exactly what you said?"

"Not exactly word by word. But I told him I still had no cook for the Transpac."

"Did you tell him you needed one?"

"I didn't have to tell him that. He knows how important a cook is in a long race."

"Did you ask him to keep on the alert for one?"

"I'm sure I made such a request by implication."

"Would you say then that you asked him in a roundabout way to hire a cook or at least to be on the lookout for one?"

"I would say that, yes. I never have to spell things out for Cully because he seems to know instinctively what is required of him."

The district attorney rose. "I object to the witness volunteering irrelevant remarks about the defendant."

"You will try to confine yourself to answering questions, Mr. Belasco," the judge said.

Donnelly stood motionless at the lectern until all the attention was refocused on him. "I have no more questions, Mr. Belasco. Thank you."

The judge looked slightly annoyed as if this somehow had spoiled his schedule for the afternoon. "Mr. Owen, do you want to recross?"

Owen changed places with Donnelly at the lectern. "Were you surprised when you learned that Mr. King had taken Mrs. Pherson on as cook?"

"I was surprised when I learned of her background and position in society. But of course, I didn't find that out until I read about it in the newspapers and saw it on TV."

"Did Mr. King call you while the *Bewitched* was en route from San Diego to tell you he was giving a woman a chance at the job?"

"He may have tried. I don't know. I was unavailable. I'd been summoned to my father's bedside in Palm Springs. He had a heart attack."

"A simple yes or no will be sufficient."

"I don't know if he called me. I wasn't home."

"I have no more questions."

Belasco started to leave the stand, but the judge held him back with a gesture. "Just a minute, Mr. Belasco. Mr. Donnelly might want to re-recross. Mr. Donnelly?"

"I have a couple of questions mainly for clarification purposes," Donnelly said. "Mr. Belasco, where were you when the *Bewitched* was on its way here from San Diego?"

"I was in Palm Springs."

"Why?"

"My father was very ill."

"Did you inform Mr. King where you were?"

"No."

"I have nothing further at this moment."

"You are free to step down, Mr. Belasco," the judge said. "I would like at this time to remind you that all witnesses are admonished to stay out of the courtroom during these proceedings except for the time they spend testifying. Was it made clear to you previously that you are to stay away from the courtroom before *and* after your testimony?"

"Yes, Your Honor."

"You are free to leave with the understanding that you may be recalled later. . . . Do you have another witness, Mr. Owen?"

"Not immediately." Owen slid an accusing look down the long polished table toward Donnelly. "I expected the cross-examination of Mr. Belasco to take up the rest of the afternoon."

"May I advise both counselors to have more than one witness available to take the stand—that is, either waiting in the corridor or at some nearby location. A good deal of time has been wasted this morning and this afternoon due to the absence of witnesses." He tapped his gavel lightly. Wood on wood was barely audible over the other sounds invading the courtroom, traffic noises through the open window, and the babble of voices from the hall, where a docent was leading her group of tourists through the memorabilia of the city's history, old wagons and cannons, display cases filled with arrowheads and shells from the kitchen midden embedded in cliffs along the shore, antique firearms and pictures. For the docent and her little troop, the courthouse was a place to relive what had happened, not to take part in what was happening behind every door with a lighted sign above it: QUIET, COURT IN SESSION.

The judge raised his voice. "We will adjourn until ten o'clock tomorrow morning. Spectators will please keep their seats until the jurors have departed. Jurors are admonished not to discuss or refer to these proceedings with anyone at all."

When the Judge returned to his chambers, he stood for a minute staring at the picture on his desk of a stout brown-haired woman holding a stout brown-haired dachshund. Both looked content with each other and with themselves. They were nice people, these two, and he really hadn't deserved either of them. But they had pretended not to be aware of this and tolerated him and made him happy.

He took off his robe and hung it in the closet, trying to figure out what Donnelly was up to. His failure to make an opening statement and the terseness of his cross-examination had the effect of making Owen's presentation seem too verbose. Brevity was one of Donnelly's favorite ploys, and juries on the whole appeared to like it, equating simplicity with truth. Truth, they thought, needed no varnish, the lily no gilding. They were wrong, of course. The truth sometimes required a great deal of elaboration, and he'd seen lilies that could have used at least a touch of gilding.

He put on his sports jacket and went out through the small reception room. Here his secretary, Krista, was on the telephone talking to her boyfriend, calling him sir so no one would catch on.

"Oh, yes, sir. Five o'clock, maybe a bit sooner, sir."

The judge never indicated that he had caught on to the deception the second time he'd heard it. It seemed to give her an innocent pleasure, which he preferred not to spoil. She was, after all, a good-natured girl and not terribly incompetent.

She smiled and waved good-bye, but she didn't hang up. The judge realized for the first time that she knew he knew and was somehow giving his blessing to her and sir. He thought, *Dammit, I don't even know sir. He might be a hardened criminal she had seen clanking down the corridor to his hearing. Their eyes met, it was love at first sight and she vowed to wait for him until he was paroled.*

He opened the door, hesitated, then turned back to his secretary. "Krista, if you need advice in handling a personal problem, kindly do not come to me."

"All right."

"Consult a professional."

"All right."

"Or better still, handle it yourself. Do what you want to do, which is what you're going to do anyway, advice or no advice."

The fog stopped drifting in from the sea when it reached the foothills of the mountains. It was motionless now, pressing down on the city like a wet gray night, dripping from the lampposts of the parking lot and polishing the leather leaves of the fig tree, which dominated the landscape.

The fig tree had been there before the parking lot, before the cars, even before the courthouse itself. Its great roots reached out like the arms of an octopus, crumbling the surface, squeezing the asphalt into submission. Occasionally some impertinent upstart suggested removing the tree, but this idea was so contrary to the city's policies that its author barely escaped a mob of protesters from such varied associations as the Chamber of Commerce, the Sierra Club, the Historical Society, the Chumash Indian Council and the downtown businessmen's garden club.

The tree remained, generating a brisk business in shock absorbers.

The judge identified with the fig tree, in its age and strength and ability to make itself felt. Seeing new fissures appear in the pavement and grow wider each week gave him pleasure even though his rheumatic old Lincoln grumbled at the discomfort.

As he was about to turn into the street, he saw Donnelly standing beside a Mercedes coupé with a dented fender, talking to his investigator, Bill Gunther. Their heads were close together as if they wanted to be sure no one overheard their conversation, an unnecessary precaution since the fog smothered sounds like an acoustical curtain.

Gunther didn't put much faith in acoustical curtains or anything else. Suspicion was an integral part of his nature and of his job. He was an ex-cop from Las Vegas, where suspicion hung low and thick over the roulette wheels and blackjack tables. In his present job he'd become very popular with the courthouse crowd. He told fat people they were getting thin and thin people they were putting on weight. He told pretty girls they were smart and smart girls they were pretty, watching with amusement the eagerness with which people swallowed an undeserved compliment.

Gunther and his boss had only one thing in common, work. Neither of them had time for or interest in cultivating close friends.

"The judge is coming," Donnelly said. "Do you suppose we should try to look less intimate?"

"We have nothing to be intimate about. Have we?"

Judge Hazeltine, who was getting more and more farsighted as he aged, had seen the two heads together. The sight disturbed him, he didn't know why. It was none of his business. They could carry their heads underneath their arms like the ghost of Anne Boleyn if they wanted to, and it would still be none of his business and violate no law that he knew about.

He guided his old Lincoln out into the street in the direction of home although the car could possibly have made the trip by itself after all these years.

Switching on the headlights, he half sang and half murmured the words of the old song:

> With her head tucked underneath her arm
> She walks the bloody tower. . . .

II

DONNELLY

*I*n high school Charles Donnelly had been voted the boy most likely to succeed. In college he was the man most likely to succeed. In law school he was second in his graduation class and finally succeeded: He married a copper heiress. By anticipating the computer revolution, he turned a great deal of copper into gold, and a millionaire at thirty, he discovered that money bored him. He went back to the practice of law, specializing in criminal cases.

He enjoyed the challenge of pitting himself against the system, and his happiest hours were spent in the law library of the courthouse, checking back through previous trials and decisions, or sitting alone in his office planning and replanning a brief.

He often worked nights, sometimes with Bill Gunther, discussing cases with him and listening to the results of investigations Gunther was in the process of making for him.

It was through Gunther that he became acquainted with Cully King.

"A black man was booked for murder tonight," Gunther said. "Did you hear about it?"

"No. Interesting?"

"Well, certainly not your usual stabbing in a barroom brawl. It was a drowning at sea."

"Who was drowned?"

"Wife of an oil executive from Bakersfield."

Gunther had a quiet voice which combined with his smooth pale skin and steel-rimmed glasses to give him a scholarly look that didn't fit the image of an ex-cop from Las Vegas. He'd come to Santa Felicia to get away from the gambling which was a way of life in Las Vegas. Here, in Santa Felicia, he was confined to betting on horses, fights, football and basketball games and an occasional election. He still lost a lot but not as much, not so often.

Donnelly said, "Did you see the man?"

"Yes."

"Get any hunches?"

"Not real hunches. More like curiosity. I can't recall a single case of a black man being arrested for drowning a woman at sea."

"Was the woman white?"

"Yes."

Donnelly paused, then said, "Find out some more details and get back to me."

"When?"

"Tonight."

"It's nearly eleven o'clock."

"You have connections. Use them."

"I was figuring on some dinner."

"Billy boy, you've just had your priorities rearranged. Work first, eat later."

Donnelly's wife had changed her name from Alexandra to Zandra, her hair from brown to blond and her figure from plump to thin. But she made no attempt to change the habit which most irritated her husband. Like many wealthy people, she had a number of small stinginesses which at first Donnelly found amusing. She haggled with shopkeepers, and when she got an $800 dress marked down to $750 she thought she got a bargain and boasted about it to anyone who would listen. She clipped coupons from newspapers and magazines for introductory offers, twofers and special-purchase items on sale. She sent the cook all over town to take advantage of these bargains.

Donnelly pointed out that her bargains were not actually bargains. "You're saving a couple of bucks on groceries and spending three or four times that much on gasoline."

Her reply was triumphant. "We have oil stock. Don't you see? . . . I'm investing. Gasoline comes from oil, and when I buy gas, I'm simply *investing*. Don't you *see*?"

"I see a semblance of logic in your argument. Unfortunately it's based on a false premise."

"What does that mean?"

"We don't own any oil stock."

"Of course we do. We must. Everyone does."

He shrugged and turned to leave. She put out a hand to stop him. She was wearing one of the flowing silk caftans she usually wore around the house. When she reached out her hand to stop him from leaving, the sleeve of the caftan slipped back to reveal her arm. It was so thin he could have spanned the upper part of it with his thumb and middle finger. Its covering didn't look like flesh but like paper wrapped around a bone to take home to a dog.

They were in the second-floor sitting room, which was smaller and more cheerful than the formal one downstairs. A trio of unseasoned eucalyptus logs burned in the grate, hissing and sputtering and oozing their vital juices at each end. Sparks flew against the screen like imprisoned birds.

He stood in front of the fire with his back to the room, to her, to their whole life together.

"You're taking those diet pills again," he said.

"This is the first evening in weeks that you've been home and you want to spoil it by—"

"How many?"

"I take one now and then. Not regularly."

"Show me the bottle."

"I certainly will not. If a husband can't trust his wife enough to take her word for—"

"How many are you taking, Zan?"

"One a day. Maybe two."

"Why?"

"You know perfectly well how easily I gain weight. I can't even walk past a chocolate éclair without putting on a pound. The pills help me. They make me feel good."

"They don't make you look good."

"How would you know? You never look at me."

"I'm looking at you now. You look sick."

She began to tremble, then to sway. She kept her balance by leaning on the back of the couch and feeling her way along it like a blind person until she reached the end and fell among the cushions.

"You filthy beast. You didn't like me fat; now you don't like me thin."

"I don't like you hooked on amphetamines."

"I'm not hooked."

"Then why take them?"

"I told you, they make me feel good. God knows I need something to make me feel good. I have no children, no husband—"

"Get yourself a hobby."

"A hobby instead of a hubby. How cute." She mimicked his flat, quiet tone. "Get yourself a hobby. Christ, no won-

68

der I look sick. *You* make me sick, not the pills."

He drew back the fire screen and poked one of the logs with his foot. It sent off a shower of sparks. One of them landed on the rug, and he stood and watched it burn, wondering with a strange sense of excitement whether it would spread and ignite the whole rug, the coffee table, the couch, the drapes, the room, the house. Then he remembered the smoke detectors which Zan had had installed in nearly every room, and he put his foot on the ember. It left just a small scar that would be noticed only by one of the anonymous maids the next time she vacuumed.

He said, "How many doctors are you conning?"

"I'm not conning anyone. I have my own personal physician, Dr. Stoddard. He believes in weight control."

"Stoddard doesn't prescribe amphetamines. So where are you getting them?"

"None of your business."

"I can find out, of course."

"Oh, sure. Put Gunther on my trail."

"Gunther has more important things to do."

But even as he spoke, he wondered if this was true. Gunther was helping him save a man's life, but Zan's life might be in almost as much jeopardy as Cully King's. Of the two, Cully had a better chance. He wanted to live; Zan seemed to have lost interest.

"Zan, please listen to me."

"No. Go away. Leave me alone. Go back to the office or wherever."

She had burrowed into the cushions with the caftan wrapped around her, as if the silk were returning to its original state, a cocoon. Only her face was visible, its pallor and hollow cheeks making her eyes look enormous. They were as gray as storm clouds.

The only sound in the room was the eucalyptus logs still fighting the fire.

Then Zan spoke, in a voice he hadn't heard for a long time, soft and sad. "Why can't we have a conversation like two nice, normal people?"

"Perhaps because we're not two nice, normal people."

"We could try."

"All right."

"Tell me what's going on in court. There was something about it on TV tonight, and I saw a picture of the murderer. He doesn't look like a murderer. Is he?"

"That's for the jury to decide."

"What do you think?"

"What I think is immaterial."

"You won't tell me?"

"It would be unprofessional."

"I bet you've told Gunther," she said. "I bet you tell him everything."

"He's my partner."

"I'm your partner, too."

"Not in the practice of law."

"Or in anything else."

She stirred inside the cocoon as if she were getting ready to emerge, to stretch her wings and fly off to some place warmer and gentler.

"Zan, for chrissake, don't cry."

"Things used to be so different."

"I'll pour you a drink. Would you like a drink?"

"I'm nervous. I'm so t-terribly nervous."

"I'm going to make an appointment for you with Dr. Stoddard."

"No. Please don't, Charles. It's just nerves. I'm just shaky, you know?"

"Yes, I do know. I've seen dozens of speed freaks, in

the jail, in the courthouse, on the streets. They all have the same look, Zan, and you're getting it."

He poured some bourbon from the decanter on the coffee table and handed the glass to her. She was shaking too much to take it, so he held it for her while she sipped. Some of it dribbled out of one corner of her mouth, and he turned his head slightly so he wouldn't have to look at her.

He said, "Does Dr. Stoddard know about the pills?"

"You keep harping on the pills. It's not the pills. I'm just nervous." She finished the bourbon and asked for more. "Aren't you drinking with me?"

"Not tonight. I have to finish some work at the office."

"We never do anything together anymore, never go to the beach club or the country club; we never even have breakfast together."

"I can't afford to sleep until noon," he said. "You used to have interests of your own, Zan, golf, tennis, bridge. Have you given them all up?"

"Tennis tires me out. And I can't sit all afternoon at a bridge table or stand around a golf course watching a bunch of bitchy women cheat on their scores. Maybe we could take a trip together, Charles. Paris or someplace exotic like Morocco?"

"When this case is ended, maybe."

"When this case is ended, there'll be another case," she said with bitter truth. "There'll be no Paris, no Morocco. Hell, we won't even get as far as L.A. Why don't you level with me?"

"All right. There probably won't be a Paris or Morocco, but I'm sure we'll be able to get down to L.A. once in a while."

"Oh, wow. Big deal."

"It's the biggest I can offer right now."

He poured her some more bourbon. This time she was able to hold the glass herself, not steadily but well enough to drink from it. The liquor didn't have the effect he'd hoped for, of making her change the subject.

She said, "A month ago, when you went to the Virgin Islands, you didn't even tell me in advance. Were you afraid I'd invite myself to go along?"

"It never occurred to me."

"Of course not. The Virgin Islands is a honeymoon spot. Why should you take me when you had Gunther along?"

"It was a business trip. We were there two days."

"Oh, a lot can happen in two days."

She made many snide references to his relationship with Gunther. He denied nothing, admitted nothing, treating her like a child whose tantrums would go away if they were ignored.

"Just answer one question, Charles, will you?"

"I'll try."

"Why *did* you marry me? Why in hell did you marry me?"

She unfolded herself from the couch, a pile of bones suddenly articulated into a skeleton. She walked unsteadily toward the doorway, and he knew where she was heading, to her bedroom and whatever drawer she had hidden the pills in—the medicine chest in the bathroom would be too obvious. He knew he couldn't stop her and he didn't try.

She walked out into the hall, her heels ticking on the parquet floor like the clock of a time bomb.

When he went back to the office, he told Gunther about the scene.

"Well," Gunther said, "why did you marry her?"

"She was very pretty and sort of defenseless. She kept phoning me, asking my advice on investing in this or that and what was the difference between a stock and a bond and so on. Finally she invited me to a party at her house. Afterward we made love in the back seat of her father's Rolls-Royce."

"Cute. Classy, too."

"Then later she told me she was pregnant. I was not only gullible in those days, I was actually rather flattered, even intrigued by the idea of having a kid. Of course, the kid never materialized and probably never existed. She didn't want children. . . . Did you ever think you might like a family, Gunther?"

"Hell, I had a family. There were twelve of us. We were always hungry, always fighting. My old lady died trying for thirteen, and my old man went off on a religious binge and disappeared into some obscure cult. Nobody ever saw or heard from him again." Gunther's laugh was bitter with remembered rage.

Donnelly nodded. When he had first rented the office, he used to have his diplomas and credentials framed and hung on the wall, a cum laude here and a cum laude there. After a few months he took them all down. They made him self-conscious, and anyway his clients weren't usually the kind to be impressed by pieces of paper printed in Latin; a lot of them couldn't read any language at all.

"I'm not smart enough to know what I want," Donnelly said. "But I'm smart enough to know what I don't want, and that's some guy sitting on my desk kicking the side of it with his heels. Can't you sit in a chair like a normal person?"

"So that's what normal people do, they sit in chairs. Anything else?"

"They show respect towards their boss."

"That part's going to be tougher, especially if the boss is in a lousy mood. I think I can handle the sitting okay. Is this right?" He turned a chair around, straddled it and leaned against the back with his chin on his forearms. "Is this how normal people do it?"

"Cut out the crap and get down to business."

"All right. I'm driving to Bakersfield tonight. I still think Mrs. Pherson sounds too good to be true. And if she sounds too good to be true, she probably is. I'll find out. I've got a date with her maid, Lucy. Lucy wants to better herself. She goes to night school, which is the reason why we've got a late date. I'm taking her to the Kern County Boll Weevil Barbecue."

"The what?"

"The Boll Weevil Barbecue is put on by a bunch of cotton growers and they don't barbecue boll weevils; they barbecue steak and ribs."

"What's the plan, to ply Lucy with food?"

"That shouldn't be necessary. She's naturally talkative, and she likes the intellectual type."

"Is that what you are?"

"The glasses help."

Donnelly leaned back in his chair and stared up at the ceiling. It was as blank as the walls except for one tiny round spot about the size of the peephole often put in the front doors of residences. He knew it couldn't be a peephole—his office was on the top floor of the building, which had a tile roof—but he was sometimes acutely conscious of it and altered his actions to meet its approval.

"I suggest you begin your trip now," he said.

"Jeez, you really are in a lousy mood. I need money."

"Use your credit cards."

"The boll weevil boys don't cotton to credit cards. . . . Hey, smile. That was a funny."

"Indeed? I have about a hundred cash. You can buy a lot of steak and beer for a hundred. And maybe a lot of Lucy."

"Not Lucy. I said, she wants to better herself."

"What's she look like?"

"Like she needs bettering. Eyes blue, hair brown, measurements nice. Oh, yes, and her father doesn't own a Rolls-Royce; he owns a Ford van. Not as classy but more comfortable."

"I'm sorry I told you about the Rolls-Royce. . . . You're going to be even sorrier if you ever mention it again."

Donnelly opened his eyes and rubbed them, but the mark on the ceiling remained unerasable. Gunther was at the door, and Donnelly called him back.

"Wait a minute. See that little circle up there just left of center?"

"Yeah."

"What do you suppose it is?"

"A bug. I mean, a bug bug, not an electronic bug."

"It never moves."

"So it's a lazy bug."

"No, it's not a bug at all. It's my conscience. I guess you'd call it my conscience."

"You have a very tiny conscience."

"It only looks tiny. In that small space I see all the thousands of eyes that have stared at me in disapproval and the thousands more waiting their turn."

"Have it painted over," Gunther said. "Or cover it with tape."

"I'd still know it was there."

"Well, what do you expect me to do about it?"

"Nothing. You're the last person in the world I'd ask to do anything about it. Those eyes are looking at you, too."

"Jeez, I can't stand all this heavy stuff. I'd better get going."

"When will you be back?"

"Day after tomorrow. I should arrive about the time court convenes."

"Good. Dr. Woodbridge will be on the stand, their pathologist. He'll spend at least an hour listing his credentials and adjusting the projector and screen. Maybe the jury will be impressed by all that, but they won't be impressed by him. He talks very slowly and hesitatingly as if he isn't sure of his facts. And of course, he isn't. Pathology is not an exact science, and there's nothing one pathologist enjoys more than to disagree with another pathologist. That's why we're paying big bucks to bring in Thorvald from Minneapolis and Nesbitt from Baltimore."

"How big?"

"Five and four respectively. Plus expenses, of course. Both are retired and have become what could be called professional witnesses. I don't begrudge them the money—they've got a lousy job."

Gunther had a narrow gap between his two front teeth, and when he blew air through it, it made an expressive hissing sound. "You're blowing a wad on this guy Cully King."

"So?"

"I can't figure out your angle. Besides, I think he's guilty as hell."

"Really? Then perhaps you should be working for the district attorney."

Again Gunther made the hissing sound between his teeth. "You usually *ask* for my opinion."

"That's right. And when I want it, that's what I'll do, ask. It will help our relationship, by the way, if you'll remember that our clients are always pure as the driven snow."

"In my hometown the only snow we saw was either gray or mud-colored. That pure white stuff is only on post-cards of ski resorts. Cully King's not ski resort. He's mud, wouldn't you say?"

Donnelly didn't indicate whether he'd heard this or not. He took out his wallet and removed five twenty-dollar bills. "Here's your money. And remember, if you get a traffic ticket, it's on you, not me."

"Why should I get a traffic ticket?"

"My point exactly. Why should you?"

"You're always coming up with a smart answer."

"That was a question, not an answer. Don't slam the door on your way out. You might disturb my little bug."

The door slammed.

Donnelly picked up the phone and called the county jail. The deputy in charge of inmates reminded Donnelly that it was late, about nine o'clock, and Donnelly reminded him in turn that an attorney was permitted to see his client at any time except during meals and linen changes, when the guards were all busy. There was no further protest.

The county jail was only two years old, and on the outside it looked very modern, a school perhaps, or a hospital or office building. Inside, it was like any other jail, the same sights and sounds, the same smell of disinfectant and of something fainter and harder to identify. The men who came to this place even for a week would never forget it, the sour smell of regrets.

The small consulting room where Donnelly waited for the guard to bring Cully King was windowless. The air blowing in from a vent near the ceiling was cold and very dry, so that almost immediately Donnelly's mouth felt parched and he wanted a drink, but there was no water cooler or drinking fountain. The only furnishing was a steel table and three chairs, all bolted to the floor.

It was ten minutes before Cully King was brought in, wearing jail fatigues and looking drowsy. "I was watching a movie and went to sleep," he said. "I already saw it three times anyway."

"I'd like to go over some things with you. Sit down."

Cully sat in the chair on the opposite side of the steel table. "I'm tired. I think they put stuff in the food to keep us quiet. Somebody told me that tonight at supper."

"Who?"

"The guy sitting next to me."

"So you stopped eating?"

"Yes."

"What happened to the rest of the food on your plate?"

"He ate it."

"What's two and two?"

"Four. But I could see for myself that he was getting sleepy the more he ate."

"You were had, Cully."

"I don't care. The food was no good anyway. I bought three chocolate bars at the commissary. Chocolate is supposed to keep you—well, you know. I don't want to lose my—my—well, you know, my abilities."

"Harry Arnold tells me your abilities are well known throughout the islands. In fact, he called you a horner. I'm not sure what the word means, but I can guess."

"It's talk for a man who fools around with other men's wives. Don't listen to Harry. He's crazy jealous."

"Why?"

"Maybe because Richie's copper like me."

"Did you have anything to do with that?"

"There's a lot of coppers in the islands. And when Harry's at work, his wife's at play. She's a slut."

Donnelly tapped the table with his fingers one at a time, as if he were playing a five-note scale up and down on a piano. "I've met Harry Arnold's wife. She's very black, Richie's more like you."

"Richie's not my son," Cully said with conviction. "I wouldn't mind if he was. He's a good kid. He treats me like some kind of hero."

"Why did you pick the Arnolds to go with you on this trip?"

"They know their business, they work hard and they're strong. This wasn't a pleasure cruise."

"You took some time out for pleasure, I'm told."

"You got that from Harry, too," Cully said without rancor. "Harry's mouth gets big after a few drinks."

"Did you take any women on board the *Bewitched*?"

"Not till Mrs. Pherson. The others were just floozies. They'd steal the smell off a goat. I wouldn't let any of them near my ship."

Donnelly was playing his five-note scale up and down on the table more and more rapidly. It was the only sign he gave of quickening interest. He said, "Repeat your story about how you met Mrs. Pherson."

"I already repeated it ten times."

"So one more won't hurt, will it? You were sitting in the bar at the Casa Mañana Hotel. Why did you pick that place?"

"It looked classy. I was sick of waterfront dives and the stink of sweat and fish. I wanted to go someplace where I could wear my new navy blue blazer and white slacks and turtleneck. I must have looked pretty good, they served me right away. After I had a couple of margaritas, a lady comes in and sits down beside me. There were other seats she could have taken, so I figured—well, what else could I figure?"

"You figured damn fast when all you had to go on was the fact that she sat down beside you. She had to sit someplace if she wanted a drink. So how come all the figuring?"

"I've been around plenty of women. It doesn't have to be spelled out to me."

"Who started the conversation?"

"She did. She said hello or hi, the usual thing."

"Was she wearing any makeup?"

"How do you tell a thing like that? All I know is she looked pretty good. I heard later she was forty, but she seemed much younger. Maybe it was makeup; maybe it was the dim lights in the bar, maybe the margaritas. Women look a lot better after you've had a few drinks. She wasn't exactly sober herself, so maybe I looked better to her, too. Maybe she didn't even realize I was black."

A guard stopped at the barred window of the door and peered into the room. Cully waved at him, and the guard waved back. The brief exchange seemed to bolster Cully's self-confidence.

"I don't need all that stuff like booze and dim lights," he said. "Women are just naturally attracted to me."

"Remember what I told you this morning, Cully. Humble, humble."

"Why should I pretend women don't like me? I say nice things to them, I do nice things. Why shouldn't they like me? . . . Do they like you?"

Donnelly thought of his last conversation with Zan. He didn't say nice things or do nice things, and she hadn't liked him for years. "No."

"You're married, though. You must have looked good to one of them once."

"Yes."

He remembered the night in the back of the Rolls-Royce. It was dark so he couldn't see Zan, but she felt all soft and round, and her skin was cool in the summer night and smelled of flowers. They weren't those picked fresh from a garden but dead ones sprayed with preservatives to make them look alive.

"You're not a bad-looking guy for your age," Cully added.

"Thank you."

"I bet there's plenty of women who'd—"

"I'm not the subject of this conversation," Donnelly said brusquely. "You are, you and Mrs. Pherson. So go on with the story. She came into the bar and sat down beside you and started talking. Then what?"

"I asked her if she wanted a drink."

"And?"

"She sort of hesitated, putting on an act of being the kind of woman who didn't drink. I wasn't fooled, especially when she ordered a double martini."

"How did she drink it?"

"What do you mean, how?"

"Fast, slow, medium?"

"It must have been fast because she ordered another pretty quick."

"Who paid for that one?"

"She did."

"Did she have it put on her hotel bill?"

"No. She paid cash. I figured her husband—she was wearing a wedding ring—had a habit of going over the bills, and she didn't want any bar tab showing up."

"How did the conversation get around to cooking?"

"I can't recall exactly, but I think she asked about good French restaurants in the vicinity. She said she liked French cuisine and did a lot of it at home. Right away I thought of Mr. Belasco because he likes French cooking best. On the spur of the moment I just asked her if she ever cooked professionally, and I told her about the *Bewitched* and the big race coming up and our needing a cook for it. She said, 'Where are you racing to?' and I said, 'Honolulu.' Then she seemed real interested. The word 'Honolulu' is kind of exciting to people who've never been there."

"How do you know she'd never been there?"

"She told me. She said she and her mother had planned to go but her mother got sick and they never made it. I said, 'Well, then, why not sign on as cook for the race? The pay's no good but the trip's great.' She said she would, just like that."

"Right away?"

"Right away."

"Without even thinking about it?"

"Maybe she thinks fast. Or maybe"—Cully attempted to look modest—"maybe she had other things in mind besides cooking. I explained that the *Bewitched* was set to leave in the morning before dawn, and it might be easier for her to come aboard that night. . . . You know."

"*I* know," Donnelly said. "Did *she* know?"

"She knew. She went up to her room, put on a coat and came down again. I waited in the lobby. I saw her standing at the desk talking to a man behind the counter. Then a few minutes later she came across the lobby, carrying her handbag and a green leather case. She was beginning to look better and better to me. I hadn't had a woman since Panama."

"Mazatlán."

"A long time anyway. We went out, got in a taxi and drove to the slip where the *Bewitched* was tied up."

"The green case, did you offer to carry it for her?"

"What do you think I am? Of course I did. But she wouldn't let me. The way she hung on to that thing I guessed something valuable was in it. Actually I didn't think much about it at all. I mean, I was getting pumped up, not having a woman since—"

"Mazatlán."

"Mazatlán. Right."

"And incidentally, watch your language in front of the jury. You were not getting pumped up, you were becoming intrigued."

"Becoming intrigued. Hey, man, that doesn't sound like me?"

"I don't particularly want you to sound like you. I want you to sound like an innocent man, a gentleman, caught in a cruel web of circumstances."

"Becoming intrigued. Is that what a gentleman would say?"

"No."

"Then why me?"

"Because you're on trial for murder. And every word you utter and every action you take, down to the merest twitch of an eyebrow, are going to be fed into the computer each of the jurors carries in his head."

Cully rubbed his eyes as if he were trying to erase images he didn't want to see. "That computer business, it kind of scares me."

"The green case Mrs. Pherson was carrying, what do you think it weighed?"

"I told you, she wouldn't let me touch it."

"So you can't estimate its weight or tell whether the contents made any kind of jangling noise, jewelry, for instance."

"She handled it real careful, gentle almost. It made me suspect there might be drugs inside."

"You thought she might be smuggling drugs?"

"Nearly every week you hear of respectable people being caught smuggling *drugs*."

"From *Bakersfield*?"

"I don't know where that is."

"It's a place where they grow oil, not coco leaves or opium poppies. Oh, yes, and cotton. They grow cotton. So they can have the Boll Weevil Barbecue."

Cully looked puzzled but didn't ask any questions. He regarded Donnelly with awe and with gratitude, and even this far into the trial he still didn't understand why Donnelly had offered to defend him without charge. Cully wasn't used to feeling either awe or gratitude, and the new role made him nervous.

Donnelly said, "The prosecution has witnesses to testify that Mrs. Pherson left the house carrying a green leather jewel case. But because something is a jewel case doesn't necessarily mean it contains jewels. The probability, however, is that it did."

"Well, I didn't know that. I swear on the Bible I didn't know."

"I believe you," Donnelly said, and for the moment he did. In a different light, a different room, he might change his mind. But right now Cully sounded and looked completely sincere, with just the right touch of reproach that anyone could ever doubt him. If the jury could see and hear him now, he would stand a good chance of walking out a free man. So much depended on his demeanor in court, and there was no way Donnelly could control that. He could advise, certainly, but he couldn't be sure the advice would or could be taken. Cully wasn't accustomed to controls. At sea he was the boss, he made the rules; on land it was hard for him to accept other people's.

"Tomorrow," Donnelly said, "will be your first real test.

The district attorney will offer in evidence pictures taken by Dr. Woodbridge, who performed the autopsy on Mrs. Pherson. His testimony will carry a lot of weight because he is the only forensic pathologist to see the actual body. The others who'll take the stand have based their opinions on what may be regarded as secondhand information, tissue slides, lab tests of blood samples and the like. The credentials of these later pathologists may be equally impressive, and their opinions equally valid, but not to a jury. The district attorney is bound to repeat this over and over, that his pathologist is the only one to believe because he was the only one to see the actual body."

"What kind of pictures will the jury be shown?"

"All kinds. The first will be of the body itself from various angles. After the clerk numbers each exhibit, it will be shown to the judge, then to me—and to you, since you'll be sitting beside me—before it is passed along to the jury. All right, when you see the initial picture, how are you going to react?"

"I don't know. I haven't seen it yet."

"You've seen dead bodies before, haven't you?"

"A few."

"How did you feel?"

Cully considered this for a moment. "I felt, I'm glad it's him and not me. And I felt very alive, you know, like going out and getting a woman. My blood was racing."

"You will be looking at pictures of a woman you are accused of murdering. That ought to slow your blood down to a crawl. And while it's crawling, you'll have time to consider this fact: Twelve regular jurors, six alternates, and the thirteenth juror, the judge, will be watching your reactions as you study the pictures."

The statement made Cully uneasy. "Well, how am I supposed to act to give them the right impression?"

"You are an ordinary man confronted with the picture of a woman drowned in the sea. Are you sorry for her?"

"Sure. Naturally."

"So you will exhibit sorrow. Turn away, shaking your head, perhaps closing your eyes. I don't suppose you cry easily."

"I don't know. I never tried."

"When was the last time you cried?"

"I think it was at a movie."

"You saw a dead person in a movie and it brought tears to your eyes?"

"No, it was a horse."

"A horse?"

"It broke its leg and someone shot it. I don't think it was fair, shooting a horse just because it broke its leg."

"Forget the goddamn horse."

"Okay."

"I want you to imagine that I am showing you on this table the blowup of a picture of Madeline Pherson's body when it was brought into the autopsy room. Remember, she didn't want to die any more than the goddamn horse did. So how are you going to act?"

"I don't see why you always get mad at me. I haven't done anything."

"Don't change the subject. The picture is here on this table. Now look at it, dammit."

"I'm looking."

"Indicate shock, sorrow, pity."

"All at once? That's going to be hard."

"One at a time," Donnelly said through clenched teeth. "Now turn your head away, shaking it slightly, blinking your eyes."

Cully did as he was told. His performance was ludicrously exaggerated as if he were on a large stage in front of thousands of people, not playing to an audience of one in a small, cold cubicle of a jail. "How's that?"

"Can't you make it more real?"

"If you make the picture more real."

Donnelly wanted to laugh but didn't. He had to keep this man under control, to avoid any camaraderie. "The pictures will be quite real tomorrow. And they will hit you. Whether or not you think you're prepared, they will hit you. And my advice is to show some emotion. Don't deadpan. I had a client a few months ago who dead-panned himself right into San Quentin, where he'll spend the next ten years. In the adjoining courtroom another murder trial was going on. It was a vicious crime committed by a vicious man. The judge in the case had decided to permit television cameras during the trial. The murderer took full advantage of those cameras. Whenever one was aimed at him, he broke into the most heart-rending sobs. Every night on the local news there was this clown crying up a storm. Both men were found guilty, but the deadpanner got ten years and the murderer got three."

"You want me to *sob*?"

"I want you to show some emotion. If you feel bad, let the jurors see it."

Both men were silent. The guard passed the window; the air conditioner whirred; someone screamed in the distance.

Cully said, "Do you always tell your clients how to act, like they had no feelings or brains or anything of their own?"

"No."

"Why me? Do you think I'm going to make a fool of myself?"

"Whether you make a fool of yourself is your business.

Whether you make a fool of me is mine, and I don't intend to lose this case because some hard-nosed smartass won't take advice."

"That's the second time you've called me that."

"There'll be others."

"I don't want to talk to you anymore."

"I'm not so crazy about talking to you either. But there are things we have to go over. What time did you and Mrs. Pherson arrive at the *Bewitched*?"

"About twenty-one hundred hours."

"Better avoid sea slang. A jury is put off by expressions they don't understand. Before I forget, there's one more thing I want you to do which may turn out to be very important. Let me see your hands."

Cully raised his hands, fingers spread apart.

"I see you bite your nails," Donnelly said. "How long have you been doing that?"

"All my life. As long as I can remember anyway."

"You'll have to stop."

"Why?"

"There isn't time to go into it right now."

"It's tough to stop doing something you hardly know when you're doing it, but I guess I can try."

"Trying's not good enough. Let your fingernails grow. Don't bite, clip or file. Now to get back to Mrs. Pherson, what time did the two of you arrive at the *Bewitched*?"

"Between eight and nine o'clock."

"What did you do for dinner?"

"Picked up a pizza on the way."

"Not very French cuisine."

"It was her idea, not mine. She said she'd never tasted pizza, and she wanted to do a lot of things she'd never done before. As it turned out, she didn't even taste it. As soon as we reached my quarters, she passed out on the bunk without even taking off her clothes. How's that for lousy luck?"

"My heart bleeds. What did you do then?"

"Ate the pizza. Had a couple more drinks. Then I slept for a few hours and got up again at three-thirty to check the engine. Once we cleared the harbor, Harry took over and I went below again for some more sleep. When I woke up, she was standing there staring down at me, the kind of stare that makes a man feel like he's being—you know, measured. It was a funny feeling because I had a blanket over me at the time, she couldn't see—"

"Go on with your story. Did she speak?"

"Not at first. I asked her what was the matter, and she said she wanted to go swimming and I was to come up and stop the boat."

"What was she wearing?"

"Same clothes as the night before; only now they were kind of beat up and wrinkled. So was she. She didn't look so good in the morning light. Also, I had a hangover."

"So she looked beat up—an unfortunate choice of words under the circumstances. Better alter it."

"Okay, she looked pale and sort of sick. She probably had a hangover, too. Maybe she figured the cold water would fix it. I explained how cold the water would be in mid-channel at that time of year, no more than fifty-five degrees. I said we were doing about twelve knots, and it would be crazy to stop the boat just so she could go swimming. She said that maybe I wouldn't have to stop it. That she could keep up, she was an excellent swimmer. I said, so are the sharks. The shark business was what changed her mind."

"Do passengers often go swimming off the boat?"

"Only when it's anchored in tropical waters and Mr. Belasco is having a party."

"So she changed her mind about swimming. What then?"

"We went to the galley, and I made some scrambled eggs and toast, and we drank some of the coffee Harry had left on the stove. We didn't talk much. There wasn't anything to say. The whole thing began to seem like a crazy idea, me and her, the French cuisine, everything."

"I'll emphasize once again how important it is for you to tell me the truth," Donnelly said. "If I don't know what really happened, I'm sunk and you go down with me."

"Why?"

"Let's look at the truth like a destination. If I don't know where this destination is, I can't prevent the prosecutor from getting there. In other words, I have to head him off at the pass."

"I'm telling the truth. I always do. The trouble is people don't believe me because of the color of my skin."

"Cut out that crap, will you?"

"It's not crap. You watch that district attorney; see the way he looks at me like I was scum."

"He looks at everybody like that. Including me." Donnelly said, then added thoughtfully, "Maybe especially me. After the scrambled eggs and toast, what did you do?"

"Relieved Harry so he could get some sleep. I saw the lady only a couple of times that day. Once she was talking to Richie, and later she was standing at the rail, watching a school of porpoises. That night we had a few drinks in my cabin, and both of us began to feel a lot better. In fact, she started to come on strong to me, and one of her earrings scratched my face. She was wearing diamond studs that screwed into her earlobes."

"Another unfortunate choice of language. No studs, no screw. Just tell the jurors she was wearing earrings."

"Anyway, the scratch hurt. I felt there was something

deliberate about it like—well, like she wanted to play rough. I don't like women who play rough, so I pushed her away."

"How?"

"Maybe I grabbed her throat."

"No maybe about it. You grabbed her throat. You'll see pictures of it tomorrow or the next day."

"I had to protect myself."

"You're going to have a hell of a time convincing a jury that a man of your size and strength had to protect himself against a woman just slightly over five feet who weighed one hundred and ten pounds. . . . What happppened then?"

"She took off the earrings and told me to keep them."

"Repeat what she said."

"I just told you. She said, 'Keep them.' "

"Her exact words are important. Just 'Keep them'?"

"Yes."

"What was she wearing?"

"Why do you harp on what she was wearing?"

"Harping is my specialty. What was she wearing?"

"Nothing."

"This woman stood there naked, removed the earrings and there was no conversation while she was doing this except 'Keep them'?"

"She wasn't much of a talker. Also, it wasn't much of a talk situation. She might have said something about being sorry she caused the scratch on my face."

"What did she call you? Mr. King, Cully, Skipper, Captain?"

"I don't think she called me anything."

"No endearments?"

"No."

"All right, she's standing there naked, taking off her diamond earrings. The jurors might find it difficult to picture this scene. For one thing, a woman usually removes her jewelry before she starts undressing."

"It happened like I said. I can't help it if they believe it or not."

"Did she take off one earring and hand it to you, then take off the other and hand it to you and so on? Or did she remove both before giving them to you?"

"What did I say the last time you asked me that?"

"I want to hear what you say this time."

Cully shook his head. "It happened last spring. That's a long time ago. You can't expect me to remember every little detail."

"Yes, I can. I do. So will a great many other people."

Cully's eyes were fixed on the door with a kind of desperate intensity as if he were willing it to open and let him out. "I can't remember."

"Maybe we should take all your answers and average them out and arrive at the truth that way, though it's a little unscientific. You don't recall the order in which she took off the earrings, but you recall her saying, 'keep them.'"

"Yes."

"What do you think she meant by that word 'keep'?"

"Keep is keep. She meant they were mine; she was giving them to me."

"It never occurred to you that she was merely asking you to keep them for her in a safe place?"

"No. Women have given me presents before. They like me."

"How many have liked you thousands of dollars' worth?"

"None until her."

"You still think she intended you to keep the jewelry for yourself?"

"Yes."

"And you acted on that assumption."

"Yes."

"By doing what?"

"First I put them in a drawer beside the bed. Then the next morning I went ashore and found a pawnshop."

"So women give you presents," Donnelly said. "Why?"

"I told you, they like me, they think I'm a good guy. Ask anyone in the islands whether I'm a good guy."

"The islands are several thousand miles away, and the only people whose opinion counts are sitting in the jury box and on the bench. They're the ones you've got to convince what a good guy you are."

Cully took a comb from his shirt pocket and ran it through his hair with quick, compulsive strokes.

"Why are you combing your hair?" Donnelly said. "You're not going any place."

"I do that when I'm nervous."

"Well, don't. I don't like it; the jury won't like it. And why should a good guy like you be nervous anyway?"

"I got the wrong color skin."

"You've got an overactive pecker, that's what you've got. And that's what might do you in."

Cully struck the table with his fist, then took four strides to the door and rapped on the window. A few seconds later the guard appeared and unlocked the door. He looked tired and bored.

Nobody said anything.

Driving home, Donnelly began to weigh once more the pros and cons of putting Cully King on the stand. It might be a necessary move since the average person believed that an innocent man would insist on taking the stand in his own defense. If everything went well—that is, if Cully was able to avoid losing his temper and taking offense at some of the district attorney's accusations and implications—he might make a good witness. In appearance and speech he was quite presentable. On the other hand, his behavior was unpredictable. He would probably do well under direct examination if he could keep from contradicting himself. But on cross-examination he might freeze up. Donnelly had seen many blacks and members of other minority groups, guilty and innocent, withdraw behind a wall of silence like children confronted with the disapproval of an authority figure.

It was hard to imagine Cully freezing up. He was more likely to become talkative. If he were lying, he would pile lie on lie like bricks until the whole thing toppled over on his head. Once Cully had been sworn in as a witness, Donnelly could do nothing to stop the proceedings, no matter how badly they were going for him. This was what bugged Donnelly the most: the thought of having no control over events or over Cully.

He took an exit ramp off the freeway past a café that catered to truckers. It made him think of Gunther. Gunther loved truck stops, claiming that they must serve the best food in town or so many truckers wouldn't stop there. He was probably parked at one right now, eating a hamburger oozing grease and bleeding ketchup and drinking a cup of dishwater coffee. He would sit quietly at the counter, looking completely absorbed in his own thoughts. No one would suspect that he was listening to several conversations simultaneously and would finally settle on one as a target and focus his ears on it, filtering out the other voices and sounds, the rattle of dishes and pots and pans, the local radio station transmitting the hysterical screams of rock singers and the nasal three-chord self-pity of cowboys riding guitars.

Gunther was a gifted eavesdropper. In addition to his

acuity of hearing, he had a genuine interest in other people, a detached interest unclouded by approval or disapproval. Just as surely as his ears focused on one thing so did his mind. He had tunnel vision, tunnel hearing, tunnel thinking, and he would eat the hamburger without tasting it and catch the odor of onions and garlic and cologne over sweat without smelling any of them.

Donnelly was irritated that he was thinking of Gunther, but Gunther would not be thinking of him. ("Donnelly? Donnelly *who*?") The fact that Gunther would not be thinking of Lucy either offered some solace.

The Donnellys lived in the house built by Zan's grandfather. It was in an old, established section of the city, off limits to nouveaux riches because no more land was available for construction and the existing houses were sold under restrictions that were illegal and hence never publicly acknowledged but were strictly adhered to. A property seldom changed owners, and when it did, the new owner would be basically the same as the old. Rich white Republicans were replaced by rich white Republicans. It was the kind of neighborhood the district attorney would like to live in and Donnelly hated. But he needed its protection as well as Zan's protection. No one questioned his background, position in life or the way he voted, although some people were surprised at the kind of client he chose to represent.

The iron gates opened at the touch of a button under the dashboard of his car and closed again behind him. He drove around the side of the house to the garage, which had once been part of the stables for the family's horses. The horses were long since gone and had been replaced by Zan's two Jaguars, a golf cart, a sailboat and the housekeeper's VW convertible.

The old three-story house was spangled with lights. Donnelly knew this was not intended as a welcome home for him but was simply the result of no one's caring enough to turn the lights off, certainly not Zan and almost as certainly not the housekeeper, whose contract stated that she didn't have to lift a finger after eight o'clock at night.

He turned off the lights in each room as he went through the hall and up the stairs. Zan's bedroom door was partly open. This was not a welcome home any more than the lights had been. She'd simply forgotten to close it.

Zan was asleep in her four-poster canopied bed, lying on her side, her hair falling across her face. She looked unreal, a wax profile on a pink satin pillow, and under a pink blanket was a collection of bones not yet assembled. (Assemble this yourself! No tools required! Amazingly lifelike! Batteries extra. Money-back guarantee!)

Her breathing was labored and irregular, fast, slow, stopping completely for two or three seconds, then hurrying to catch up.

"Zan?"

A tortoiseshell cat curled up at the foot of the bed began to purr at the sound of a voice. But the purring was purely reflexive and no more a welcome than the lights left on or Zan's door left open. If he touched the cat, it would get up, arch its boneless back and move away. If he touched Zan, she would wake up moaning.

On the table beside her bed was a glass half filled with water and a bottle of capsules. He picked up the bottle and read the label. "Nembutal 1½ grains, Dr. Casberg." Dr. Casberg's office was in Westwood, and he had issued the prescription to Sarah Killeen, the name of the Donnellys' housekeeper.

Donnelly had no way of knowing how many capsules Zan had swallowed, but obviously it was enough to counteract the amphetamines. Zan was no longer a human being. She had become a battleground in a war between amphetamines and barbiturates, and the battleground was already strewn with dead and dying cells.

He stood looking down at her, feeling the terrible responsibility of doing something he was incapable of doing, saving her life.

"Zan, don't," he said in a whisper. "Don't kill yourself like this. I never meant to hurt you in any way. I wanted to love you. I don't know what happened. But please don't do this to yourself."

He put the bottle of Nembutal in his pocket. Then he began a systematic search of her bureau and desk drawers, looking for other containers of pills and capsules, not sure what the names would be either of the drugs or of the doctors who'd prescribed them.

Zan's drawers were as confused as her life. The housekeeper and maids had probably been instructed not to touch them. Panty hose and nightgowns were entangled with slips, pieces of costume jewelry, bottles of perfume, golf socks, handkerchiefs, keys, letters, bras, cachets. He found twenty-nine containers of different drugs prescribed by a number of different doctors. There were also two soiled unlabeled envelopes containing capsules which were probably street drugs. He put them all in the pockets of his jacket, Dexedrine, Desoxyn, Plegine, Percodan, Valium, Tenuate, Seconal. He had no plan what to do with them except check out the various doctors named. The only name he recognized was that of Zan's own doctor, who had prescribed the Percodan. The checking would have to be done by either himself or Gunther since he couldn't afford to let the office staff start any further gossip.

He began walking across the room, and with each step

he took, the plastic bottles clicked against one another in his pockets. He felt like a burglar. He had, in fact, committed an act of burglary. He refused to think of the consequences of his act or to consider putting the stuff back in her drawers and letting her go on her way, undisturbed. He felt he must make an attempt to stop her destructiveness. Talking did no good. Self-control, willpower, discipline, these words had never meant much to her; now they meant nothing. Direct action was necessary. Her sources of supply must be dried up. It would be easy enough to contact the doctors whose names were on the labels and give them a warning. The street drugs in the envelopes were another matter. How had she gotten hold of them? She avoided even driving through those sections of the city where drug transactions were routine. In fact, she seldom left the house, so her supplier must be someone who could deliver them to her, a maid, a gardener, a mechanic at the foreign car service garage, an operator at the beauty salon where she had her hair and nails done, a clerk in one of the dress shops, a grocery deliveryman.

He closed Zan's door and went back down the stairs, past the library with his collection of lawbooks, the formal dining room, where the bouquets on the long mahogany table were changed daily though no one had eaten there for years, the family dining room, the kitchen and, at the end of the hall, the housekeeper's quarters, a bedroom, sitting room and bath.

He knocked on the door. A dog barked and was ordered to be quiet.

"Who is it?"

"Charles Donnelly."

"It's after eight o'clock."

"I know."

"I'm off duty. My contract specifically states that I am

not obliged to perform any services after eight o'clock."

"I merely want to ask you a question, Mrs. Killeen."

She unlocked and opened the door but didn't invite him inside. Instead, she stepped out into the hall, pushing a little black dog back into the room with her foot. Before the door closed again, Donnelly had a glimpse of a steamy scene from a porn movie.

"It is precisely eleven o'clock, Mr. Donnelly. Surely you recall the terms of my contract."

"Surely I do. I wrote it."

"Well?"

"I went in to say good night to my wife. She was asleep. On the table beside her bed was a bottle of one-and-a-half grain Nembutal which had your name on it and the name of a doctor in Westwood."

She was immediately on the defensive. She pulled her plaid bathrobe up around her throat, tightening the belt with a yank. She was a tall, heavyset young woman with a slight Celtic accent.

"Of course, it had my name on it, Mr. Donnelly. The capsules were prescribed for me. I pulled a muscle in my back when I was helping my sister in Westwood move and I had trouble sleeping. My sister's doctor prescribed Nembutal."

"How is it they were in my wife's room?"

"She asked me if I had something to help her sleep, so I gave them to her."

"Is that all?"

"What do you mean by *all*?"

"Is that all you gave her?"

"Yes."

"Did you ever, at her request, provide her with any other controlled substance?"

"I see what you're getting at," she said, giving her belt

another quick yank. "The answer is no, I'm not her supplier. I know, the whole staff knows, that she's on something. She acts like a lunatic."

"That is not the proper way to refer to your employer."

"I'm off duty."

"If you find it offensive to work for someone who acts like a lunatic, send in your resignation and I'll be glad to accept it."

She recognized a bluff when she saw one and merely smiled. "Oh, I'm quite happy here. Unpredictable behavior is what one expects in domestic service."

"Where is she getting her supplies, Mrs. Killeen?"

"Judging from the bulges in your pockets, you've seen the bottles. So have I. She's getting the stuff from doctors. And if you think you can stop her, you're wrong. Put the lid on one, she'll find others. There are hundreds of doctors in this town. Some of them own planes and helicopters and yachts, and you don't get those by swabbing throats and bandaging knees."

"Thank you," he said. "Good night, Mrs. Killeen."

"Good night, Mr. Donnelly."

She went back into her room, where the little black mongrel had settled in her chair in front of the television set.

"I don't have to be nice to him if I don't want to," she told the dog. "I'm off duty. Anyway, these damn fags shouldn't get married in the first place."

III

The
DISTRICT
ATTORNEY

*I*t was 10:00 A.M.

The jurors' notebooks had been distributed, and everyone in the courtroom was in place except the judge. He remained in chambers, talking to his old friend Quentin Woodbridge. Woodbridge was a tall, spare man about sixty with a semicircular fringe of white hair surrounding his bald pate like a broken halo.

The two men played bridge together twice a week at the University Club. These games were intensely serious. Shoptalk was forbidden. Any conversation was limited to the barest essentials, opening and closing amenities and a rehashing of the game at the bar afterward.

District Attorney Oliver Owen belonged to the same club, but the two men avoided him. Owen was chatty. Silence seemed a challenge to him, a hole to be filled. And he filled it, with trivia, jokes, gossip, political comments and anecdotes about his family. If the jokes had been funny, the trivia interesting, the comments astute and the family stories less boring, he might have been excused on the grounds of his youth (he was forty) and inexperience (he was a latecomer to bridge and refused to believe anyone could take it seriously).

Woodbridge sat on the judge's desk, keeping his hands in his pockets the way he often did, as if he were cold. The judge knew this wasn't the reason.

He said, "Well?"

"It's time to go in."

"I didn't ask you what time it was, Woody. I asked you how you were feeling."

"Me? Fine."

"How fine?"

"Fine enough."

The judge was quiet for a few seconds. "Does Owen know?"

"I didn't tell him."

"He has a way of finding things out."

"If he knew, he would have said something to me, also to everyone else in town. So the assumption is he doesn't." Woodbridge got off the desk. "The bailiff's waiting for me in the hall. I'd better be going."

"Take it easy."

Eva Foster noted the time, 10:09, and the bailiff made the announcement: "All rise. Superior Court in and for the county of Santa Felicia is now in session, Judge George Hazeltine presiding."

Quentin Woodbridge was duly sworn and took his place on the witness stand, carrying several pages of notes to refresh his memory. He consulted these notes frequently as he listed his credentials in a slow, halting voice.

Owen didn't hurry him. He liked the sound of all those university degrees and titles and honors, as if he somehow had a share in them because the doctor was his witness.

"You are a forensic pathologist, Dr. Woodbridge?"

"Yes."

"Would you kindly explain to the jury exactly what a

forensic pathologist is, as opposed to an ordinary pathologist?"

"A forensic pathologist has degrees in both law and medicine."

"Where did you obtain such degrees, Dr. Woodbridge?"

"My law degree is from the University of Southern California in Los Angeles. My medical degree is from Johns Hopkins University in Baltimore."

"Before either of those you had a Bachelor of Science degree, did you not?"

"Yes."

"Where did you obtain that?"

"The University of Michigan."

"The University of Michigan," Owen said.

At her stenotype machine Mildred Noon made a note of the repetition. It was a device called echoing, used by attorneys to allow time for framing the next question. The device aggravated the difficulties of accurate court reporting, and before the trial began, Mildred had sent a friendly note to Owen and Donnelly urging them to avoid it and other annoyances like overlapping, speaking when someone else was already speaking, thus preventing the verbatim reporting required by law. Donnelly had ignored the note. Owen acknowledged it with a note of his own: "Mrs. Noon, for your information, I never echo. And if overlapping is caused by opposing counsel, it is not my responsibility."

Owen continued. "While at the University did you receive any scholastic honors?"

"I graduated magna cum laude."

"And were you elected to any scholastic society or fraternity?"

"I have a Phi Beta Kappa key."

"And later at medical school did you receive any similar honor?"

"Yes."

"And what is that called?"

"Alpha Omega Alpha. It is given only to the top graduates in medicine."

"Are you a member of any professional organizations?"

"Yes."

"And what are they?"

"The American Medical Association and the American Bar Association."

"Did you ever serve in the armed forces, Dr. Woodbridge?"

"Yes."

"What branch?"

"The United States Navy."

"In what capacity?"

"I was an internist at the Naval Hospital in Bethesda, Maryland."

"Was it during your service as an internist that you decided to specialize in pathology?"

"Yes."

"How did this come about?"

"There was an opening in the homicide investigation department, and I was given the opportunity to fill it."

"Have you subsequently had other positions in this line of work?"

"Yes."

Donnelly said, without rising, "In the interest of saving time and getting on with the evidence, defense stipulates that Dr. Woodbridge is well qualified."

"The prosecution is entitled to submit a full account of Dr. Woodbridge's education, experience and expertise," the judge said. "Opposing counsel will be afforded similar opportunities when the time comes. Please continue, Mr. Owen."

"Thank you, Your Honor. Dr. Woodbridge, how long did you remain at Bethesda Naval Hospital?"

"Five years."

"During these five years did you publish any medico-legal articles?"

"I coauthored one paper and was a contributor on three others."

"Where were these published and in what year?"

Woodbridge shuffled through his notes. He had used the same ones during a dozen trials, and he should have been able to read them off quickly and easily. But his hands trembled, and everything seemed so long ago and irrelevant. Why was he here in this somber poorly lit room trying to find the names of obscure journals containing outdated information?

After three or four minutes his lower lip began to quiver like that of a child about to cry.

The judge, watching him from the bench, saw the signs of weariness in his old friend and declared a morning recess before the usual time of eleven o'clock. As the courtroom began to clear, he leaned down and asked Woodbridge to come to his chambers.

On his way to the judge's chambers Woodbridge's gait was unsteady, and he had a curious sensation of watching himself, an old man shuffling back through the years, trying to find things and people that didn't matter. Had they ever mattered, these endless rows of dead bodies? Had they ever mattered, these unread reports on un-mourned, unremembered people?

In chambers Woodbridge lay down on the leather couch without waiting to be asked.

"You said you felt fine," the judge said.

"I said fine enough."

"How much is enough?"

"Enough to get through another day. Look, George, I'm just tired. I'm tired of courtrooms and trials, I'm tired of attorneys. God knows I'm tired of dead bodies."

"I have to say this, Woody, so listen to me. I think you should stop working."

"And do what?"

"Do what? You don't have to do anything."

"There are sixteen waking hours in a day. How do I spend them?"

"You might try improving your bridge game."

"My bridge game wouldn't need improving if my partner would read my signals correctly."

"I do not consider a kick under the table a legitimate signal."

"Nor do I. The kick was involuntary."

"Oh. Sorry." The judge hesitated. "Do you get spasms like that often?"

"You stick to legal questions, George. Leave the medical stuff to me."

"It wasn't intended to be a medical question but a personal one, a friend showing interest in a friend."

"Nonsense. You were prying." Woodbridge sat up. "Actually quite a few people have occasional spasms, even dead ones. I knew in advance, of course, that bodies will sometimes move when a muscle contracts. But the first time it happened it damn near scared the pants off me."

Both men laughed, more as a release from tension than from amusement.

Woodbridge said, "Crazy, isn't it? A couple of old codgers on their last legs like you and me being asked to decide

whether a healthy young man like Cully King will live or
die."

"You're wrong, friend. We're not deciding the life or
death of Cully King. You're only a witness; I'm only the
judge."

"Oh, come on, George, everyone knows the judge is
the thirteenth juror."

"Only twelve ballots are cast."

"Right. But you can slant a case one way or another."

"Only at the risk of being overturned on appeal. I might
take such a risk if I were completely convinced of the
guilt or innocence of a defendant. In this case I have no
such conviction. I'm staying out of it. I'm an observer."
He rose from his chair, looking down at his legs. They
were without doubt his last legs, but they were also his
first ones, and he had a certain respect, even affection
for them, especially when they were well concealed be-
neath his trousers and he could imagine the strong muscles and tanned skin of his youth.

"What the hell," he said. "Let's lighten up. How about
a drink? Are you supposed to drink?"

"No. Are you?"

"No."

"So let's have at it. Will scotch do?"

"Scotch," the doctor said, "will do wonders."

Oliver Owen called his wife, Virginia, from one of the
two telephones in the attorney's room.

"Is that you, Vee?"

"I don't see who else it could be, Oliver."

"A maid, cleaning woman, your sister. One can't be too
careful."

"I don't have a maid or cleaning woman, and my sister

109

lives in Stuttgart. So yes, I guess it's me."

"I won't be home for lunch. Judge Portelli has asked me to eat with him. We'll probably go someplace where they serve wop slop."

"Don't talk like that. You love Italian food. By the way, the school just called. They're having an emergency teachers' meeting this afternoon—something about vandalism—and they're sending all the kids home at noon. It's ruined my schedule. I'm supposed to do my stint as a pink lady at the hospital."

"The boys are old enough to be left at home by themselves."

"Not if you want a home to come back to."

"That's absurd. They're the best-behaved boys in town. . . . I have an idea. Why don't you drop them off here on your way to the hospital? They can spend some time in court watching their old man in action. They might get inspired."

"Fine," Vee said, and hung up, somewhat depressed at the thought of the boys spending the afternoon at a murder trial. They might get bored, they might get ideas, but the last thing in the world they'd get was inspired.

Vee replaced the telephone on the small white desk in a corner of the kitchen. This corner was her own personal space. Sitting in the stenographer's chair in front of the typewriter she'd used in college, she felt that she was a real person, quite apart and distinct from Oliver and the boys. The corner was as private as a voting booth, and she could mark her ballots any way she chose.

She was a small, pretty woman with lively brown eyes and dark hair that was as tightly curled as a poodle's and could never be beaten into submission with a brush. During her fifteen-year marriage she and Oliver had three sons. In their father's presence the boys had beautiful manners even at the table and addressed their elders as ma'am and sir. Away from home they were unmitigated hellions, noted for their provocative mischief at school, at camp and on field trips. Vee often felt that they didn't belong to her at all, that she had merely been used as a vessel and then put in dry dock.

When the boys' transgressions were reported to her, she kept them to herself, knowing that if she told Oliver, he would either express disbelief or else manage to blame her in some way.

On Sundays Vee went to church with what she called her four boys. They were a handsome, dignified group, looking as if they might be posing for the cover of a church magazine. During hymns they sang lustily, except for Chadwick, whose voice was changing and who'd been instructed by his father to keep quiet and merely open and close his mouth at the proper times. So Chadwick opened and closed his mouth. A careful observer might have noticed that the openings and closings were some-what exaggerated like those of a patient in a dental chair. But most of the congregation thought Chadwick, with his light brown curls and angelic blue eyes, was the picture of an ideal son. It would have been difficult for any of them to imagine Chadwick putting epoxy glue in the hair of the girl who sat in front of him in social studies class.

When word of the incident reached Oliver, he went to the principal's office in righteous indignation.

"My son Chadwick does not even know of the existence of such a thing as epoxy glue."

"Then he can't have been paying much attention in chemistry class," the principal said.

"In the unlikely event that the story turns out to be true, there must be a logical explanation for it."

"I'd like to hear one."

"The girl's hair was probably long and bushy and impaired my son's view of the blackboard, so he took steps to correct the situation."

"Most ingenious."

"Oh, yes, he's a very clever chap."

Chap wasn't the word the principal would have chosen, but he didn't bother arguing. A lawyer was a lawyer.

Chadwick was warned, the epoxy glue confiscated from his locker and the girl's parents dropped their damage suit because their daughter's new short hairdo was very becoming.

When the school janitor found graffiti written in semi Latin all over the walls of the boys' lavatory, suspicion fell immediately on Jonathan. No detective work was required to bolster this suspicion: Jonathan was one of only three students taking Latin, and the other two were girls.

PRINCIPALIS SCREWAT OMNES GIRLS IN OFFICIO

The accusation was close enough to the principal's deepest feelings to make him deal harshly with the culprit. Jonathan was forced to scrub the lavatory walls with a toothbrush and to write "*mea culpa*" 1,000 times on the blackboard. Jonathan wrote the words 999 times, figuring no one would bother to count, and no one did. It was a small victory in a large war, but Jonathan boasted about it to his brother Chadwick, who told his brother Thatcher, who told his teacher, who told the principal. Jonathan returned to the blackboard for 1,001 more *mea culpa*'s.

On learning about the whole thing in a letter from the principal, Vee confronted Jonathan in his bedroom.

"That was really stupid, Jonathan."

"Yes, ma'am."

"You might just as well have signed your name to the graffiti."

"I thought of that, but—"

"What am I going to do with you, Jonathan?"

"You could always bat me around the room a little."

"You know I can't bat you around the room. You're bigger than I am."

"Sorry about that. I guess we'll have to think of something else. Maybe we should tell my father and make it his problem."

"God, no."

"Or we can build a rack in the backyard. You know, one of those devices they made to torture people by stretching them. That way we could kill two birds with one stone. I'll get tall enough to make the basketball team and you can satisfy your lust for punishment."

"I don't have any lust for punishment."

"Whatever."

"Promise me you'll never write any graffiti again."

"Yes, ma'am. Or should that be no, ma'am?"

"Just say you promise never to write any graffiti again."

"I promise never to write any graffiti again," Jonathan said, adding silently, *in Latin*.

The youngest boy, Thatcher, was Oliver's favorite. Since Thatcher showed no literary, artistic, athletic or musical ability, it was decided he should become a lawyer. After graduating from law school, he would spend a year or two in some prestigious law firm, then run for Congress, distinguish himself in the House or Senate, and ultimately, if the political climate were right, make a bid for the presidency.

Thatcher already had what Oliver considered a promising start. He could recite the names of all the Presidents in order, and frequently did, with oratorical flourishes that could make the halls ring, the audience cringe and former Presidents toss in their graves. Repeat performances were given at his parents' dinner parties, school and church socials, Kiwanis picnics and Republican fund-raisers. It was, perhaps, not much of a talent, but some Presidents had started with less.

One morning, after the boys had left for school, Vee suggested to her husband that it was time for a change.

"Oliver, don't you think Thatcher should break in a new act?"

"A new act? It's not an act, my dear woman."

"Well, whatever it is, people are probably getting sick of it."

"People getting sick of hearing the names of their own Presidents recited by a boy whose name might well be added to that list someday?"

"Do try to be objective, Oliver. How would you like it if you had to listen over and over to little Wendy Morris recite all the constitutional amendments?"

Oliver's coffee cup, on its way to his mouth, stopped in midair. "The constitutional amendments, constitutional amendments. Why, Vee, that's a marvelous idea, splendid. I'm surprised I didn't think of it myself. A list of the constitutional amendments is the next logical step. Let's see, how many do we have now?"

"Too many," Vee said. "Many too many. I mean, Thatcher is only ten years old."

"When I was ten, I could recite whole pages of the Bible. Yes, I can see Thatcher now, standing in front of an audience, his small voice pronouncing the great truths of our Constitution. Can't you picture it, Vee?"

"Yes. Oh, yes, I can picture it." Vee slapped some jam on an English muffin and hoped she would be forgiven, not only by Thatcher but by God and future audiences.

"And dates should be included, of course," Oliver said. "It's too bad Thatcher has trouble with numbers, but we'll manage. Vee, my dear, I sometimes underestimate you. You are as smart as you are pretty."

Coming from Oliver, this was the equivalent of a passionate declaration of love, but Vee was not moved to respond in kind. *I should have kept my big mouth shut. Poor Thatcher, it will take him weeks to learn the amendments, and he'll never get the dates straight. He has a rotten memory. I wonder if any of our Presidents had rotten memories.*

Oliver's dream flowed on, unimpeded by flotsam or jetsam or common sense. "By the time Thatcher applies for admission to law school he'll have an edge. And he'll need it, what with all the minorities the schools of higher education are being forced to accept nowadays."

"Oliver, don't you think Thatcher is getting a little old to be shown off in public like this?"

"Shown off? Encouraging my son to remind people of their great American past cannot be construed as showing him off. And don't forget, my dear, it was *you* who suggested the constitutional amendments. Doesn't that fill you with pride?"

"Not really." She was filled instead with guilt and the disturbing prospect of going through life branded as the woman responsible for Thatcher's memorizing the constitutional amendments and passing them along to countless captive audiences throughout the city.

During the recess Donnelly also made a telephone call. Since he intended it to be kept private, he passed up the phones in the attorneys' room and used one of the public booths in the hall.

"Ellie? This is Charles Donnelly. I'll be brief. I want you to get your boss to come down to courtroom number five between now and noon or this afternoon between two and four. Yes, I know he's busy. But this is literally a matter of life and death. Remind him he owes me one, a big one. All I ask is that he sit in the courtroom and observe. Then I'll get back to him later. I repeat, it's a matter of life and death."

Dr. Woodbridge returned to the stand and continued listing his credentials. The jurors, who had come back from their coffee break fairly alert, now lapsed into a kind of stupor. They didn't know what terms like "board accreditation" meant, and when it was explained, they didn't much care and were inclined to side with Donnelly's request for cutting out this kind of time wasting. Juror No. 3, the cement finisher Paloverde, accustomed to hard work in the open air, fell asleep in the close atmosphere of the courtroom and woke up only at the sound of a commotion in the hall. Even the heavy carved oak door, three inches thick, failed to smother the noise of a woman screaming.

"—where I was consultant to the Veterans Administration Hospital in Sawtelle."

"That's in California?"

"Yes."

"Please speak up, Dr. Woodbridge," Owen said, but the judge interrupted.

"Hold everything, please." He nodded to Di Santo, his bailiff, and Di Santo went out into the corridor. Three or four minutes later he returned, his face red and moist. Semicircles of sweat were staining the underarms of his shirt. He approached the bench, wiping his face with a handkerchief.

"There's a deranged woman in the hall," he told the judge in a whisper.

"Get rid of her."

"She won't go. She wants to come in here."

"Why?"

"She claims someone here robbed her and she wants to make a citizen's arrest."

"Did you tell her there's a trial going on?"

"That's what I was trying to do when she—when she —when she—" He leaned closer to the bench. "She spit in my eye. I've never been spit in the eye before. It's humiliating. How do you defend yourself against a thing like spit in the eye?"

"Go out there and get rid of her."

The bailiff turned to obey, but before he was halfway to the door, a woman staggered into the courtroom. Two men, a deputy and a man in work clothes, had been attempting to restrain her by hanging on to her arms. But she slipped out of their grasp and left them holding an empty coat. She came screaming past the first row of spectators right into the well.

"There he is!" She shook her fist at the counsel's table. "He robbed me. He took my pills. Arrest him! Arrest him!"

Donnelly didn't move or even blink. He sat like a marble man while a bailiff and a deputy grabbed his wife from behind. She hadn't stopped to dress, only to put on slippers and a coat over her pajamas. The coat lay on the floor near the doorway like the cast-off skin of a snake.

"I want him arrested. He's trying to kill me. He took away the pills that are keeping me alive."

"Have a deputy drive her home," the judge said to Di Santo.

One of the spectators opened the door, and Zan was half dragged, half carried out into the hall. As the door closed, there was an eerie silence, as if she had fainted or been knocked unconscious.

For the first time since the trial began the jurors started

to talk among themselves in court. The touch of madness seemed to have drawn them together in a closed circle like pioneers attacked by Indians.

The judge pounded his gavel for attention.

"We will have a ten-minute recess." After the jurors and most of the spectators had filed out, he spoke quietly to Donnelly, "I'll see you in chambers, Mr. Donnelly. . . . Mr. Donnelly?"

"Yes," Donnelly said. "I'll be there."

"You can use my door."

"Thanks."

The two men went out the door behind the bench, past the evidence room into the judge's chambers. Donnelly crossed the floor carefully as if it had been mined.

"Your wife seems pretty upset," the judge said.

"Yes."

"I haven't seen her for two or three years. Has she been ill?"

"Yes."

"She looks as though she should be in a hospital."

"Yes."

"I gather you don't want to discuss the situation. . . . Well, I have to. An incident like this must not occur in my courtroom again."

"I am not responsible for my wife's actions."

"If what she said is true, you're responsible for this particular action, aren't you?" When Donnelly didn't reply, the judge added. "Did you confiscate her pills?"

"Yes."

"Why?"

"So she couldn't get at them."

"That sounds as if more than one kind of pill was involved. What's she been taking?"

"Uppers in the morning, downers at night, sometimes both at the same time, anytime."

"She ought to be getting help. Confiscating her pills won't do it. You'd better call her doctor and have him go over and see her."

"I did. He's probably there now wondering where she is. Thanks, by the way, for having her driven home. I'll pick up her car if I can find it."

"What are you going to do about her condition?"

"Whatever is possible," Donnelly said. "Which isn't much. She doesn't qualify for legal commitment. Putting her in a drug abuse prevention center requires her consent. So does entering her in a convalescent home. Are there any other options?"

"Give her back the pills and hire round-the-clock nurses to dole them out and keep an eye on her. I'm not speaking now as a judge but as a concerned observer."

"Thank you."

"About the only action I can take legally is declare a recess until this afternoon, giving you a chance to go home and straighten things out. It's too early to go back into court. I said ten minutes, didn't I?"

"Yes."

"We have half of it left. Sit down."

Donnelly sat in the chair on the other side of the judge's desk. The judge was staring at him over the top of his spectacles.

"Tell me, Donnelly. Do you believe in genetic programming?"

"To some extent."

"You know what? I'm beginning to go for it hook, line and sinker. I mean, I'm strongly tempted to believe that you and I were genetically programmed to be here together in this room at this minute discussing this subject. Does that strike you as crazy?"

"Debatable, certainly."

"It has nothing to do with religion or anything like that, just genes, DNA, some mechanism we haven't yet discovered and probably never will. There isn't time." He removed his spectacles and put them on the desk. "Do you suppose you and I were programmed to have a drink at this point?"

"I could suppose that, yes."

"Well, I'm not one to fly in the face of fate or kismet or DNA." The judge for the second time that morning brought out the bottle of scotch and two glasses. "I wonder if I'm programmed to become an alcoholic."

"It seems unlikely at your age."

"I guess I'll just have to wait and see. Cheers."

"Cheers."

Zan's Jaguar was not in either of the parking lots across from the courthouse, so Donnelly began walking around the block. He found the car near the front entrance parked on a yellow curb. The doors were unlocked, the key was in the ignition and Zan's purse lay on the front seat. The sight of the abandoned car affected him more than her appearance in court or even the scene with her the previous night. It was strangely symbolic. The key in the ignition seemed to be waiting for someone to take charge, and the purse on the seat an invitation to someone to assume ownership. Zan couldn't take charge or own anything, not even herself. She had been exchanged for some plastic bottles and two dirty envelopes.

Without even touching the car he went back into the courthouse, called his office and told his receptionist to meet him at the front entrance immediately. Then he went outside again to wait.

He sat on the concrete and metal bench at a bus stop. He had never before sat at a bus stop or given one more than a passing glance or wondered about the people waiting there. A teenaged Mexican boy was reading a book on computers while a pensioner dozed under a straw hat.

At the other end of the bench was a young black woman with two small children. She had a paper bag on her lap with flowers sticking out of the top. The children were sharing a box of Cracker Jack. They stared at Donnelly with the frank, friendly curiosity of the very young.

"Hello," Donnelly said.

The mother's arm shot out with the speed of a karate expert and pulled both the children toward her.

"Don't you speak to no strange men, you hear?"

Donnelly's emotions seemed to be rising closer to the surface with each of the day's incidents. Normally he would have ignored the woman's remark, probably would not even have heard it or taken it personally. Now it bothered him. What did she mean by a strange man? Did she mean a stranger? Or did she feel instinctively that he was strange?

"I'm sorry," he said. "I didn't intend—"

"Pertaining to myself, I don't speak to no strange men neither."

The paper bag on her lap rattled; the flowers nodded their heads; the children continued eating Cracker Jack.

"I'm sorry," he repeated, and there was something in his voice that brought the old man out of the past and the teenager out of the future. They both looked at him disapprovingly as though he were an unwelcome intruder from the present.

The clock in the courthouse tower struck the third

quarter of the hour. He sat on the flagstone steps of the entrance and watched a pigeon drink from the fountain. It was a day of firsts. He had never before watched a pigeon drink. It dipped its bill in the water, then threw its head back like a man gargling.

He wondered how long he was genetically programmed to sit on the courthouse steps and watch a pigeon drink.

Shortly before two o'clock District Attorney Owen arrived for the afternoon session with his three sons, Chadwick, Jonathan and Thatcher. They were big, handsome boys who bore a strong resemblance to their father. Bailiff di Santo had been forewarned and set aside three seats in the front row. He solemnly presented each boy with a notebook and a ballpoint pen, the same kind the jurors used.

Thatcher, the youngest, construed his notebook and pen as gifts and thanked the bailiff with a fine, firm handshake. The other two eyed theirs with suspicion.

Chadwick said, "What's this for?"

"To make notes," the bailiff told him.

"Notes like about what?"

"The trial. What's going on, et cetera."

"Nothing's going on."

"Court hasn't convened yet. When court convenes, you will see the American judicial system at work."

"Jeez," Jonathan said. "This is worse than school. I thought we came here for fun."

"This is not," the bailiff said, "a fun place."

The boys were the center of attention until the jurors returned to their seats. Dr. Woodbridge took his place in the witness box, and the judge reentered through his private door.

Dr. Woodbridge began showing his long list of blown-up pictures of the body of Madeline Pherson. The pictures were shown to the defense counsel, the judge and then the jury. Spectators caught only a glimpse of them, which considerably disappointed the boys.

Chadwick picked up his pen and wrote: "This is not a good example of the American system of justice on account of I can't even see the pictures. What's so judicial about that?" At this deprivation the boys began to protest in whispers until their father turned and scowled them into silence.

It was Jonathan who seconded his older brother's opinion: "This is a rotten example of the American judicial system on account of I can't even see the evidence."

The idea of communicating by note caught on and there was a flurry of exchanges:

O. O. should let his hair grow longer so his ears won't stick out.

The judge looks snockered.

Watch the way that clerk shakes her boobs when she walks.

O. O. is boring.

One of the jurors in the front row is asleep.

So am I. I am writing this in my sleep.

That's what it looks like, you morron.

I vote we split. People are going in and out all the time so no one will notice.

Are you nuts? O. O. will miss us.

He'll miss Thatcher. You and me can split and Thatcher can stay.

I wanna split too I'm just as bord as you are You gotta take me along.

Shut up and write the names of the presidents backwards. Ha ha ha.

If you leave me here I'll cry.
Jeez he wil too. And O. O. will take his side.
O.K. we all stay. and die like heroes.
I don't wanna die. If you make me die Ill cry.
Dying's too good for you you little shit.

The district attorney turned again toward the spectators and saw his boys diligently writing in their notebooks. He felt pride rising up through his chest like gas.

Jonathan saw the expression on his father's face and interpreted it correctly.

He wrote:

He's going to brag about this at his club. We better start paying attention. Who's on trial?

The black guy.

Do you think he's guilty?

How would I know? I never saw him before.

O. O. thinks he's guilty.

O. O. thinks everybody's guilty.

Jeez, what if he wants to see our notebooks afterwards?

We'll tell him he'll have to get a search warrant.

In case he does we got to have something to show him.

Such as what?

Do we think the black guy is guilty or not?

Chadwick wrote: "A man is innocent until proven guilty by the evidence. Evidence must be based on facts. I don't have any facts, so maybe he is and maybe he isn't."

"This," Jonathan wrote, "is a baffling case because I don't know anything about it. I've never seen a dead body except in movies and TV. I'd like to become a pathologist so I could see a real dead body (providing the pay is right)."

Thatcher wrote, "My dad is the best districk atturny in the world so the black guy is guilty. I saw a dog on the lon. I want a dog. Why don't we by a dog?"

During the course of the afternoon the boys learned a number of interesting facts.

The body of the woman bore numerous contusions, abrasions and lacerations. ("Hell," Jonathan said, "my body's got those all the time.")

The woman had four broken ribs, three on the left side, one on the right. ("Hey," Chadwick said, "remember when Thatcher broke two ribs falling out of a tree and cried for a year?")

The woman's lungs contained only a small amount of salt water. Lungs are seldom filled with water in drowning victims. ("I bet I swallowed more than a small amount when I was learning to surf," Chadwick said. "You never did learn to surf," Jonathan replied.)

The cause of the woman's death was asphyxsia caused by immersion in water.

Each of the boys wrote their verdicts in their notebooks.

Guilty   Chad Owen
Guilty   Jon Owen
Gilty   Thatcher Hamilton Owen, Esq.

When court adjourned at four-thirty, a deputy in plain clothes drove the boys home in a sheriff's car.

Thatcher asked the driver, "Are you a real cop?"

"Pinch me and find out."

"I might get arrested."

"You bet. For assaulting an officer."

"I hope," Jonathan said, "you get life."

"I don't want life. I don't want—"

"Oh, shut up, you little shit. With any luck they'll give you the gas chamber."

Thatcher protested. "I'm sick of being a little shit."

"Cheer up," the deputy said. "Eventually you'll grow up to be a big shit."

It was a bad day for Thatcher. The amendments were sprung on him that night after dinner while the family was still sitting at the table.

"Thatcher and I," Oliver announced, "will now adjourn to the library."

Vee sighed audibly, the two older boys exchanged wary glances and even Thatcher, not noted for his acuity of senses, smelled something in the wind.

"Why?" Thatcher said.

"Because we have an important matter to discuss."

"Why?"

"Stop repeating why like some idiot parrot," Vee said. "Just go and get it over with."

As a favor to his brother—who would, of course, be expected to pay it back in full plus extras—Jonathan tried to change the thrust of the conversation. "I wonder if parrots understand what they're saying when they talk, also other members of the parrot family, cockatoos, macaws, budgerigars, cockatiels, et cetera, et cetera."

"Be quiet." Vee's voice was so sharp that all four males stared at her as if she were a robot who had suddenly acquired the power of speech. Then the two older boys started clearing the dishes from the table without being told, and Thatcher and his father retired to the library, where Oliver explained the object of their meeting.

"What's an amendment?" Thatcher said.

"An amendment is something added to the original to alter it, usually for the better."

Thatcher considered this thoughtfully. "You mean like a lady going to a doctor to have her boobs made bigger?"

"No. No, I would not place a constitutional amendment in the same category as the amplification of a lady's bosom."

"What's a bosom?"

"You are beginning to annoy me, Thatcher."

"I can't help it. I'm supposed to know these things if I'm going to grow up and be President."

"Very well. Mathematically speaking a bosom equals two boobs."

"I heard Mom talking on the phone about a lady called Betty who had her—"

"Thatcher."

"Yes, sir."

"Shut up."

"Yes, sir."

"Now, our mission is to memorize the amendments to our Constitution."

"What's a constitution?"

"The law of the land. The first ten amendments are generally referred to as the Bill of Rights."

"The *first ten*?" Thatcher repeated. "Holy moly, how many tens are there?"

"There are two tens plus six. To wit, twenty-six constitutional amendments. I'll read you the first one. Listen carefully. Are you listening carefully, Thatcher?"

"Twenty-six. Holy gophers."

"Amendment One has to do with restrictions on the powers of Congress. It reads as follows: 'Congress shall make no law respecting an establishment of religion, or prohibiting the free exercise thereof; or abridging the freedom of speech, or of the press; or the right of the people peaceably to assemble, and to petition the government for a redress of grievances.' December fifteenth, 1791. Do you understand that, Thatcher?"

"No."

"Do you understand any of it?"

"No."

"Why not?"

"Too many big words."

"They may seem big to you now, son, but as you memorize them, they will shrink."

"How much will they shrink?"

"Thatcher, I am becoming exasperated."

"I know. Your face is getting red. Mom says when your face starts to get red, we better get the hell out."

Oliver looked genuinely shocked. "That's quite impossible. Your mother doesn't use profanity."

"Not when you're around."

"Perhaps you misunderstood her."

"No. She used short words. They might have been big to begin with and they shrinked."

"Shrank. Shrink, shrank, shrunk."

"Yes, sir."

"Now, to get back to the amendments, what was the purpose of Amendment One?"

"I don't know."

"Was it to restrict the powers of Congress?"

"I guess so."

"There, you're catching on already. I knew you would. Now repeat after me: Congress shall make no law—"

"Congress shall make no law . . . I wonder if there's a law about dogs. I think they should pass a law making everybody buy a dog. I saw a dog on the courthouse lawn that was real cute and fuzzy. Why don't we buy a dog?"

"I don't want a dog."

"What if Congress passes a law *forcing* you to get one?"

"I would obey such a law, of course, but—"

"*Oh, wow.* Think of it. All of us with dogs, Mom and you and Chad and Jon and me, me with the biggest because I'm the smallest. Oh, wow. Me and my big dog could beat up on Chad and his littlest one. And all the kids in the neighborhood could take their dogs to school and we could have fights at recess. Oh, wow."

Oh, wow. Oliver echoed the words silently and stared up beyond the library window toward the heavens. God, as usual, was elsewhere.

Later that night, when Vee and Oliver were about to retire, Vee was brushing her hair, and Oliver his teeth. He was a diligent brusher, ten rotary strokes at the front and back of each tooth, the brush held at a forty-five-degree angle to remove plaque at the gum line.

He came out of the bathroom and stood behind Vee at her dressing table. "Does my face really turn red when I'm mad?"

"Fifty-seven, fifty-eight. Yes."

"And did you actually tell the boys that when my face turns red, they'd better get the hell out?"

"I might have said something of the sort."

"Why?"

"It seemed like sensible advice."

"Couldn't you have phrased it another way?"

"Like what?"

"Like, 'Boys, when your father is provoked, kindly remove yourselves from his presence.'"

"I could have phrased it like that, but I didn't. The boys respond better to simple language. 'Get the hell out,' is more vivid and compelling than 'Kindly remove yourselves from his presence.' Don't you agree?"

"Unfortunately, yes."

He put his hands on her shoulders while she finished brushing her hair. In the soft pink light of the twin boudoir lamps she looked very pretty and almost as young as when he first met her, the day he graduated from law school.

She had come to the graduation party with someone else, and he'd brought another girl. It was love at first sight. They were married as soon as Oliver took a job with a law firm. Vee worked for the first year, up until the day before Chadwick was born.

Vee enjoyed her children, accepting their various phases and faults as she accepted changes in the weather. She knew perfectly well Thatcher would be lucky if he got into college, let alone law school, Congress and the presidency. She knew, too, that eventually Oliver would come to his senses, and they could have a nice, normal life.

Meanwhile, there were the amendments.

He told her about Thatcher's idea of a new amendment making it mandatory for each person to own a dog.

"How sweet," Vee said.

"Not really."

"Oh, but it is. You know how Thatcher's always going up to strange dogs and petting them."

"Oh, yes, I know. I paid for the thirty-six stitches on his hand last year. Besides, the object of Thatcher's proposed amendment doesn't involve petting but rather the staging of boy-dog fights on the school grounds."

She laughed. He didn't.

"I'm beginning to doubt," he said somberly, "that Thatcher is presidential timber."

"He won't be eligible to run for another twenty-five years so you might as well stop worrying about it for now and come to bed. Whose turn is it to switch off the lamps?"

"Yours."

"I thought it was yours."

"All right, mine."

She got into bed, and he switched off the lamps and joined her.

They lay together in the darkness, their bodies touching but separated by Thatcher and the amendments and the dog, by the trial and the pictures of the dead woman and the smiling brown face of the man who may have killed her, by Vee's broken vacuum cleaner and the fettucine Oliver had eaten for lunch.

Vee said, "How did the boys behave in court?"

"Very well except for a few whispers. I confess to being disappointed in their notes on the proceedings."

"Maybe you expect too much."

"More than that. I sometimes get the feeling I'm out of touch with my sons."

"Sometimes you are, Oliver. But we all drift in and out of touch with each other throughout our lives."

She put her head on his shoulder and smiled with her mouth against his skin. He was such a big, beautiful man she often wondered how she'd been lucky enough to land him.

IV

The CLERK

*B*efore court resumed the next morning, the judge summoned Court Clerk Eva Foster to his chambers.

The judge was wearing the half glasses that divided his face into two parts contradicting each other. The upper part was the broad intellectual forehead and grave little eyes. The lower part had the puffy cheeks and full pink lips of an older Thatcher.

Eva had on a new knit dress, an unfortunate choice for the occasion.

"Sit down, Miss Foster."

"Yes, sir."

The judge studied her over the tops of his glasses, then put his head back and studied her through the bottoms of the glasses to achieve a balanced view.

Finally he spoke. "District Attorney Owen brought his three sons to court yesterday afternoon. The two older boys were quite noticeably—ah, noticing you, or shall I say ogling you?"

"Boys that age will ogle anything that moves."

"And you *do* move, Miss Foster. Quite well, if I may say so."

"Is my work satisfactory, sir?"

"Yes, yes indeed. You're always right in there pitching,

bringing in the evidence, knives, guns, garments, et cetera. Which brings me to the point."

"What does?"

"Garments. Your garments."

Eva looked down at her dress, which had cost her a week's salary and been advertised in *Vogue*. "You don't like this dress?"

"I like it fine. It's very becoming."

"Then what's this all about? I fail to see—"

"*He* saw. Mr. Owen, that is. And what he saw was two of his boys ogling you. So of course, he had to ogle you also in order to determine what they were ogling. Understandable, really. Parental responsibility and all that. At any rate he reached a conclusion."

"Indeed?"

The top half of the judge's face seemed to be fighting the bottom half, with the fight ending in a draw.

"Consarn it, Miss Foster, all this ogling wasn't my idea. I'm just the middleman."

"What conclusion did Mr. Owen reach?"

"He feels—that is, he opines, believes, whatever—that you do not wear undergarments designed to bind, confine, restrain—"

"I know what 'bind' means, Your Honor. 'Bind' is what the ancient barbarous Chinese did to the feet of their little princesses. They bound their feet to prevent them from growing normally so the poor creatures were never able to walk. Those barbarians believed that only peasants should find it necessary to walk. It was a cruel, inhumane, dreadful thing to do."

"Oh, for goodness' sake, Miss Foster. I am not asking you to bind your feet. I simply want you to wear a bra."

Eva sat in deliberate silence, looking around the room.

It was as contradictory as the judge's two-part face. Dignified rows of red and gold lawbooks were topped by a stuffed great horned owl with one of its glass eyes missing and a dead mouse squeezed between its claws. The formal mahogany desk was scarred with cigarette burns and scratches from the seashells the judge collected on his morning beach walks. The latest pile of seashells gave the room the pervasive odor of fish.

"The bailiff," Eva said, "has a potbelly."

"I'm aware of that, Miss Foster."

"Have you asked him to wear a girdle?"

"No."

"Why not?"

"A potbelly is not as ogleable—oglible—consarn it, a potbelly is not as seductive as certain other parts of the anatomy. Also, he wears a belt around it."

"Only to keep his pants up."

The judge was beginning to regret having brought the subject up. "It would be very difficult for me to ask my bailiff to wear a girdle."

"You didn't seem to mind asking me to wear a bra."

"On the contrary. I hesitated; I weighed the pros and cons; I mulled over it a long time."

"If you had mulled a little longer, you would have realized that this is clearly a case of sexual discrimination."

"But it isn't discrimination. It is simply a recognition of obvious sexual differences. The bailiff's potbelly is not in the same category as your chest."

"Cases of sex discrimination can go all the way to the Supreme Court."

"Oh, Lord," the judge said. His day had started out so well. The sun was shining; he'd eaten a good breakfast; nobody was mad at him. Now suddenly he was coming up before the Supreme Court on charges of sexual discrimination. "Couldn't we forget this conversation, Miss Foster?"

"I could if you could."

"It never happened. Right?"

"Right. But in case it happens again, I shall have no hesitation in bringing the matter to the attention of the National Organization for Women."

"You wouldn't by any chance consider a compromise?"

"You mean wear half a bra? That doesn't sound feasible. In fact, it might have quite the opposite effect of the one you're seeking by proving to be a turn-on for certain kinky types. Do you understand?"

"Yes yes yes."

"Also," Eva said, "you can't buy half a bra. I would have to buy a whole bra and cut it in two, which would make it impossible to fasten."

"I didn't suggest half a bra, Miss Foster. I suggested a compromise, something in the nature of—well, a rather snug-fitting chemise."

"I haven't seen a chemise in years."

"Then perhaps you might choose outer garments that don't follow so precisely the contours of the human form. Would you consider such a compromise?"

"Oh, yes. I would consider such a compromise blatant discrimination."

"Very well, the subject is closed."

"Thank you, sir. And I'll try to walk out very, very carefully so as not to attract any—"

"Oh, go bind your feet, Foster," the judge said.

At ten minutes to ten the deputy brought Cully King in from the county jail. In jail Cully wore what the other inmates did, but on trial days he was allowed to dress in his best clothes, navy blue blazer, gray slacks, white shirt and a blue tie which he'd bought in Mazatlán at a waterfront stall. The tie bore the picture of a yacht painted by an expatriate American artist from a picture Cully showed him of the *Bewitched*. Nobody would have recognized the *Bewitched* from the painting, but any sailor could see it was a ketch, and the artist insisted it was one of his finest works for a mere twenty-five dollars.

Neither Donnelly nor the DA had arrived yet, and except for the bailiff and a few early court watchers, Cully and Eva were alone.

"We'll be late starting this morning," Eva told Cully. "I upset the judge by being right. He can't stand other people being right this early in the morning, so he'll probably need time to soothe his ego."

"I don't care if he's late. I'm not going anywhere." Cully smiled, a rather grave, sweet smile that made him look very young. "Are you going anywhere?"

"Not for a while. I'm taking my vacation at Christmas. I'm not sure yet where I want to go."

"My islands are very beautiful at Christmas. I would like to be home for the holidays."

"With your wife and kids?"

"She's not my wife. We never got married. Maybe they're not my kids either, but I support them all, so they treat me like a King. . . . That's a joke. Get it?"

"I got it."

"Why don't you ever smile? I thought it was a pretty good joke."

"Tell me about your house."

"Not much to tell. Not much of a house. Small, crowded, not too clean when you compare it with a ship. My brother-in-law lives with us. He's a bum, but he's a good dancer, and Louise likes to go dancing. Me, I can't dance unless

I'm drunk. Maybe I can't dance then either, but I do it. I'll do practically anything when I'm drunk." He paused for a moment. "If I ever murder anybody, it'll probably be my brother-in-law. I've thought about it a lot."

"You mustn't talk like that," Eva said. "People might overhear and get the wrong impression."

"Why should they? My brother-in-law has nothing to do with the woman I took on board as cook."

"Are you still sticking to that story?"

"It's true."

"It doesn't sound true."

"I can't change what happened."

"Mr. King, you must learn how to present yourself as an innocent person. An innocent person doesn't talk about the possibility of murdering his brother-in-law."

"All right, I won't talk about it. I'll still think about it, though."

"Listen. What I mean is, you can't just go around telling the truth. You've got to make it sound truer than truth."

"Are you making fun of me?"

"No."

"I think maybe your are."

"No. I'm trying to help you."

"Why?"

"I don't know."

Cully lapsed into a puzzled silence. He sat with his hands on the table, rolling a pencil between the thumb and forefinger of his right hand back and forth along the palm of his left hand. Against the lighter skin of his palm the calluses stood out like pebbles on a beach.

Eva liked these hands, which were so different from Donnelly's, always too carefully manicured, and from the judge's, gnarled by arthritis, and the bailiff's, with their pale, puffy fingers, one of them nearly strangled by his wedding band. Cully's were lean, strong hands you could depend on to get things done, to provide and protect.

She looked down at her own hands, small and thin, and she had a sudden, very disturbing impulse to put one of them in Cully's and let it lie there.

For nearly a minute her breath caught in her throat, then had to race to make up for lost oxygen. She wondered what was the matter with her and whether she should talk to somebody sensible like Mildred. After years of trial work Mildred had a sixth sense about the guilt or innocence of a defendant. She would know whether or not this man was a murderer.

"I like your dress," Cully said.

"Why?"

"It's a great dress. It fits you great."

"I hate it," Eva said, "I hate it. I'm never going to wear it again."

Bill Gunther came in swinging his battered old briefcase. He looked as though he had spent the night in a clothes dryer that had twisted his suit, torn a button off his shirt and tumbled his hair. Actually he'd been on the road from Bakersfield since midnight, caught in a dense tule fog which had slowed traffic almost to a standstill. His steel-rimmed spectacles seemed to have brought along a sample of tule fog, and Gunther's attempts to wipe the lenses clean with his sleeve had been futile.

He pulled a tie out of the pocket of his coat and put it on. Then he ran his hands through his hair, using his fingers like the teeth of a comb. He had needed a haircut at the beginning of the trial, and he still did. The total impression he made was that of a man who had more important and profound things to think about than clothes and grooming.

"It is customary," Eva said, "to dress at home."

"I wasn't at home."

"I bet you weren't."

"In fact, I haven't been home for so long I've forgotten my address. You don't happen to have it lying around someplace, do you?"

"No. Try phoning your mother."

"I'm fresh out of mothers."

He put his briefcase on the table. It gave off a faint but identifiable odor of used underwear and dirty socks, so he transferred it to the floor. Then he turned to Cully.

"How'd things go yesterday?"

"Not so good, I think. Maybe even bad."

"How bad?"

"That doctor made it sound like I strangled her and punched her in the ribs. It didn't happen that way."

"If it didn't happen that way, they can't prove it did."

"Maybe they can if Dr. Woodbridge keeps using words nobody else can understand."

"Wait'll Donnelly gets to him. Woodbridge will be using four-letter words like H-E-L-P."

"You like this man Donnelly?"

"He's the boss. He pays my rent, buys my beer, so sure I like him."

"But you're not his real friend?"

"I don't even know where he lives."

"My, my, your memory is feeble this morning, Mr. Gunther," Eva said. "You can't remember where you live and you can't remember where your buddy lives. Did you have a bad night?"

"The worst."

"You dropped a bundle at your bookie's."

"Oh, butt out, Foster. I'm discussing evidence with our client."

"Then try lowering your voice. Some of these court watchers have twenty-twenty hearing."

The district attorney came in with his chief investigator, Deputy Bernstein, followed a minute later by Donnelly.

Donnelly looked perfectly groomed as always. His gray silk and wool suit matched the gloss and color of his hair. With it he wore a white shirt, a Harvard tie and a Phi Beta Kappa key. The key was legitimately his, but he was not a graduate of Harvard. Urged by his New England family to go west and stay there, he came to California and enrolled at UC Berkeley. Here, in the less restrictive atmosphere and more equable climate, he flourished.

"Good morning, gentlemen," Donnelly said. "Did you sleep in your clothes, Mr. Gunther?"

"I didn't sleep in anything."

"Really? You must tell me about it later. Much later."

Gunther shrugged, picked up his briefcase and went to his customary seat inside the well but at the railing, away from the counselors' table.

Donnelly unpacked the papers he had brought, legal pads filled with the letters, numerals and squiggles that passed for writing and a copy of the local morning newspaper with an account of yesterday's proceedings. It was a fairly accurate report, and Donnelly gave it to Cully to read.

As he read, Cully's face was impassive, but his hands trembled slightly. "They make it sound like I'm guilty."

"Tomorrow's will be better," Donnelly said. "I think the jury's getting saturated with medical terms."

"Why do you think that?"

"They haven't been taking as many notes as they did previously. They're ready for simpler language. So am I."

* * *

"All rise, Superior Court in and for the county of Santa Felicia is now in session, Judge Hazeltine presiding."

It was ten-fifteen.

Eva Foster recorded the time in her notebook, Mildred Noon sat poised at her stenotype machine and Dr. Woodbridge was escorted back to the witness box by the bailiff. The courtroom had the communal warmth of a barn, but the smell was different. This was the smell of people under stress.

The judge watched the bailiff as he returned to his seat, noting that his potbelly seemed to be increasing and his khaki shirt was strained to the limit. He looked like a man whose chest had started to fall down and then was caught in the nick of time by the leather belt of his trousers. A girdle might not be such a bad idea, the judge thought. He took a long, deep breath, swished it around in his lungs for a minute, then exhaled and spoke.

"Mr. Owen having completed his examination of Dr. Woodbridge, we are now ready to hear Mr. Donnelly's cross-examination. Are you ready for the cross-examination, Mr. Donnelly?"

"Yes, Your Honor."

Donnelly took his place at the lectern, facing the witness. His manner and voice were grave.

"Dr. Woodbridge, my name is Charles Donnelly. If, during the course of this cross-examination, any of my questions seem too personal, even hostile, I beg your forgiveness in advance. Any doubts cast will not be on your integrity but on certain conclusions you've reached. Although we are on opposing sides in this case, we both are interested in establishing the truth. And in any quest for truth, verbal blows are often exchanged. I regret this, but

I must fight for what I believe in. Would you accept an apology in advance, Doctor?"

"Oh, certainly." Woodbridge felt a tic in the left corner of his mouth. If he'd been alone, it would have expanded into a full smile. He'd known Donnelly for years, and this was one of Donnelly's favorite tricks, presenting himself to the jury as a Boy Scout who must stoop to dirty tricks in the interest of justice.

"Dr. Woodbridge, you said yesterday that the cause of Mrs. Pherson's death was asphyxia."

"I did."

"Can you give us a short and simple definition of 'asphyxia'?"

"I can make it short, but I can't make it simple since a rather complicated process is involved."

"Short will do."

"Asphyxia is oxygen starvation due to the obstruction of breathing passages."

"Can this obstruction of breathing passages be caused by a number of things?"

"Yes."

"Can you name some, please?"

"Accident first comes to mind, as when a person attempts to swallow a piece of food, usually meat, that is too large and the food gets lodged in his throat. Another cause is disease, such as a tumor or a violent allergic reaction to some food like shellfish which causes the throat to swell. Smothering, another cause, can be accidental, as when an infant gets entangled in its bedclothes, or deliberate, such as a pillow held against the face. Hanging, the use of a ligature around the neck, rope, wire, belt, is a not uncommon method of suicide. Another cause of asphyxia is the use of hands applying pressure to the windpipe and larynx, in other words, strangulation."

The wail of a siren just outside the windows silenced the doctor, and he shook his head at the futility of trying to compete.

When the siren faded, Donnelly said, "Haven't you omitted the most important cause of asphyxia, Dr. Woodbridge?"

"Not by intent. I was about to add drowning when I was interrupted."

"Yesterday afternoon the district attorney emphasized the fact that very little water was found in Mrs. Pherson's lungs. In most cases of drowning are the lungs filled with water?"

"No. Very seldom."

"Can you give us, as briefly as possible, the actual mechanism of drowning as when, for instance, a person falls overboard from a boat?"

"The person would begin to fight for his life, probably start yelling for help and thrashing around in the water. During this struggle for survival, water enters the throat and windpipe, causing the mucous membranes to produce more mucus in self-protection. This mucus combines with the water to form a viscous substance rather like soap lather but sticky and tenacious. This may be combined with vomit as well, and the victim strangles on his own body fluids."

"Can we conclude that the cause of death is not water in the lungs, as is commonly believed?"

"No, it is not."

"What if the fall from the vessel is not accidental but intentional?"

"Water would still be ingested and the reaction of the mucous membranes would be the same."

"It is a commonly held belief that a drowning person

will come to the surface three times. Is this correct?"

"No. The body might not come to the surface at all and never be recovered. This is especially true in fresh water."

"Why?"

"The human body is heavier than fresh water."

"What about salt water?"

"Salt increases the body's buoyancy. If there is a large amount of salt, such as in the Great Salt Lake of Utah, a person becomes so buoyant that it's difficult to swim."

"Does the temperature of the water have any effect on survival time? Strike that. . . . Dr. Woodbridge, you stated yesterday that in your opinion Mrs. Pherson died of asphyxia due to strangulation."

"I did."

"You further stated that the strangulation resulted from the use of hands."

"Yes."

"You based your opinion on two grooves found on the front of the throat approximately the size of thumbs."

"That was the main basis, yes."

"You also stated that these grooves had been made premortem—that is, before death—did you not?"

"Yes."

"Do you know what time Mrs. Pherson's death occurred?"

"No."

"Can you tell within an hour?"

"No."

"Within two hours?"

"Not for a certainty, no."

"Why not?"

"The fact that the body had been immersed in water about fifty-five degrees makes it difficult to determine the exact time of death."

"Yet you contend that the grooves found on Mrs. Pherson's throat were made prior to death. How certain are you of this?"

"One hundred percent. Or almost one hundred percent."

"Almost." Donnelly spoke the word slowly, letting it hang in the air like a cloud of doubt. "In the field of medicine as in other sciences, new facts are coming to light every day, are they not?"

"Yes."

"Do you try, Dr. Woodbridge, to keep up with current advances, new theories, new facts, which are printed in various publications?"

"I try. But currently there are so many medical publications that I would have to choose between reading them all and carrying on my own work."

"Is the special field of cold-water rescues relatively new?"

"I believe so."

"Have you done any reading on this subject?"

"Not a great deal."

"Not a great deal. Does that mean a small deal?"

The district attorney got to his feet. "I object, Your Honor. Dr. Woodbridge's qualifications were well established at the beginning of his testimony. All this prying into what he has or has not read I construe as badgering."

"I don't," the judge said. "Overruled. Repeat your question, Mr. Donnelly."

"I'll rephrase it. Have recent studies done in the field of cold-water drowning contradicted some long-held notions?"

"Long-held notions are being shot down every day in almost every scientific field. Can you refer to a specific case, please?"

"One well-publicized case happened last year near

Seattle. Two boys were playing on a frozen lake when the ice broke and one of them fell in and was submerged. His companion tried to rescue him, but he, too, fell in and was submerged. The frantic barking of the boys' dog drew attention to their plight. More than an hour elapsed before the body of the first boy was brought out of the lake. No signs of life were evident, but the paramedics went to work anyway, as they're trained to do whether or not the task seems hopeless. In this case the boy was revived and actually started breathing on his own. A short time later he died. However, during that long submersion in that icy water he remained alive, his metabolism so slowed that he was in a state of suspended animation. Do you recall this case, Doctor?"

"Yes."

"What was your reaction when you first read or heard about it?"

"I felt very pleased at the resourcefulness of the human body."

The unexpected answer broke the tension, and a hum of appreciation and amusement drifted across the court-room. Donnelly was annoyed at losing the attention of the audience, but he realized it was to his advantage, and he pursued the subject.

"Do you remember, Dr. Woodbridge, how long the boy was submerged before being brought out of the lake?"

"I believe it was at least an hour."

"What was the body's mechanism that saved him, if only for a short time?"

"The term you used seems to be an adequate description for the layman, suspended animation. The lowering of the body temperature and slowing of its metabolism decrease the brain's need for oxygen."

"Are there other such cases on record of people surviving a previously unheard-of time of submersion?"

"Yes."

"Well documented?"

"Yes."

"What was the common denominator?"

"The low temperature of the water."

The tic at the corner of Woodbridge's mouth picked up its beat. He knew what was coming. He could see it in Donnelly's eyes and in the way the district attorney had moved forward in his chair, ready to go into action like a runner listening for the starting gun.

"Dr. Woodbridge, could such a thing have happened to Madeline Pherson?"

The district attorney jumped to his feet. "I object, Your Honor. Witness is being asked to speculate. I object further to this whole line of questioning, or shall I say answering, since defense attorney seems to be delivering a medical lecture to the doctor."

"Witness is not required to answer the question," the judge said.

"Let me ask a hypothetical question instead," Donnelly said. "Suppose such a thing had happened to Mrs. Pherson, could not the grooves on her throat and the lacerations and contusions on her body have occurred *after* her submersion in the water?"

Donnelly didn't even wait for an answer. None was necessary. He turned a page of his notes as if it were the final page of a book.

Glancing at the wall clock, he saw that it was 11:16, later than the usual morning recess time but early for the lunch break. He decided to ask for the break, allowing the jury nearly three hours to ponder the question *Could such a thing have happened to Madeline Pherson?*

* * *

With forty-five extra minutes for lunch Eva Foster decided to go home. She lived in a three-story Victorian house with her father, Frank, her stepmother, Dora, and Dora's teenaged son, Pete. Her father had changed jobs many times, and wives four times, but he clung with obstinate affection to the old house in spite of the office buildings and apartments built up around it.

Eva headed for her room on the second floor, avoiding the two steps that creaked and the worn place in the upstairs hall carpet which people were always tripping over. Nobody did anything about the worn carpet. It was as much a part of the old house as the dumbwaiter that moved noisily on its trolley back and forth from the kitchen to the third floor.

In her bedroom she glanced at herself in the full-length mirror attached to the closet door. Then she took off the knit dress, flung it on the patchwork quilt bedspread and put on a loose-fitting cotton shirtwaist. It was a nice, sensible dress, the kind she should have worn in the first place. Every office in the city had one exactly like it walking around with some anonymous female inside.

On her way back downstairs she noticed that the worn place in the hall carpet had two new worn places, one on each side, made by people wanting to avoid the original. Eventually there'd be a whole row of them growing across the hall like fungi.

She found her stepmother in the kitchen, making a salad and watching a game show on television. The show seemed to be a continuous laugh track, interrupted by occasional snatches of dialogue.

Dora's high, sharp voice pierced the sound track like a stiletto. "What are you doing home?"

"I live here."

"What?"

"I . . . live . . . here."

Dora turned off the television, frowning as all the jolly people left her life as abruptly as they had entered. She had the kind of blond prettiness people always referred to in the past tense. "You know what I mean," Dora said. "You didn't get fired, did you? God knows it's a contagious disease around this place."

"I didn't get fired," Eva said. "Court adjourned early."

She opened the refrigerator door and took out a can of tomato juice and an apple.

Dora was watching her suspiciously as if she weren't quite sure she had been told the truth. "Why?"

"Why what?"

"Why did it adjourn early?"

"It was a technical matter."

"I wish you'd tell me what's going on once in a while. My bridge club is coming this afternoon, and they're dying to hear some inside information about the case."

"I can't give you any inside information."

"Why not? You must have an opinion on whether the man is guilty or not. My goodness, you're right there."

"I'm right there now. But I wasn't right there when the woman died."

Eva stood at the kitchen sink, drinking the tomato juice and looking out at the liquidambar tree that separated the house from the apartment building next door. In the noon sun its giant leaves shone brilliant orange-red as if they were bursting into vibrant new life. But every year her father reminded Eva gloomily that this was not life but death. And pretty soon the leaves would begin to drop and curl up crisp as taco shells. Then her father would get up early in the morning and rake them into a pile to be crushed into the trash can. Her father was very neat.

"I bet the others do," Dora said.

"What others do what?"

"The ones who work in the courtroom. I bet they go home and tell their families everything."

"You can read in the newspaper everything you're supposed to know."

"But all the girls in the bridge club will know the same thing, and I won't have anything extra to tell them."

"If your friends want to know what goes on in a courtroom, they should come and find out for themselves. It's a free show."

Eva peeled the apple and cut it into quarters.

"I turned off the TV so we could talk," Dora said. "And now you have nothing to say."

"Not about the case, no. We could discuss the weather."

"I'll have enough of that when your father gets home. He'll tell me what the temperature is in Paris, Bangkok, Hong Kong, you name it. And we hardly ever go further than Los Angeles. It beats me how a man fifty-six years old can want to read the surf reports every night in the paper, the size of the swells, what direction they're coming from and the intervals between waves. It really beats me, a man who's never been out of the country or on a surfboard in his life wanting to know the temperature in Hong Kong and the size of the waves at Zuma Beach. Don't you think that's odd?"

"I haven't thought about it. What is the temperature in Hong Kong, by the way?"

"Why?" Dora said coldly. "Are you going there?"

"I might."

"If you didn't spend all your money on clothes, you could afford to."

"Maybe I'll win a free trip. That's it. You could go on one of those quiz shows you're always watching and win a free trip to Hong Kong. You wouldn't want to take the trip yourself because you don't like Chinamen so you give the ticket to me. And before I even get there, I'll know the temperature. How does that sound?"

Dora's plump pink face looked fretful like a disappointed child's. "I wouldn't dream of giving you the ticket. Either I'd sell it or I'd take the trip myself, Chinamen or no Chinamen. And speaking of spending all your money on clothes, what happened to your dress?"

"What dress?"

"This morning at breakfast you were wearing a new knitted dress."

"I changed."

"I can see that. But why?"

"I wanted to."

"You must have had a reason for wanting to."

"I decided it wasn't suitable for a courtroom."

"Surely they don't tell you what to wear."

"No."

"Then why not look as attractive as you can? That dress made you almost sexy."

Eva knew what was coming: It was up to a woman to look as sexy as possible because one never knew when Mr. Right was going to come along. Or even Mr. Half-Right, since a woman who'd reached Eva's age couldn't afford to be choosy.

It was Dora's favorite theme, and she played it like a virtuoso. "You remember that nice Mr. Weatherbe your father brought home from the office for dinner Saturday night? Well, he asked your father about you and sent his best regards. It's a sign he's interested in you, even though you sat there like a dead clam all through the meal."

"How do you tell a dead clam from a live one?"

"Dead or alive, that isn't the point. Mr. Weatherbe is a very presentable man. He dresses well—that part should certainly appeal to you—he has nice teeth and not a trace of dandruff."

"How could he have dandruff when he's bald?"

"His hair is thinning a little on top. You can't call him bald."

"I can. I just did."

"When are you going to get it through your head that you're no spring chicken anymore. You can't be so picky. Goodness gracious. what are you waiting for?"

Still standing at the window, Eva watched the liquid-ambar tree dazzling to death in the sun. "Not that it's any of your business, but I'm waiting to fall in love."

"Fall in love? That's silly."

"Why?"

"People can't expect to just fall in love. They have to go out and look for it, work at it, not sit around the dinner table acting like a—"

"Dead clam."

"Yes, a dead clam. That's what I said, and I won't apologize for it. Mr. Weatherbe's hair may be thinning a bit on top, but he earns a very good salary. And the fact that he asked after you must mean he's interested." Dora stabbed at an oil-slick lettuce leaf. "So you're waiting to fall in love. I can't really believe you said that."

"Believe it."

"You're sure you don't have one of those things they call a father fixation?"

"I doubt it."

"Let's hope you're right. One of my friends was saying the other day how funny it was that Frank had had four wives and through all four of them you were still occupying the same bedroom you had when you were a child instead of going out and getting a place of your own, which you could well afford to do if you didn't spend so much money on clothes. Not that I object to having you here, but you'd think with all that blabbing you do about women's independence you might go out and get some place of your own. Why don't you?"

"Inertia," Eva said. "All us dead clams suffer from inertia. And I'd appreciate it if you didn't bring up the subject of Mr. Weatherbe again. He may earn a good salary, but he's a conceited ass who suffers from logorrhea."

"What's that?"

"Look it up."

"There you go again. Whenever you're losing an argument, the only thing you can do is flaunt your superior education."

"I can think of something else to do," Eva said. "But it wouldn't be legal."

She spent the rest of her lunch hour looking in shopwindows, buying an umbrella for Mildred Noon's birthday and finally going into a bookstore and asking for a map and some literature about the Caribbean islands.

She was a steady customer at the store, and the middle-aged woman behind the counter greeted her by name.

"Going on a cruise, Miss Foster?"

"I might someday."

"I've never been to the Caribbean myself. But I have a friend who took one of those cruises that was supposed to be like the Love Boat on TV. A love boat, my eye. In the first place most of the passengers were women, and the only men on board were the crew."

"And in the second place?"

"There was no second place. What do you think she

went on the cruise for? It was an expensive mistake. She would have done better to join one of those health clubs."

"Thanks for the advice."

"There at least you'll be surrounded by men and you can start scouting. It's amazing what poor judges of character women are. They use their eyes and ears instead of their brains. They might as well say eeny meeny miny mo."

Eva stared down at the map in her hands. It had begun to quiver, as if someone had opened a door and let the wind in. She felt no draft.

Eeny, meeny, miny mo, catch a nigger by the toe.

Had the woman chosen these words deliberately? She seemed to be looking at her in a peculiar way. Perhaps she knew all about the trial, had even been one of the anonymous court watchers, had seen Cully talking to her, smiling, admiring her dress.

She started to refold the map, but it wouldn't fold, and the woman took it out of her hands. "Here, let me do it."

"Thank you," Eva said.

"Personally I think the best way to meet men—or women either, for that matter—is to buy a dog. People who walk dogs always get acquainted with each other. Have you noticed that?"

"Yes."

"Actually, I think dogs are a lot smarter than people. When dogs want to get acquainted, they just walk up to each other and sniff around a little, and they're either friends or enemies right off the bat. Wouldn't it be nice if people felt free to do the same?"

"I guess so."

"Aren't you feeling well, Miss Foster?"

"I'm all right."

"Maybe you've been working too hard. You know, it's

funny, but in all the years you've been coming in here I've never known what you do for a living."

"I work for the government."

"Aren't you lucky. I hear they have great health insurance coverage. And the pensions! If I could get a pension like that, I'd make a point of living forever."

"I'll take the map," Eva said. "And the paperback on the Virgin Islands."

"Want me to put them in a bag for you?"

"No, thanks, there's room in my purse."

"What a lovely purse," the clerk said. "What's it made of?"

"Alligator."

"I thought alligators were on the endangered species list and people weren't allowed to use their skins."

"That used to be true. But now alligators are farmed and the use of their skins is legal."

Eva paid for the book and map and went back out onto the street.

She arrived in the courtroom ten minutes early, but Cully was already seated at the counsels' table. Bailiff di Santo stood at the back of the room, talking to a pensioner who divided his time between the courthouse and the library in the next block.

"My game plan is simple," the old man told Di Santo in a voice that defied walls. "Here today, there tomorrow. The courthouse is livelier, but the seats in the library are more comfortable. These benches in here would bend an elephant's ass."

Eva sat down at the table she shared with Di Santo. Cully smiled at her but waited for her to speak first.

"You're early," she said.

"Yes."

"Where do they take you for lunch?"

"Back to the jail. We have our big meal at noon. The

food's okay. There are rumors they put something in it to kind of calm everybody down, but if you're hungry enough, you don't care."

"It wouldn't be legal for them to do that."

"Do you think that would stop them?"

"Of course. Don't you?"

Cully shrugged and turned away.

"I have to believe in our judicial system," Eva said. "I'm part of it."

"So am I, right now."

"I keep forgetting. I guess that sounds pretty crazy, but it's true. When we're sitting here talking like this, I keep forgetting we're not two ordinary people having an ordinary relationship."

"Two people like us could never have an ordinary relationship whichever way the trial turns out. Even if the jury finds me innocent, you'll never be sure."

"Yes, I will. I told you, I *believe* in the system."

He made a funny sound through his teeth that could have been interpreted as almost anything, a parent hushing a child, the beginning of a curse or a simple exhalation of air.

Eva took the paperback out of her purse and began to read:

The Caribbean Sea is dotted with many islands. One hundred of varying sizes are designated as the Virgin Islands, east of Puerto Rico. Of volcanic origin overlaid with limestone, these islands have a tropical climate. The only source of water is rainfall, which is collected in cisterns. The islands belonged to Denmark and were purchased from the Danes in 1917 by the United States as a strategic move to help protect the Panama Canal.

All-year population is sparse, but the islands, especially the three largest, St. Thomas, St. John and St. Croix, are a haven for tourists, especially in the winter months. The main harbor at St. Thomas is a favorite port of call for oceangoing yachts.

It was Columbus who discovered the islands in 1493 and named them in honor of St. Ursula, whose 11,000 virgins died in defense of their chastity. A hundred years later Sir Francis Drake renamed them in honor of Elizabeth I.

"I could have told you anything you wanted to know about my islands," Cully said. "You didn't have to buy a book about them."

"I just happened to see it lying on the counter and picked it up. I'm still trying to decide where to go on my vacation."

"Books like that don't always give you the whole truth. They tell about the blue sea but not the lack of fresh water. They describe big, beautiful beaches without mentioning the big, beautiful bugs."

"How—how big?"

"Size isn't so important. It's the real little ones that bite the worst. A woman like you would be better off going to a city like New York to see the shows and the museums and stuff like that."

"How do you know what a woman like me would like?"

"For one thing you have a very fair skin, which means you don't spend much time outdoors."

"My job keeps me inside. I like a lot of things besides art galleries and museums. Boats, for instance. I love boats, and I never get seasick. I'd like to go someplace on a boat someday."

As soon as the sentence left her mouth, she regretted

it. It seemed to fall between them like a wall, and when he spoke again, his voice was barely audible. "Why did you say that?"

"Say what?"

"About wanting to go on a boat. Did you mean an ordinary boat or a yacht like the *Bewitched*?"

"I didn't mean anything special. I was just remarking that I've always wanted to go someplace on a boat or ship, whatever's going."

"The last woman I took someplace on a boat didn't get there. If she had, none of us would be in this courtroom. But here we are. Take a train." His lips stretched in a caricature of a smile. "You'll be safer on a train, especially if you don't pick up strangers in the bar."

Court resumed at 2:11.

Dr. Woodbridge, back in the witness box, appeared refreshed after the long lunch break. He even managed to give his cross-examiner a friendly nod as Donnelly went to the lectern with his sheaf of papers.

The bailiff, who'd already announced the opening of the afternoon session and returned to his seat, now rose again and quickly approached the bench.

He spoke in a whisper. "One of the jurors is missing."

"You might have stopped me when I was saying, 'Let the record show.' "

"I didn't notice. She sits in the back row, number eight, and she's real little."

"Name?"

"Mrs. Latham."

"Well, all we can do is wait." The judge raised his voice and addressed the audience. "One of our jurors has apparently lost her way to the courthouse. Rather than declare a recess I will simply ask you to wait a few minutes

161

for her arrival. Until that time you are free to converse among yourselves."

Nine minutes passed before an elderly gray-haired woman came bustling into the room. Her hair was uncombed, and the neat, prim front she'd presented the preceding sessions of the trial had disappeared. She wore a grease-stained nylon jacket with "Olympics '84" across the back of it and a pair of soiled denim slacks with the right leg folded up to mid-calf.

The judge frowned at her over his glasses. "You're late, Mrs. Latham."

"Yes, sir. My grandson's bicycle had a flat tire."

"And how did that affect you, Mrs. Latham?"

"I was on it."

The judge consulted his bailiff in a whisper, then spoke to the elderly woman again. "You live at One fourteen Gaviota Avenue?"

"Yes, sir."

"And you rode a bicycle all the way down here?"

"Had to. My car was stolen from the jury parking lot this morning. When I went out to drive home for lunch, there it was, just an empty space where I'd left my car. It's un-American to have your car stolen right next to the courthouse with the police station a block away. The place must have been crawling with cops and deputies and judges and bailiffs, and right in front of all their noses someone breaks into my car and hot-wires it and drives off."

The district attorney's objection was loud and immediate. "Your Honor, I protest any further remarks on the part of this juror in open court, and I request a consultation at the side bar."

Both counsel and the court reporter gathered on the right side of the judge, who swiveled his chair around to face them.

The district attorney explained his objection. "Her remarks indicate a possible bias against law officers and may constitute grounds for her dismissal."

"Nonsense," the judge said. "She's mad. You'd be mad, too, if you had to ride a bicycle all the way from Gaviota Avenue."

"I feel that the least you can do, Your Honor, is to question her in chambers and ascertain whether she will be able to render a fair and impartial verdict."

"If that's the least I can do, I'll do it. I always do the least I can. Have you any further instructions for the bench, Mr. Owen?"

"No, sir."

"Good. Go and sit down." He tapped the gavel lightly. "Court is recessed for five minutes. Jurors may retire to the jury room except for Mrs. Latham. Mrs. Latham, I will see you in chambers."

Mrs. Latham was beginning to enjoy her first taste of the limelight. She was a very tiny woman, accustomed to being ignored in shops, pushed to the end of the line in grocery stores and seeing only the back of the person in front of her at parades. She followed the judge out of the room, trying to straighten her hair as she walked.

"Please sit down, Mrs. Latham."

"Yes, sir."

"Are you prejudiced against police officers, Mrs. Latham?"

"Not until this morning when I went out to get in my car and it wasn't there."

"Previous to that, you never had any grudge against officers of the law?"

"No, sir. I never have. I'm a true blue American, top to bottom."

"Do you feel any resentment over being asked to serve on this jury?"

"Oh, no. I haven't anything else to do."

"Did you report your stolen car to the police?"

"Yes, sir."

"Were you satisfied with their response?"

"They were polite, but they didn't give me much hope."

"It's not police business to offer hope. You'll have to go to a church for that."

Mrs. Latham was allowed to continue as Juror No. 8.

The long delay in the start of the afternoon session prompted Judge Hazeltine to make an apology which turned out to be a still further delay. He derived a certain satisfaction from this. He wasn't going any place, so he didn't care how long it took to get there. And it was quite pleasing to see the district attorney grimly crossing his arms on his chest and Donnelly white-knuckling the sides of the lectern.

"Shakespeare wrote eloquently of the events and conditions which make life difficult to bear. Among these he listed:

> The oppressor's wrong, the proud man's
> contumely,
> The pangs of disprized love, the law's delay.

"What was true several hundred years ago is true today. The judicial process is long and slow. And as many judges in many courts have done before me, I proffer an apology. . . . Mr. Donnelly, you may continue your cross-examination of Dr. Woodbridge."

"Thank you, Your Honor," Donnelly said, "for bringing Hamlet's soliloquy to our attention."

"Oh, was that Hamlet? I thought it was Lear. You see, at one time or another I memorized all the soliloquies of Shakespeare. It hardly mattered who said what. The memorization was a form of punishment back in the days when schools were schools and not diploma factories. If a student was caught chewing gum or talking out of turn, he was forced to stay after school and memorize a soliloquy. Yes, now that I think of it, I believe it was Hamlet. The slings and arrows speech, right?"

Mildred Noon leaned toward the judge and said with only the slightest movement of lips and larynx, "Do you want me to put all this in the record?"

"Why not? I'm saying it, aren't I?"

"Yes, but you may not want to be reading it in the transcript."

"On the contrary. This trial needs a touch of class. Why must everything be downgraded to the lowest common multiple?"

"I don't know. But—"

"Slings and arrows, Mildred. Slings and arrows. Now back to work."

So back to work it was, and everything was put on record. Mildred had a vague hope that the printed word might help obscure the fact that the judge had spent more of his lunch hour drinking than eating.

Donnelly said, "May I proceed now, Your Honor?"

"Certainly. I told you that before."

The judge settled back in his chair, the district attorney unfolded his arms and Donnelly released his grip on the lectern and picked up one of the papers from the sheaf in front of him.

"Dr. Woodbridge, you have stated that Mrs. Pherson, in your opinion, died of manual strangulation. Correct?"

"Yes."

"Your use of the word 'opinion' suggests that given the same set of circumstances, another person might come to an entirely different conclusion. Is this possible?"

"It's possible that different pathologists might reach somewhat different conclusions. But I believe they would all have to agree that strangulation was involved in Mrs. Pherson's death to some extent."

" 'To some extent.' Is that what you said?"

"Yes."

"Your use of the phrase seems to be a backing down from your original statement that Mrs. Pherson died of manual strangulation, does it not?"

"I modified my original statement by making it clear that it was my opinion."

"Are you by any chance suggesting that pathology is not an exact science but an interpretive one, involving opinions instead of facts?"

"It is both, I believe."

"Comparing pathology with mathematics, for instance, when mathematicians are confronted with the numbers two and two, there is unanimous agreement that they add up to four, is there not?"

"Yes."

"No difference of opinion is involved, no ifs, ands or buts?"

"No."

"Would you therefore call mathematics an exact science?"

"On such a simple level I would also call pathology an exact science. When a group of pathologists is confronted with a cadaver, there is unanimous agreement that it is a dead body."

The audience purred with amusement. The sound reminded Donnelly of the tortoiseshell cat that lay across the foot of Zan's bed, purring in its dreams, oblivious of everything but itself.

Irritation sharpened Donnelly's voice. "You are the first

pathologist to take the stand, Dr. Woodbridge. Do you think there will be others?"

"I'm sure there are others scheduled."

"Do you think they'll agree with your opinion about the cause of Mrs. Pherson's death?"

"I object," the district attorney said. "Witness is being asked to form a conclusion without any foundation."

"Sustained."

"I withdraw the question," Donnelly said, satisfied. It had already been answered.

"On what do you base your opinion that manual strangulation was involved in Mrs. Pherson's death 'to some extent'?"

"First, there were the grooves left on her throat by thumbs."

"*In your opinion*, left by thumbs. What else?"

"Broken bones in the larynx. This is not a matter of opinion or interpretation. A broken bone is a broken bone."

"These bones which define the larynx, how would you describe them?"

"I'm not sure I understand the question."

"Are they large or small bones?"

"Small."

"Are they strong, sturdy bones?"

"No."

"Are they fragile?"

"Quite fragile, yes."

"Are these bones often damaged in victims of strangulation?"

"Both their position and composition make them vulnerable."

"Vulnerable to pressure?"

"Yes."

"Pressure of any kind?"

"Yes. But in this case, as in others like it—"

"You have answered the question, Dr. Woodbridge."

"Am I not allowed to qualify my answer?"

"Since you've qualified most of your other answers, you might as well qualify this one as well."

"I move that remark be stricken from the record," the district attorney said. "Once again counsel is trying to harass and intimidate the witness."

"Strike it," the judge said. "Kindly refrain from further lapses of this nature, Mr. Donnelly."

"I'll try, Your Honor."

"In my court you get no brownie points for trying. Succeed."

"Yes, Your Honor. Dr. Woodbridge, how many bodies of strangulation victims have you autopsied?"

"I'm not sure."

"Can you give us an approximate figure?"

"I could give you a more specific figure if you will give me a more specific time period. Do you mean, since I have been employed in Santa Felicia County?"

"I'll limit the question to that time."

"Then my answer is, maybe a dozen."

"And did these bodies have marks on the throat like those found on Mrs. Pherson?"

"Similar."

"Marks on the throats of *maybe* a dozen victims of strangulation *similar* to those found on that of Mrs. Pherson, who, in your *opinion*, died of manual strangulation. Is that right?"

"Well, I—"

"Or fairly right? Or even a little bit right?"

The district attorney was on his feet again. "Once more this witness is being badgered."

"You have been warned previously, Mr. Donnelly," the judge said. "Continued disregard of the court's warnings could result in contempt charges, a fact of which you must be aware."

"Yes, Your Honor. But I don't consider what I said to be badgering."

"In this courtroom, Mr. Donnelly, it's what I consider that's important."

"Yes, Your Honor."

The judge frowned. He had an itch between his shoulder blades which was impossible to scratch, even if he hadn't been on the bench, and an itch inside his head as well, caused by the change in Donnelly. In previous trials Donnelly had gotten away with murder—in every sense of the word—by remaining scrupulously polite, smoothing the edges of even his sharpest questions with "if you please," "by your leave," "begging your permission." He was like an expert skater gliding across the ice so quickly it didn't have time to break. That was changed now, not a great deal but enough to be apparent to someone who'd seen him in action previously. He was still skating, but there were cracks in the ice.

Donnelly continued his cross-examination. "Dr. Woodbridge, I would like at this point to examine another of your opinions—that is, that Mrs. Pherson's bruises were inflicted before death. You stated your belief that the bruises were premortem, did you not?"

"Yes."

"Occurring before death?"

"Yes."

"Is it possible for bruises to occur postmortem, after death?"

"When the heart has stopped pumping blood through the vascular system, the blood will obey the laws of gravity and settle in the most depressed areas of the body and the surrounding skin will appear bruised."

"Then your answer is yes?"

"A qualified yes."

"Is it possible for the bruises on Mrs. Pherson's throat to have occurred after death?"

"I don't see how it would—"

"I didn't ask whether you saw how. I asked if it was possible."

"It's possible but not probable."

The doctor's tic had become more noticeable and almost as regular as the tick of a clock.

"Suppose we accept the idea that the bruises occurred before death," Donnelly said. "How long before death?"

"I don't know."

"Could the bruises, in fact, have been on Mrs. Pherson's throat before she even came on board the *Bewitched*?"

"It's possible."

"Can you think of anything to rule this out?"

"Well, for one thing, she was seen by a number of people, at the hotel, in her suite, in the bar, at the desk, as well as by the crew of the *Bewitched*. And none of them, to my knowledge, has mentioned seeing such bruises."

"Now, without bothering the clerk to bring back some of the pertinent exhibits, could you indicate on your own throat the relative position of the bruises on Mrs. Pherson's throat?"

"How do you want me to do that?"

"With your thumb and forefinger."

"They were approximately here."

"Let the record show," Donnelly said, "that Dr. Woodbridge is indicating two areas underneath the collar of his shirt."

The doctor's hand dropped back into his lap like a wounded bird.

"Do you have any bruises on your throat, Dr. Woodbridge?"

"No."

"Would I be able to see them if you had?"

"No."

"Why not?"

"They would be covered by my collar."

"Do you know what Mrs. Pherson was wearing when she left the hotel?"

"No."

"What was she wearing when you first saw her?"

"Nothing."

It was a simple word, stating a fact already known to the audience, but it had a curiously shocking effect. There were sharp intakes of breath and uneasy stirrings, as if the woman had been stripped of her clothes before their eyes.

"Under what circumstances is an autopsy routinely performed?"

"When a person who has not previously been ill is found dead, or when there are obvious signs of violence, either self- or other-inflicted."

"When a victim of violence is brought into your lab, what is the initial procedure?"

"Certain steps are taken which will help the police identify the victim."

"Such as?"

"The body is measured and weighed, fingerprints are taken, and, of course, photographs."

"Were these things done in the case of Mrs. Pherson?"

"Yes."

"And what were the measurements of her body?"

"I'll have to consult my notes."

"Please do."

The neat sheaf of papers Woodbridge had brought into the courtroom the previous day was now beginning to look as crumpled and untidy as the doctor himself. "Do you want me to read my original notes or the somewhat amplified and edited version of my secretary?"

"Whatever's shorter."

" 'The body is that of a female Caucasian, well cared for, age approximately forty, blue eyes, brown hair, five feet two inches in height, a hundred and nine pounds by weight.' "

"Then she was a small woman?"

"Smaller than average, yes."

"Before you make any actual incisions in the body, are other tests done?"

"Blood samples are taken."

"For what purpose?"

"To determine whether the person was suffering from acute or chronic disease."

"Anything else?"

Woodbridge threw a glance at the district attorney which was neatly intercepted by Donnelly. He ran with it.

"Dr. Woodbridge, was one of the tests performed in order to establish the presence of alcohol in Mrs. Pherson's bloodstream?"

"Yes."

"What was the result?"

"Point-one-four percent."

"What does this mean?"

"That she'd had a few drinks."

"It's been well established that the woman was drinking.

172

What is important for the jurors to know is how much."

"I can only give you the figure my tests indicated."

"Very well. I have here, Dr. Woodbridge, a chart issued to clarify the actual meaning of a blood alcohol test. Will you please examine this chart, Doctor? It consists of only a single page."

Donnelly took the page to the witness box and stood while the doctor read it. About four minutes passed. During this time there was no noise in the room, but the silence seemed to be filled with vibrations. It was the kind of silence peculiar to a courtroom, a pulse of expectation.

"Are you familiar with this chart, Dr. Woodbridge?"

"Not this particular one. I've seen others like it."

"Can you explain its purpose to the jury?"

"The chart shows how many drinks a person of a certain size must consume over a certain period of time in order to reach a certain level of blood alcohol."

"Then body size is a determining factor in the test results?"

"Yes."

"Will you please study the chart and see if the figure point-one-four percent occurs?"

"It's here."

"What does this indicate in terms of body weight and drinks consumed and in what time period?"

"It shows how much alcohol will be found in the blood of a person weighing a hundred twenty pounds who has consumed six drinks within a period of two hours, each drink consisting of one ounce of eighty-six-proof alcohol, such as those served in a bar or restaurant, or a twelve-ounce bottle of beer."

"At what alcohol level is a person legally drunk in the state of California?"

"Point-one-zero percent."

"For those of us with short memories will you please repeat Mrs. Pherson's weight?"

"A hundred nine pounds."

"And her blood alcohol content?"

"Point-one-four percent."

"The chart in front of you indicates some of the behavioral results of various blood alcohol percentages. Can you tell us how the chart describes the behavior of people with point-one-zero percent—that is, legally drunk?"

"Their inhibitions and judgment are seriously impaired."

"What about point-one-five percent?"

"The behavior pattern is not given for that particular figure."

"Then what is the next figure?"

"Point-two-zero percent."

"And how does a person behave at this level?"

"Point-two-zero percent indicates a probable problem drinker who is not fit to drive for up to ten hours after the last drink."

"And Mrs. Pherson was probably in between these two, factoring in her body weight of a hundred and nine, eleven pounds lighter than the hundred-twenty-pound example. Is that correct?"

"Very likely."

"Would you say Mrs. Pherson was drunk?"

"This chart is based only on averages and there is—"

"And her inhibitions and judgment seriously impaired?"

"No doubt there was some degree of impairment."

"And would you say that a person unaccustomed to drinking might have more severe behavioral reactions than someone who drinks regularly?"

"This is not my field of expertise."

"I've spent most of the day trying to locate and pin down your field of expertise and getting equivocal answers like 'maybe,' 'to some extent,' 'possibly,' 'in my opinion'—"

"I object," the district attorney shouted. "Such an acrimonious and malicious statement is inexcusable."

"Strike the defense counsel's remarks," the judge said. "Once again I am reminding you, Mr. Donnelly, that you are an attorney in this case, not the judge. You might mull over the following facts: In the county of Santa Felicia there are five Superior Court judges and seven hundred and seventy-five attorneys."

"I didn't know that, Your Honor."

"Once in a while I get lucky and come across something you don't know, Mr. Donnelly. Have you any more questions for this witness?"

"I would like to continue after a brief recess."

"Recess of fifteen minutes is hereby declared."

The judge and jury and most of the spectators left the room. Eva would have liked to stay behind and talk to Cully, but he was deep in conversation with Donnelly, so she, too, went out into the corridor.

Sitting on a bench directly under the QUIET, COURT IN SESSION sign was a middle-aged, grim-faced man wearing a black suit. He had on dark glasses, mirror-coated to reflect the images of other people and obscure his own. It was not the first time Eva had seen him sitting in the same spot, sometimes talking, sometimes with his head bowed as though he were praying or counting the tiles in the floor or simply listening to what everybody else was saying. He never went in or out of the courtroom.

As Eva was about to pass him, the man rose and approached her, holding his arms rigidly by his sides.

"Miss Foster?"

"Yes."

"I have watched you in court, so I know who you are."

"I haven't seen you there."

"Oh, no. I'm not allowed to go inside. But when the door opens, I look in to see what's going on."

"Why aren't you allowed inside?"

"I was subjoined as a witness. They tell me it's common practice to keep witnesses away from the courtroom before and even after testifying. But it's very unfair. I want to be in there hearing what they're saying about her. I want to be able to stand up and tell everybody what a good woman she was, a good, God-fearing woman."

"You're—are you her husband?"

"Yes."

"You'll get a chance to speak when your turn comes, Mr. Pherson."

"That's not soon enough. I hear people talking in the corridor, so I know what's going on inside there, the vilification, the lies. She never drank, never touched a drop of liquor in her life. And God knows she'd never go into a bar by herself and pick up a man, a black man. Lies, lies, a crazy quilt of lies patched together by that murderer."

"Please lower your voice, Mr. Pherson, or the bailiff will ask you to leave."

He stared at her as if for a minute he'd forgotten she was there, a person, not a blank wall to bounce words against. "You're his friend."

"The bailiff and I have known each other for a long time, but that doesn't—"

"No, the other one, the black man. I've seen you talking to each other before court begins, leaning towards each other, smiling, very friendly, very cozy. What do you whisper in his ear?"

"I never whispered anything in his ear."

"I've seen you whisper in that black ear of his. Back home we have a mushroom called a tree mushroom, and it looks like a black ear, and it's shiny, slimy."

"Hanging around the corridor like this isn't good for you, Mr. Pherson."

"Well, I'll give you something to whisper in his slimy black ear. Tell him—tell him that if he's found innocent, he won't be free, never, ever. I'm going to get him. If he tries to run away, I'll track him down no matter how far and fast he runs."

"I think you'd better go home and rest, Mr. Pherson."

"My home is far away."

"Where are you staying while you're in town?"

"The Biltmore. I have a room on the beach. At night I lie awake and listen to the sea, where he threw her after he violated and strangled her."

"None of that has been proved."

"It has to me. He drugged her with liquor and took her down to that boat and ravished her, then stripped her of her jewels and threw her overboard. I'll get him for that. I'll get him if it takes the rest of my life. Tell him. Tell him for me."

The sympathy she'd felt for him at first was beginning to dissipate. "Delivering death threats to a defendant is not part of my job, or anyone else's around here."

"I tried to tell him myself, but the deputy wouldn't let me near him. I wrote him a letter at the jail, but I don't think he got it."

"The mail there is censored. A threat like that wouldn't be allowed through."

"Then it's up to you."

He put his hand out and touched her arm. Its coldness almost instantly penetrated the thin fabric of her sleeve, and she took a step back as if to evade the touch of death.

"I think you should go home to Bakersfield, Mr. Pherson, and wait there until the district attorney is ready to put you on the stand."

"He's ready now. I'm going to be next."

"Then you'd better start calming down. Do you have any kind of tranquilizer to take?"

"My wife and I have never believed in chemical dependence."

"A lot of your beliefs may be shot full of holes before this is over. If I were you, I'd use all the help I could get."

He took off his glasses, and for the first time she saw his eyes, dark and bitter and rimmed with red.

"You're talking to me as if I were a silly old fool. I'm not a silly old fool, Miss Foster. And I meant what I said. I'll get that black bastard if it takes the rest of my life."

He returned to the bench and his original posture, head bowed, hands folded. But she knew now he was neither praying nor counting floor tiles. He was planning. And he wasn't a silly old fool; he was a dangerous man.

She went back into the courtroom. The bailiff was standing beside the window, talking to a young woman who'd been hired by the local television station to do sketches of the defendant and judge and jury since cameras were not allowed.

Cully was sitting at the counsel's table, alone.

He appeared to be in a good mood. "How are things in the outside world?"

"The same."

"That bad?" When she didn't respond, he said, "Hey,

that's a joke. There's no law against smiling once in a while."

"What at?"

"At me."

"I don't smile unless I feel like it. Women used to be expected to smile all the time in order to feed a man's ego, but no more."

"Why not?"

"Women realized that we are just as important, even aside from procreation, as men. We are just as intelligent, just as skillful, and what we may lack in strength we make up for in endurance."

He seemed stunned by her barrage of words. "Hey, wait a minute. I didn't ask you to smile at me that way. I got a lot of women who'll smile at me that way. What I meant—I only meant it wouldn't hurt you to laugh a little when I make a joke."

"All right. Ha-ha."

The oak door of the courtroom opened with the languor and ponderous combination of weight and justice. A man peered inside, identifiable as a tourist by his Bermuda shorts, Panama hat and Japanese camera slung around his neck. He kept the door open long enough for Eva to catch a glimpse of Pherson pointing a long, skinny finger in her direction. Cully's back was to the door, so he didn't see Pherson and wouldn't have recognized him if he had.

"Her husband is here," Eva said.

Cully looked genuinely puzzled. "Whose husband?"

"Mrs. Pherson's. He's going to be testifying against you."

"How can he testify against me? He doesn't know me."

"He knew his wife. He'll say she never drank and she was the last woman in the world who'd go into a bar and pick up a man."

"It's what she did."

"He'll never believe it. At least he'll never admit it. Isn't that just like a man? If he admitted his wife would do something like that, he would consider it a reflection on him, and people might think he wasn't giving her what she wanted."

"Maybe he wasn't giving her what she wanted."

"So you did, I suppose?"

"I offered Mrs. Pherson a chance to try out as a cook for the race to Honolulu because she said she knew a lot about French cuisine and that's what Mr. Belasco likes."

"She probably never cooked a meal in her life. The Phersons had a housekeeper and a maid, according to the transcript of the preliminary hearing. That transcript is available to you. Haven't you read it?"

"I tried. It was too full of lies, bad things I never did. I am not like that man in the transcript. I am me, I think I am a nice person. I wouldn't do bad things like that."

"Tell it to Mr. Pherson."

"Did he—you know, talk much about me?"

"Enough."

"What did he say?"

"He wants you punished."

"How?"

"Any way at all so long as you end up dead."

"So he wants me dead." Cully's voice showed no surprise or fear, only a kind of weary bitterness. "They all do. Look at them."

By this time the spectators were coming back into the courtroom. The bailiff propped the door open and stood by as they returned to their seats, the artist with her sketchbook, the crime reporter from the local paper, tourists accidentally caught up in the excitement, an entire class of seventh graders with their teacher, retired white-collar workers and housewives seeking to kill an afternoon or a man.

Cully had twisted around in his chair to look at them. Now he turned back to face the table.

"They all want me dead," he repeated.

"Not all of them. In every trial the court watchers are divided in opinion. Some of them are on your side."

"How can you tell?"

"There's a lot of body English used in a courtroom, nods, smiles, grimaces, frowns."

"That lady in the front row, is she drawing a picture of me?"

"She's been doing pictures of all the people connected with the case."

"I saw her staring at me during recess." He seemed to have forgotten Mr. Pherson and all the others who wanted him dead. He looked pleased and slightly embarrassed. "I wonder if she'd let me see it when she's finished."

"She might not even be drawing you."

"I bet she is. That's why she stayed during recess, to study my features because all she can see of me while the trial is going on is the back of my head. Do I look all right?"

"You look . . . fine."

"Should I turn around and let her see me better?"

"No. No, I think she's seen you."

So have I, Eva thought.

She had seen a child-man, naïve, self-centered, crude, who could forget that he was on trial for his life at the prospect of seeing a sketch of himself. She felt a rush of blood up the side of her neck into her head. Conflicting emotions expanded and contracted her veins and beat on her temples.

"Miss Foster, could you try and fix things so I get to

see the picture? I mean, if it's nice. I don't want to see any ugly picture of me. If she thinks I'm guilty, she might draw me ugly. I'm not ugly, am I?"

"No."

"She might even draw me good-looking. Do you suppose she might draw me good-looking?"

"I don't know."

"I'd sure like to see that picture. Could you fix it for me?"

"No."

"Why not?"

"I don't want to."

He blinked, as if someone had shone a sudden light in his eyes. "You sound funny, like you have something against me."

"The only person I have anything against is myself."

"Then why won't you do a simple thing like asking the lady if I can see the picture? I might want to get copies made to send back home to my wife and kids."

"You said—you told me you weren't married."

"I call her my wife; she calls me her husband; the kids call me Papa. It's easier that way and no harm done."

"No harm done, is that what you think?" All her blood seemed to have accumulated in her head, leaving her lower limbs numb and her hands cold and clammy. She leaned toward him and said in a hoarse whisper, "Take your goddamn picture and shove it."

He looked bewildered, and she felt somehow that she had injured a defenseless creature who didn't understand what he had done wrong.

"Listen," she said. "It's just that I can't do anything like what you asked me to. It's not allowed."

"No, that's not the reason. It's because you hate me. Why?"

"I don't hate you."

"You sound like it."

"Look, you and I aren't even supposed to be talking to each other, let alone about things like love and hate."

"I never said anything about love."

"I meant emotions, feelings in general. I meant—"

"I know what you meant," Cully said.

Donnelly and Gunther had come in, and Gunther stopped in front of Eva's table and slung his briefcase on the polished surface.

"Foster, you look guilty. What have you been doing, plotting to overthrow the government? Yes? No?"

"None of your business."

"I'd like to be in on it. I'm bored. My soul cries out for a little excitement."

"Tell it to shut up."

"Mr. Gunther," Donnelly said, "kindly remember that Miss Foster is inclined to interpret such personal remarks as sexual harassment."

"Have I been harassing you sexually, Foster?" Gunther said.

"No."

"Has anyone?"

"No."

"You wouldn't really mind if they did, would you, Foster?"

She looked up at the two men. They both were smiling. So was Cully.

Before the warning buzzer sounded the end of the recess, District Attorney Owen talked to his witness at the bottom of the spiral staircase leading to the clock tower.

Owen was reluctant to criticize the older man, but for the sake of his case he felt he had to.

"You weren't very sure of yourself up there," Owen said. "In fact, you let Donnelly push you around."

"I did the best I could."

"All that stuff about cold-water drowning, you never mentioned any of it to me."

"It's a relatively new field."

"I think you should have told me. It would have given me a chance to be better prepared. In a case like this surprises can be disastrous. . . ."

"It seemed unlikely that Donnelly knew about or would try to use this cold-water rescue stuff."

"What are the chances that Mrs. Pherson died the way he suggested, *after* she was in the water?"

"My guess is one in a million."

"Then it didn't happen?"

"No."

"Why are you so positive now when you were so hesitant on the stand?"

"I'm not under oath. And I'm not facing Donnelly." A gust of cold air circled down the spiral staircase, and Woodbridge shivered. "It's his righteousness that scares me. He comes riding in on a white horse to rescue an underdog, some Mexican or black or prostitute, and he doesn't care how much shit the horse scatters or whose fan it hits."

The fifteen-minute recess which stretched to half an hour had apparently agreed with Donnelly. He took his place at the lectern, this time without notes except for a single sheet of yellow paper from a legal pad. He watched almost benevolently as Woodbridge returned to the stand.

"Dr. Woodbridge, I would like to call your attention to people's exhibits numbers seventeen and nineteen. Miss Foster, are those available?"

"Right here, sir."

Number 17 was a picture of the right profile of Madeline Pherson, showing only her head. Number 19 showed the left profile.

"Did you have occasion to examine Mrs. Pherson's ears, Dr. Woodbridge?"

"Yes."

"Was there anything peculiar about Mrs. Pherson's ears?"

"Not peculiar, no. I saw that they'd both been pierced for earrings."

"Is there any tearing of the flesh such as might be caused by someone yanking earrings off during or after the commission of a crime such as robbery or murder? It's a not uncommon injury among victims of violence. To repeat the question, was there any evidence that Mrs. Pherson's earrings had been forcibly removed?"

"No."

"What do you deduce from this?"

"That she took them off herself."

Over the district attorney's objection, Woodbridge's answer was allowed to stand.

"To pursue an entirely different line of question, Dr. Woodbridge, can you tell us the state of your health?"

"My health?"

"Yes. Do you have good health, fair, bad?"

"Fair."

"Are you suffering from any chronic condition which might interfere with the performance of your job?"

"I believe my job performance is satisfactory."

"I will repeat the question and ask you to give a more responsive answer. Do you suffer from any chronic physical ailment which might impair your ability to perform your job?"

"I don't think so."

"You are not sure?"

"The only way I can answer that without going into detail is to say that I am qualified to do my work properly."

Donnelly approached the witness stand. "Will you take this piece of paper and hold it out two or three feet in front of you?"

"I object, Your Honor," Owen said. "I see no purpose in this line of questioning, no relevance to this case."

"The purpose and relevance will emerge in a moment, Your Honor," Donnelly said. "If you will direct the witness to do as I requested—"

Before Donnelly could finish the sentence and the judge could rule on the DA's objection, Woodbridge stretched out his hand, took the piece of paper and held it at arm's length. Then he turned his head away as if he didn't want to see what was happening to the paper. It was shaking, slightly at first, then increasing to the point where the paper crackled.

"Are you nervous, Dr. Woodbridge?" Donnelly said.

"No."

"Your hand is trembling. Is there any reason for this?"

"Yes."

"Can you tell us what that reason is?"

Owen folded his arms across his chest in a gesture of self-defense, afraid something was going to happen but not knowing what it could be.

The judge knew. "Mr. Donnelly, is it necessary to pursue this line of questioning?"

"I believe that Dr. Woodbridge's answer will have some bearing on his previous testimony. I need not remind Your Honor that the phrase 'beyond a reasonable doubt' is of great importance in a criminal trial."

"That's right, Mr. Donnelly. You needn't remind me."

"Then may I repeat the question to Dr. Woodbridge?"

"Go ahead."

"Dr. Woodbridge, you stated a minute ago that you were not nervous," Donnelly said. "You have participated in many criminal prosecutions and have established a reputation for coolness and composure. Why are your hands trembling now?"

The doctor's answer was slow and almost inaudible. "I have Parkinsonism."

"Will you speak a little more loudly so the jurors are sure to hear you?"

"I have Parkinson's disease."

"Would you explain what that is?"

"It is a degenerative disease affecting motor function—that is, body movements."

"Are these movements involuntary?"

"Yes."

"The medical term for this is resting tremor, is it not?"

"Yes."

"Do you have akinesia or bradykinesia—that is, slowness of movement?"

"Sometimes."

"Do you also have an increase of rigidity?"

"Yes."

"Speech difficulty?"

"Sometimes."

"What causes all this?"

"They don't know why people get Parkinsonism."

"What I meant was: What causes the symptoms?"

"A lesion in that part of the brain that controls body movement."

"Can this lesion of the brain cause confusion?"

"It may cause what is mistaken for confusion because

it sometimes affects the ability to control speech."

"Does this lesion of the brain impair the ability to think, to make judgments, to assess facts?"

"No."

"Are you being medicated for your disease?"

"Yes."

"Does the medication impair you in any way? Does it cause confusion or uncertainty?"

"No. No. I am not confused. I can think—" He crushed the sheet of paper and threw it on the floor. "I can think per—I can think perfect—perfectly. My mind . . . very clear."

The district attorney's objection and the judge's gavel sounded simultaneously.

"Court is adjourned until tomorrow at ten o'clock," the judge said. "The jury is admonished not to discuss this case with each other or anyone else and not to read or watch any news coverage pertaining to this trial."

Woodbridge stepped down from the stand, wiping his face with a handkerchief. He confronted Donnelly at the lectern.

"You son of a bitch."

"Sorry," Donnelly said. "But I didn't cause your illness, I merely brought it to the attention of the jury in the defense of my client."

"How far will you go to defend a client?"

"Any distance the law allows."

"Well, before you ride that white horse of yours too far," Woodbridge said, "make sure it's a Thoroughbred."

He walked away, and Donnelly watched him. He didn't know exactly what Woodbridge meant by the white horse, but he didn't care. He had made his point.

In the minds of some of the jurors, perhaps all of them, there would be a reasonable doubt. "Beyond a reasonable

doubt" and "to a moral certainty" were the most important words in the instructions the judge would give the
jury before it began deliberations.

The moral certainty part would be more difficult. What
it basically amounted to was a gut feeling whether a defendant was innocent or guilty.

Gut feelings were hard to reach and alter. They were
composed of bits of the past and pieces of the present,
sights and sounds and smells processed into a mass in the
middle of the gut. This mass could be benign or malig-
nant; it could not be digested.

He saw Woodbridge walk from the courtroom, very
slowly, as if his illness, once out of the closet, had gained
weight and gravity. Donnelly felt a certain pity that he'd
had to kill a part of Woodbridge in the interests of justice.
Cully's life or death wasn't the real issue. Donnelly himself
had died a hundred times so far that year and would die
a hundred more.

Life and death didn't matter. It was the judicial system
itself that mattered, the system of justice for all. If that's
the white horse he was riding, it was a Thoroughbred.

As always at the end of a day the courtroom emptied
quickly. Within five minutes the only people left were
Cully and the bailiff and Eva and the woman artist who
was still sitting in the front row putting the finishing touches
on a sketch. The woman looked up as Eva approached.
"Am I overparked?"

"No. I just wanted to ask you if Mr. King could see the
sketch you've done of him. Would you mind?"

"Not at all. Here it is."

"*You* show it to him."

"Don't you even want to see it?"

"No," Eva said. "I don't want to see it."

V

The
WITNESSES

*D*uring the night a marine layer unfurled over the city, draping the clock tower of the courthouse and smothering its chimes. The hours, unseen and unheard, ceased to exist until the sun burned a hole in the fog. Then the prodigal parrot, the main occupant of the tower, woke up and began to groom its feathers, using the oil from its preen gland. While it prepared itself for the day, it kept a sharp eye on the sheriff's van, which was unloading its prisoners for the morning's trials. The bird swooped down on the men, its free flight mocking their shackles.

The hours came back to life. Eight. Nine. Ten o'clock.

In courtroom 5 the man who stepped up into the witness box gave his name as Tyler Winslow Pherson. He lived at 300 Garden Grove Avenue, Bakersfield, and was the executive vice-president of the Valley Oil Corporation. In response to the district attorney's question, he said that the deceased woman had been his wife, Madeline.

"We were married for eighteen years," Pherson said. "Madeline was a wonderful woman, devoted to the service of others, children, the elderly, the handicapped. She raised large sums of money for many charities. She spent months learning braille so she could translate books for the blind, and in her work at Hospice she counseled families of the terminally ill. She was a woman who loved God and was loved by Him. I don't understand how He could have let this terrible thing happen to her."

"We all sympathize with your plight, Mr. Pherson. But in order to proceed with the trial, I must ask you to confine yourself to answering my questions."

"How could He have let it happen to a woman like Madeline? Why?" He looked down at Cully. "Why? Why did you kill her?"

Donnelly jumped up to object and the judge began pounding his gavel, but Pherson did not see or hear.

"How many others have you killed? How many others will you kill if they let you go?"

"You will be found in contempt, Mr. Pherson," the judge said, "if you continue in this vein."

"I have a right to know. I have a right."

"The defendant also has a right to a fair trial conducted under the rules of—"

"Rules. The rules are all in favor of that murderer. Aren't there any rules to protect the memory of my dead wife?"

"If you cannot contain yourself, Mr. Pherson, I must ask you to step down and return at a later time."

Owen was careful not to show it, but Pherson's outburst suited his purpose. His remarks might be stricken from the record, but the jury wasn't likely to forget them or his anguished face when he made them.

Owen said, "Do you feel capable of continuing your testimony, Mr. Pherson?"

"Yes. Yes, I'm all right."

"I'd like to establish some facts about the family background. For instance, do you have any children?"

"No. We were never blessed."

"Are there any close family ties?"

"Madeline had a very deep relationship with her mother."

"Does her mother live in Bakersfield?"

"No. She died in March. She and Madeline had been planning a trip to Hawaii when her mother became ill. Madeline took it very hard. That was the reason I wanted her to go on a vacation. I thought a change of scene would be good for her, cheer her up. The irony of that haunts me day and night, the irony that I should be responsible for her death while trying to help her. She didn't really want to go anywhere. It was my decision. I'm used to making decisions; I'm used to being right." He shook his head. "This time I wasn't right. God help me in my terrible wrongness."

"Will you please just answer my questions, Mr. Pherson?"

"Yes. Yes, all right."

"Did Mrs. Pherson inherit anything from her mother?"

"A small amount of real estate, an insurance policy, some treasury notes and the heirloom jewelry which for generations had been passed on to the oldest daughter. The insurance on them was outdated, and Madeline intended to have them reappraised and reinsured. I don't know their current value."

"Do you think they were worth a considerable amount of money?"

"Yes."

"In what way did Mrs. Pherson obtain these jewels?"

"Her mother's lawyer handed them over at his office."

"In a container?"

"Yes."

"Were you present?"

"Yes."

"Can you describe the container?"

"It was about the size of a makeup case, covered with embossed green leather with a large old-fashioned lock.

I carried it out to the car for her, and she sat with it on her lap all the way home. She didn't cry or make a fuss, but it was not a happy time. During her mother's illness she remained cheerful and supportive. Now it was all over. Perhaps she was thinking, as she sat with the case on her lap, that she would be the last owner of the jewelry since there was no eldest daughter to pass it on to, no daughter at all. It was the end of the line."

"So you persuaded her to take a vacation, get a change of scene?"

"Yes. She chose the San Diego area. My secretary made the necessary travel and hotel arrangements, and I drove her to the airport. She called me when she arrived. She sounded quite cheerful. It was the last time I heard her voice."

"That will be all for now, Mr. Pherson," Owen said. "Thank you."

Donnelly rose and went to the lectern for the cross-examination. "Mr. Pherson, you said your wife sounded cheerful when she called you. Did this surprise you?"

"I was happy about it."

"Yes, but were you surprised?"

"I thought it would take longer for her to snap out of her depression and begin to enjoy life again. So my answer is, I was pleasantly surprised."

"Did she ever talk of suicide?"

"No, never."

"I believe you stated that Mrs. Pherson counseled the terminally ill and their families, did you not?"

"Yes."

"Wouldn't the subject of suicide come up naturally in the course of these conversations?"

"When I said she never mentioned suicide, I meant in

regard to herself. Such a thing would never have occurred to her."

"Even though she was, according to your testimony, in a state of depression after her mother's death?"

Pherson sat in silence, motionless except for his eyes, which moved slowly up and down the two row of jurors, establishing eye contact with each person.

"My wife did not kill herself. She was murdered."

The words were spoken not in the loud, abrasive tone of his previous accusations but with quiet dignity and utter conviction.

Donnelly's objection was routine. Pherson's words would be stricken from the record, but they would remain in the memories of the jurors, no matter how solemnly the judge would later instruct them to lay aside their emotions and base their decision solely on facts. They wouldn't do it; juries seldom, if ever, did. Facts had a way of being pushed out of shape or out of sight.

And the fact was that Madeline Pherson had gone into that bar not to raise funds for charity, not to translate books into braille, not to counsel the terminally ill. She had gone into that bar to drink double martinis and pick up a stranger.

The judge said, "Do you have any further questions to ask this witness, Mr. Donnelly?"

"Not at this time, Your Honor."

"You are excused for now, Mr. Pherson. Counsel will notify you if you are needed again. Meanwhile, the same rule applies to you as to all the other witnesses in this case. None of you is allowed inside this courtroom until the conclusion of the trial. And you are reminded not to discuss your testimony with any other witness."

"Pardon me, Your Honor," the district attorney said.

"My next witness hasn't arrived yet from San Diego. It's a four- to five-hour drive or longer, and I don't expect him until about one o'clock. The situation is my fault. I anticipated that Mr. Pherson would be on the stand for a longer period."

"All right. Instead of the usual morning recess, we will take the lunch break now and reconvene at two o'clock."

Cully was sitting on the edge of his chair, hands on the table in front of him with the fingers knotted together like oiled ropes. Donnelly sat down beside him and began to repack his briefcase. "Well? Anything wrong?"

"Did she really do all those good things?"

"Yes. Gunther checked it out."

"But that wasn't like the woman who started talking to me in the bar. She wasn't trying to save my soul, I can tell you that. She was coming on to me."

"So you say."

"She came on strong to me. I swear she did. Maybe the police made a mistake and the body they found wasn't hers but somebody else's."

"She was positively identified by her husband and the housekeeper."

"I saw a movie once about a lady with a split personality who—"

"Forget it. Mrs. Pherson was a nice, wholesome, healthy woman."

"Then why did she come on to me like that?"

"Maybe you're irresistible."

The courtroom was empty by this time except for the two men and the bailiff standing at the door, waiting for the deputy to come and take Cully back to jail.

"About those scratches on your cheek, was she in such a fury of passion she scratched you with her fingernails?"

"No. No, it didn't happen that way. What happened was she grabbed me and one of her earrings scratched my cheek."

"Which earring?"

"I'm not sure. I mean, there was a whole lot going on and we were both drunk, and who can remember a little thing like which earring?"

"The jury likes to know little things like that. They may swallow the big stuff whole like the whale swallowed Jonah, but they can get pretty picky about small details that don't add up or can't be remembered."

"Okay, let's say it was the left earring."

"Let's not say anything until we reconstruct the scene."

"Like how?"

"Walk toward me and grab me the way Mrs. Pherson grabbed you."

"That would look funny. People might think—"

"The jury's out of the room, and they're the only ones whose thinking should concern you. Go ahead. Grab. Do it."

"No."

"Come on. Just pretend you find me irresistible, so in a fit of passion—"

"No. It would make me look funny, feel funny."

"Why? Pretend we're enacting a scene from a play."

"I'm not a playactor."

"Grab me, you son of a bitch."

The bailiff turned at the sound of a raised voice. "Anything the matter over there?"

"No," Donnelly said. "We were just discussing how irresistible Cully is to women." When the bailiff's attention had returned to the hall, Donnelly added, "Not only to Mrs. Pherson but to our own little Eva. The way she looks at you with those hot little eyes of hers is enough to roast a turkey. Don't you feel the heat, turkey?"

"No."

"This sudden attack of modesty doesn't suit your style, Cully." Donnelly had finished putting all his papers back into the briefcase. Now he snapped it shut but made no move to leave. "By the way, I have a letter for you. It was addressed to me, but the enclosure is for you."

"Who's it from?"

"Your wife." Donnelly put the letter on the table, but Cully didn't pick it up or even glance at it. "Don't you want to read it?"

"No."

"I think you'd better. It's often helpful to get somebody else's slant on things."

"Louise has only one slant."

The letter was neatly typed and punctuated and contained only two misspellings.

"Louise didn't type this," Cully said. "She can't type. Her brother did it for her. He probably urged her to send it, too. The son of a bitch hates me."

"Ah, yes, your brother-in-law, the one you'd like to murder."

Cully blinked in surprise. "Who told you that?"

"Miss Foster. She thought I ought to warn you not to make such remarks because people might get the wrong impression. Or the right one, whatever."

"I wouldn't have told her if I thought she was going to blab it all over."

"She didn't blab it all over. By telling me, she was trying to protect you. Oh, yes, she's quite the tigress, Little Eva is. And you, amigo, are her cub."

"I'm not. I won't be. I refuse."

"Cubs don't have a choice," Donnelly said. "Read your letter."

There were two sheets of paper inside the envelope. One was a request to Mr. Donnelly, Esquire, to pass the enclosed to Cully King.

Dear Cully:

I hope you're doing okay because I certainly am not. I need money. You can't expect me to live on nothing while you're going around murdering people. Thanksgiving is coming pretty soon and what have I got to be thankfull for, with a husband in the cooler and me with nothing to wear? Whether you are innosent or guilty the least you can do is to send me the money Mr. Belasco paid you. It won't do you any good where you are, getting free room and board and maybe even color TV.

That was as far as Cully read. He threw the letter on the floor. "Belasco never paid me."

"I know. I asked him not to, and he agreed."

"What'd you do a crazy thing like that for?"

"The money is being kept for you. That way you can, more or less legitimately, claim to have no assets. If you have no assets, a public defender will be appointed for you in case something happens to prevent me from continuing your defense. If or when you get out, you should have enough to tide you over while you pick up the pieces of your life."

"I don't want to pick up any pieces. Nobody wants me out anyway."

"A lot of people do."

"Not for my sake they don't. Louise wants me out so I can go on supporting her and that louse of a brother of hers. Pherson wants me out so he'll have a chance to kill me. Eva Foster probably has some crazy idea like wanting to marry me. Oh, sure, they all want me to get out."

"So do I."

"With you it's because you'd hate to lose the case."

"No. It's because I'd hate to lose you."

It took a minute for Cully to understand. When he did, his whole body tightened as if preparing to strike.

"Think about it," Donnelly said.

"You're crazy."

"No. I've been planning for some time to quit this business and go up to my ranch in Idaho. I'm sick of the law, the victims and the victimizers. I'd like to be surrounded by nice, normal creatures, horses, dogs, cattle. I doubt there is a God, but if there is, these must be His creatures, not us. They accept the world and each other. They're not always planning, scheming, fighting to get to the top where there's no place left to go but down. A river flows through the ranch, loud and ferocious in the spring when the ice pack starts to melt in the mountains. In the fall it flows gently. But no matter what season, each drop of water is different. It's not like the sea, where every wave seems to be the same, monotonous as death. A river is alive, fresh, vital. I must have felt that way when I was a child, but I can't remember, I can't remember."

"I don't have to sit here and listen to this crap."

"Yes, you do. You have no choice. You are an accused murderer, which considerably limits your choices."

"Everyone has rights."

"The rights of an accused murderer exist mainly on paper and in the lofty minds of idealists. You are sitting here quietly listening to your attorney. If you make any move to protest, if you get loud or contentious, the bailiff will come over, then a deputy, two deputies, and you're in handcuffs and irons. Accused murderers aren't free to do what they want to do. They sit and listen to their attorneys, whether that attorney is reading the weather report or making a reasonable proposition. That's what this is, a reasonable proposition."

"Not to me."

"You said you didn't want to pick up the pieces of your life. Well, neither do I. I have to walk away from the past. Walk with me, Cully."

The bailiff yawned, shifted his weight from one foot to another, checked his wristwatch with the clock on the wall and thought of a Reuben sandwich with cold beer and hot apple pie.

"Consider it carefully," Donnelly said.

"There's nothing to consider, you hear? Nothing."

"You'll be looked after the rest of your life."

"Some life, stuck on a ranch in the middle of nowhere with a queer and a bunch of cows and a river instead of the sea. That's not for me. I want to be a free man or a dead one."

"Surely I deserve some return on my investment. Face the facts, Cully. The odds against you right now are about ten to one. If I can turn them around, you'll owe me your life. And remember, I didn't get you into this mess. You did it all yourself."

"I didn't. It was *her* fault. I think she planned the whole thing. She intended to jump overboard, and she did. And like you made the doctor admit on the stand, she could have possibly been unconscious and something in the ocean made those marks on her throat."

"Bullshit," Donnelly said. "They're your marks. You choked her."

"What for?"

"The jewels."

"I only got five hundred dollars for the earrings."

"The other jewels, the ones in the green leather case."

"I don't know anything about that case, I swear it."

"You lie as naturally as you breathe, so I won't ask you what you did with it or how you expect to dispose of jewels, whose description will be known to every gem dealer and pawnshop owner in the country."

A suffusion of blood gave Cully's face a purplish hue. "I can't dispose of what I ain't got."

"What you ain't got," Donnelly said, "is anyone who believes you."

"It's your job to make them believe me."

"Most lawyers would expect big bucks for a job like that. All I expect is gratitude."

"I'm fresh out of gratitude."

"Think about it, the way your future looks from here. Even if you're found not guilty, you can never wash off the smell of this trial. You won't be considered an innocent man; you'll be considered a murderer who got away with it. Naturally you'll never get another job in your field. What yachtsman would entrust his boat to a man with your reputation? When you choked Mrs. Pherson, you killed two people, you and her. You're through, Cully. What you think is just a curve in the road ahead is the end of the line."

Donnelly drove home feeling light-headed and weak, like a man recovering from a long illness.

His life had always been a series of blueprints, carefully planned, precisely drawn. Now, in one brief interlude, a door had been opened, and the blueprints scattered all over the room. There was no way to retrieve them and put them back in order.

He parked in the garage. Both of Zan's cars were in their usual place, but there was a smell of exhaust fumes in the air and the hood of Zan's Jaguar was still warm.

He went into the house by the back door. The house-keeper, Mrs. Killeen, was on the telephone in the kitchen. She hung up as soon as she saw him and got to her feet, straightening the prim white collar of her pink uniform.

"Are you home for lunch, Mr. Donnelly?"

"If it isn't any trouble."

"I like to be informed in advance. However, I can always toss something together in an emergency."

"Simply coming home to one's own house can hardly be described as an emergency."

"*I* plan ahead."

"So do I," Donnelly said. This was true until an hour ago. Now everything had blown up and away, and the flight both scared and elated him.

"Your wife is upstairs in her sitting room," Mrs. Killeen said. "She's in a good mood, by the way, so don't wreck it."

"Is that an order, Mrs. Killeen?"

"Merely excellent advice. But then lawyers are more inclined to give advice than to take it, so I might as well keep my mouth shut."

"A very good idea."

The door of Zan's sitting room was open, but he knocked anyway so he wouldn't startle her. She sat at her small bird's-eye-maple desk, writing a letter. She was dressed for a fall day in town, in a tweedy beige suit almost the color of her hair. The bulkiness of the suit gave her added weight and fresh makeup concealed her pallor.

"Why, Charles, what a nice surprise."

"For me, too. You look very well."

The steadiness of her voice and hands made him wonder what kinds of pills she'd taken that morning and which doctor she had conned into prescribing them.

"I'm just writing to my brother, Michael, to tell him my news. Or rather, our news."

"I didn't know we had any news."

"Oh, but we do. You just haven't found out about it yet."

She laughed. It was a pleasant sound with none of the latent shriek that could be heard in most of her laughter.

"Are you ready for a great big surprise, Charles? I should really make you guess, but it would be cruel to keep you in suspense."

"I could stand it."

"Anyway, you'd never guess. It's too wonderful, really."

"Tell me."

"We're going to have a baby."

The shock wave that hit him subsided almost immediately, leaving him with the realization that she couldn't be talking about her own pregnancy—she was, after all, over forty, in poor health and chemically addicted—she was referring to adoption. Even this seemed very remote. She could never qualify, and neither could he. But she looked so happy, and there were so few happy moments in any life, that he didn't want to spoil it for her until he had to.

"I think it's just what we need, Charles. Something to bring us together, give us a common interest. We've been growing apart, and a baby will give us something to plan for, the nursery and clothes and christening and—"

"Where will we get this baby, Zan?"

"I heard about an obstetrician in town who arranges such things."

"For money?"

"For money, naturally, to pay him for his work. He

brings together unwanted babies with wanting parents, that's his motto."

"Is that where you went this morning, to see this doctor?"

"Yes."

"Did you give him any money?"

"No. He'll have to see you first in order to make sure you're a wanting parent. . . . You are, aren't you, Charles?"

"I think we should discuss the subject before coming to a decision. We'll have to wait until this case I'm on is finished. Then we'll sit down and talk."

"When will the case be finished?"

"I don't know."

"Weeks? Months?"

"Possibly."

"But the doctor's expecting to hear from us tomorrow."

"I'm afraid he won't, Zan. You've waited twenty years before considering adoption, you can wait a little longer, build up your health and energy and be ready to face the responsibility of having a child. It's a big step. Whether it's up or down needs further extrapolation."

"Extrapolation." She picked up the sheet of letter paper she'd been writing on and began to fold it over and over again until it was pleated like a fan. "That's a fancy word for no, isn't it?"

"It means we must assess the situation."

"Haven't you guts enough to come right out and say no?"

"If that's what you want me to do, very well, no. You can't assume responsibility for a child in your present state of health."

She took the little fan she'd made out of the note paper and started waving it slowly back and forth across her face. All her movements were slow. Since he didn't know what kinds of pills she'd taken, he wasn't sure whether this uncharacteristic languor meant that they were wearing off or increasing in effect. There was even a very faint possibility that she hadn't taken anything more addicting than a dream.

"I am a wanting parent," she said.

"Today you are. What about tomorrow?"

The word didn't have the effect on her that he thought it would.

"Tomorrow I'll go down and see the doctor and tell him what an important case you're working on so you couldn't come in person but you wanted him to know how eager you are to have a child. Tomorrow," she repeated. "Just think, tomorrow there might be a baby waiting to enter our lives."

"Your life," he said. "Not mine."

"You don't have to share it, Charles. You wouldn't make much of a parent anyway. You have no more feeling than a turnip. I may have a thousand faults, but at least once I was able to love, and I will again. There are years and years of love stored up inside me."

"What's the name of this doctor, Zan?"

"I won't tell you."

"All right. Maybe I can find it in the yellow pages under 'Children for Sale.' "

"You're going to ruin things for me, aren't you?"

"This particular thing, yes."

"Why? Do you hate me so much?"

"No."

"Every time I get an idea you shit on it."

"This isn't an idea," he said. "It's a fantasy. I don't know when or where it started, but I know where and when it's going to end. Here. Now."

"It's not a fantasy. I want a child."

"At the moment that's probably true. But tomorrow

you might want a chimpanzee. You can probably get one for about the same price."

The first witness of the afternoon session gave his name as Alfred Elfinstone, assistant hotel manager of the Casa Mañana, San Diego.

At first his testimony seemed likely to be as undramatic as his appearance. He was small, neat, discreetly dressed and spoke with a pronounced British accent. He'd picked up the accent during his service at the hotel chain's London branch, and he'd clung to it through the years as a symbol of civilization in a world without rules, manners or syntax.

Yes, he had been on temporary duty at the desk when Mrs. Pherson registered during the afternoon. She was a nice-looking, dignified woman, wearing sturdy, sensible shoes of the kind British women wore for striding across the moors, a sight Mr. Elfinstone had never seen but could picture from reading the novels of Jane Austen and the Brontë sisters.

Mrs. Pherson, he recalled, had handed him a green leather case to put in the safe for her. "It appeared to be a jewel case, quite old except for the lock which was brand-new, or looked that way to me.

"Later," he said, "she came back to the desk and retrieved the green case without explanation. At least, if there was an explanation, I didn't understand it."

"It? What's *it*?"

"What she said."

"Which was?"

"That she intended to do something she'd never done before in her life and would assuredly never do again. Then she laughed. She had a most pleasant laugh, bubbly but controlled, like fine champagne."

"You didn't tell me this in our previous conversations, Mr. Elfinstone. Why not?"

"I just remembered it a minute ago."

"Were you puzzled by her remarks?"

"Not frightfully. I usually don't pay much attention to what people say. It's what they do that counts."

"And what did she do?"

"Took the elevator up to her suite. A few minutes later she came down again, walked across the lobby and joined a man."

"Is the man now sitting in this courtroom?"

"I'm not sure. I didn't pay much attention to the man. I was more interested in the way the green leather case clashed with the blue and white coat she was wearing. Well-groomed ladies avoid this sort of thing."

Owen smoothed away the frown wrinkles between his eyebrows. He didn't like surprises in general. In particular he didn't like the kind of witness who suddenly remembered things on the stand and blurted them out without consultation.

Elfinstone was scratching his left temple as if trying to conjure up more surprises.

He did. "Now that I come to think of it, I recall asking her what she meant to do. She said she couldn't tell me, it was a secret and, if anyone found out, they might try to stop her. *I* wouldn't, I told her. I believe in people reaching for the brass ring, seizing the day. *Carpe diem.* As I watched her cross the lobby, I thought *Yes, the little lady is going to seize the day.*"

"Then, as far as you could tell, Mrs. Pherson did not appear to be despondent?"

"My word, no. Happy as a lark, she was. I'm no ornithologist, but I believe larks are presumed to be happy because they sing a lot. Mrs. Pherson was not singing, of course, it being a hotel lobby. But she might have been singing inside herself, as it were."

"Yes. Thank you, Mr. Elfinstone. I have no more questions."

"Are you ready to cross-examine this witness, Mr. Donnelly?"

"Yes, Your Honor."

"Then go ahead."

Donnelly exchanged places with Owen at the lectern.

"Mr. Elfinstone, how many years have you been in the hotel business?"

"Over twenty years."

"During this time have you had any experience with guests checking in and subsequently committing suicide?"

"Alas, yes. Yes, indeed, though we try to keep such things private. People tend to avoid rooms where a tragedy has taken place."

"In your years of experience have you observed that potential suicides exhibit similar behavioral patterns?"

"No."

"Some were obviously despondent, were they?"

"Yes."

"And some quite cheerful?"

"Yes."

"Did others have a calm, pleasant manner?"

"Oh, yes. Lull before the storm, you know."

"Are you saying, in other words, that you couldn't pick out a potential suicide on the basis of appearance and behavior?"

"If we could do that, we would steer them to an establishment run by our competitors."

Mr. Elfinstone was becoming a hit with the audience, and both he and they would have liked the scene to continue. But Donnelly had no more questions, and the judge told Mr. Elfinstone he could step down.

He stepped down, satisfied that he had done his duty and harmed no one. He didn't believe in the death penalty.

The testimony of Isaac Stoltze and Angelina Gomez took up the rest of the afternoon.

Stoltze was the bartender on duty when Mrs. Pherson went into the bar and sat down beside Cully King. He was a reluctant, if not a hostile, witness. The payment allotted to him by the state would not cover the loss of a day's wages and the expense of driving up from San Diego. In addition to the financial aspect, being a witness interfered with his principle and practice of noninvolvement. He minded his own business and did his job well, and if other people had done the same, he wouldn't be here on this witness stand with people staring at him as if he were the one who'd done something wrong.

The state might as well have saved its money. Stoltze could not positively identify the pictures of Mrs. Pherson or the person of Cully King, didn't recall what or how much they had to drink or whether they went out of the bar together.

Angelina Gomez was a plump, pretty young woman with a face round as a dumpling and eyes like black grapes. It was her first experience as a witness and her first trip north of Los Angeles. She had driven up from San Diego with Mr. Elfinstone, who assured her that there was nothing to worry about, that all she had to do was tell the truth. His assurances made her more and more nervous. The truth kept wandering in and out of her mind like a lost child, never pausing long enough to be identified.

The strain proved too much for Angelina. She sobbed

into Mr. Elfinstone's handkerchief, drank the coffee he'd brought along in his thermos and used his rearview mirror to reapply her makeup. By the time she reached the courtroom she was composed, and the truth was standing quite still in a corner of her mind.

She told the district attorney she was the housekeeping maid assigned to the south wing of the fourth floor of the Casa Mañana. After guests checked into the hotel, she said, they usually unpacked or partly unpacked, then left their rooms to go down for a walk on the beach or to wander through the *tienditas* on the ground level. During this time she was expected to make sure everything was tidy, ashtrays washed and soiled towels replaced. Angelina was doing just that when Mrs. Pherson unexpectedly returned to her suite.

"Let's just pause here for a minute," Owen said. "Did you enter the room during Mrs. Pherson's absence?"

"Yes."

"Had she unpacked?"

"Yes, sir. Everything was hung up in the closet or put away in drawers. She was a tidy lady. All I had to do was replace a couple of towels she had used."

"The clothes that were hanging in the closet, had they been put there carefully?"

"Oh, yes, just like they were for sale in a store, all zipped and buttoned on their hangers to keep their shape."

"Just where were you when Mrs. Pherson came back unexpectedly?"

"In the bathroom. I offered to leave and come back later, but she said no, it didn't matter because she was going right out. So I finished tidying up the bathroom, replacing two towels. I heard her talking to herself in the bedroom. At least I guess it was to herself. There wasn't

213

anybody else there. It was like when you're dressed to go out and before you leave, you look in the mirror and say, 'Hey, looking good.' "

The audience appreciated this more than Owen did. He was suspicious of Mexicans anyway, and he wondered if she'd deliberately brought up the business of standing in front of a mirror making approving remarks before leaving the house. Everyone did it, of course. He wasn't the only one. And he certainly never said, "Hey, looking good."

"Did she sound happy, Miss Gomez?"

"Oh, yes, real happy, like maybe she'd had a couple of drinks."

"Did you listen to what she was saying?"

"I had to listen. I was there. You can't open and close your ears the way you can your eyes."

"What did you hear?"

"Something like, 'You always wanted to go to Hawaii, and now you get to go.' Stuff like that. I didn't think anything of it. A lot of people would like to go to Hawaii, me included. I never even saw Santa Felicia until this afternoon."

"Then she seemed to be looking forward to the trip, is that right?"

"Sure. Why not?"

Owen had no further questions, and Donnelly did not cross-examine.

Court was adjourned for the weekend.

On Friday night the two older Owen boys, Chadwick and Jonathan, were allowed to go to a high school football game.

Thatcher, the youngest, knew what was in store for him. He could see the constitutional amendment booklet sticking out of his father's coat pocket, so he hung around the kitchen as long as possible, even going so far as to help his mother stack the dishes in the dishwasher.

"I feel sick," he told Vee. "Like I got something serious."

"Really? What do you suppose it is?"

"Chicken pox."

"I don't see any spots."

"Right here on my arm."

"That's your poison oak from last week."

"Or maybe I got Rocky Mountain spotted fever."

"That comes from ticks not found around here."

"Then how about endometriosis?"

"Will you spell that for me?"

Thatcher was as easily trapped as a butterfly. He had picked the word up while eavesdropping on a conversation between two lady teachers, and he'd copied it in the corner of a notebook, thinking it might be useful someday. This was the day. He took a scrap of paper from his pocket and read aloud the carefully printed letters.

"Endo meet me oasis."

"That sounds serious," Vee said.

"It is. I think I ought to go to bed and watch TV."

"I think you think wrong. Your father is waiting for you in the den."

"But I feel weak and dizzy. Things are floating in front of my eyes."

"You have no fever, your color is good and you ate two helpings at dinner."

"But what if I really got that disease? It could be fatal."

"Not as fatal as what you'll get if you don't drag yourself into that den. And for your information, by the way, endometriosis is a disease of the womb, and boys don't have wombs."

"I could be an exception. Nobody ever X-rayed me."

Vee closed the dishwasher with a bang. "Beat it, Thatcher."

"Okay. But you'll be sorry if I'm terminal."

"We are all terminal, Thatcher. However, at the moment you're more terminal than most, and endometriosis has nothing to do with it. Your father doesn't like to be kept waiting."

Vee switched on the dishwasher, wiped her hands on her apron, found out she wasn't wearing one and reached for a towel.

"Thatcher, I want you to do me a favor."

"What's in it for me?"

"What's in it for you? Joy in bringing happiness to someone, pride in your ability to show compassion to another human being."

"How much is that in dollars?"

"One."

"What's the deal?"

"Be patient with your father. You know how proud he is of you and how much he loves you."

"If he loves me so much, how come I'm not at the football game? If I'm too young for football, I'm too young to memorize the amendments."

"Oh, come on, Thatcher, be reasonable."

"I'm reasonable. It's everybody else that isn't."

"A buck is a buck. Take it or leave it."

"All right, it's a deal. What do I have to do?"

"Be nice to your father. The case he's prosecuting is very important to him, and he's working so hard he needs to get his mind off the law."

"The amendments," Thatcher pointed out in a deadly reasonable voice "*are* the law."

"Oh, you know what I mean. Make an effort to memorize at least some of them. Give it the old college try."

"I'm only in the sixth grade."

"So give it the old sixth-grade try. Will you do that for me, please?"

"No. I'll do it for a buck."

Vee gave him a hug and kissed the top of his head. She loved this boy who was so much like his father as deeply as she loved the father who was so much like his son.

In the small, book-lined den Oliver Owen sat in the red leather chair in front of the fireplace. The leather was actually vinyl, and the fireplace was a gas grate, but the books were real and read.

Thatcher sat on the floor, arms clasped around his legs, chin resting on his knees.

"Wouldn't you be more comfortable in a chair, Thatcher?"

"No." Then, thinking of the dollar, Thatcher added, "Dad."

"Very well, we'll get right down to business. What are the first ten amendments called?"

"The Bill of Rights."

"Good. You remembered."

"I don't remember what they are, though, except the one about how we should all carry guns around."

"That's not quite what it says, Thatcher. We'll get back to that later. For now let's go through some of the other amendments to give you some idea of what's ahead. Let's look at Amendment Thirteen. Like the other amendments, it is indicated by a Roman numeral—in this case an *X* followed by three ones. In Roman numerals an *X* is a ten, and three ones add up to what?"

"If I had a computer like all the other kids—"

"You don't need a computer to add ten and three, especially when I've already told you the answer, which is thirteen."

"I was just going to say thirteen."

"Amendment Thirteen reads as follows: 'Section One. Neither slavery nor involuntary servitude, except as a punishment for crime whereof the party shall have been duly convicted, shall exist within the United States or any place subject to their jurisdiction. Section Two. Congress shall have power to enforce this article by appropriate legislation.' December eighteenth, 1865."

Thatcher chewed thoughtfully on the hangnail on his left thumb. "Does that mean we can't have slaves?"

"Yes."

"Why not?"

"Because slavery is wrong."

"Why?"

"Don't ask stupid questions, Thatcher. Figure it out for yourself. Would you like to be someone's slave, having to obey orders, to work without salary or allowance?"

"No, but I wouldn't mind having one of my own. Man, think how great it would be having a slave to do all your chores, pick up your clothes and do your homework and beat up on the kids you don't like. Wow, wouldn't that be super?"

"No, it would not be super, Thatcher. It would be immoral and illegal, and the possession of a slave would make you hopelessly dependent."

"I already am, Chadwick says. Wow, when I think what my slave could do to that creep—"

"Let's stick to the subject. At the time, 1865, there were actually some arguments in favor of slavery. And certainly some results of the Thirteenth Amendment were not adequately foreseen by its creators. I refer to the excessive proliferation of the black race in the last hundred years."

"Maybe a slave could even go to school for me and take my exams. And Friday nights he could stay home for me while I went to the football game. Boy, oh, boy, when I get to be President, I'm going to bring back slavery."

"Shut up, Thatcher."

"Why?"

"Because you—because I—because. Just because."

"That doesn't sound like a legal argument to me."

"It may not be legal, but I suggest you obey it. *Now*."

"Okay, okay. This wasn't my idea anyway."

"*Now*."

Thatcher darted out of the room like a freed slave. With a sigh Oliver returned the amendment booklet to his pocket. Then he leaned back and closed his eyes.

When Vee came in half an hour later, she found him asleep. She leaned down and kissed the top of his head just the way she had kissed the top of Thatcher's, with the same mixed feelings of pride, joy and resignation.

"Oliver, dear."

He awoke with a start. There were no slow, sweet awakenings for Oliver. His eyes snapped open, ready to confront an enemy. "What's the matter?"

"Your office called. A man named Harry Arnold has been trying to reach you. He's at five-five-five-one-eight-one-eight."

"All right. Thanks."

"Do they have to disturb you like this on a weekend?"

"Harry Arnold is my most important witness in this case. I've got to find out what he wants."

Harry's wants were simple: two plane tickets back to the Virgin Islands for him and his son, Richie. He was sick of waiting around for his turn in the witness box; he was sick of Santa Felicia, as he was sick of the climate, the people, the food.

"I want to go home," Harry said.

"That's impossible."

"What if I just do it anyway?"

"If you leave now, while you are under subpoena, the court will order you to be brought back, and in addition, they could fine you a considerable sum of money or even put you in jail. My advice—"

"Who asked for it?"

"—is to stay put and consider this a little vacation. The Judge's allowance for your food and shelter has been very generous."

"Some vacation, stuck in a crummy motel and my son, Richie, hanging out at the waterfront most of the time. It's a rough place for a fifteen-year-old, bums, winos, pushers. Sure, he hangs around the waterfront at home, but everybody knows him, and he ain't the only black, like he is here."

"I'm putting you on the stand Monday morning. We've already discussed in detail the questions I'm going to ask you. After I've finished my questioning, the defense will cross-examine. Then I might decide to reexamine, and the defense will very likely recross. You've been advised of all this before."

"What comes after that recross stuff?"

"You may be requested to keep yourself available for further questioning later in the trial."

"Jeez almighty, I could be here till Christmas."

"A murder trial is not conducted for the convenience of witnesses. You may consider it bad luck to have been in that particular place at that particular time, but eventually you may come to realize it was good luck because it enabled you to help justice prevail."

"I don't want to be a witness. I didn't see nobody kill nobody."

"You told me you heard screams in the night. That makes you the last person to hear Mrs. Pherson's voice."

"Maybe it wasn't her voice. Maybe it was the radio."

"Richie will testify that he, too, heard the screams."

"Why'd you have to drag a kid his age into it?"

"I didn't drag him; I didn't drag you. That's just the way it happened."

"It could still of been the radio."

"You also told me Cully King was drinking heavily and that he has a reputation for violence when he's drunk."

"A lot of my friends do."

"An hour or so after you heard screaming you went up on deck to check a loose cable and you saw Cully King throw some clothing overboard."

"It could of been trash."

"What's the matter, Harry? Up until now you've been pretty positive about the woman's screams and the clothes being thrown overboard."

"I want to go home. I don't like it here. I don't like the way my kid is acting, hanging out with those bums at the waterfront and him only fifteen."

Owen thought of his own son Chadwick, barely a year younger than Richie but a mere child in comparison. He said, "You're lucky, Harry, to have a responsible, hard-working son like Richie."

"No luck about it. I brung him up like that."

"Be at my office at nine o'clock Monday morning," Owen said, "and don't bring Richie. He's not allowed in the courtroom except during his time on the stand. Nine o'clock and be prompt."

"Who says?"

"The state of California says."

There was a long silence, then Harry's voice, tight and high as if it had squeezed past clenched teeth: "I'll be there."

Harry hung up and replaced the telephone on the bed-side table. Propped up against two pillows, he looked like a huge man with a barrel chest and overdeveloped deltoids that made him appear neckless. Below the waist he was small and scrawny. All of him was black, the purplish black of the native West Indian. He could climb a mast with the agility of a monkey climbing a coconut tree and slide down again without a drop of blood on his calloused hands. Like Cully King, he'd gone to sea as a boy, but he lacked Cully's brains and perseverance and remained semiliterate. He couldn't or wouldn't adapt to computers. They reawakened superstitions long buried, and their language was that of a hostile and barbarous tribe.

He turned on the television set and watched an old movie until Richie came home. It was after ten.

"Where you been?" Harry said.

"Out."

"Where is out?"

"The opposite of in."

"That supposed to be funny?"

"Maybe it wasn't."

"It wasn't. So start over. Where you been?"

"Hanging around."

"Hanging around where, who, what for?"

Richie sat down in the only upholstered chair in the room. He was taller than his father, and lighter-skinned, but he had equally heavy shoulders and arms. He was always growing into or growing out of things. The happy medium passed as quickly as any moment of happiness.

He pulled at the hairs of the seedling mustache on his

upper lip to stimulate its growth while his father watched in disapproval.

"You should wash your face better," Harry said. "So you been out hanging around, huh?"

"Yeah."

"What part of out and what part of around?"

"I was drifting. You know, doing this and that."

"What's a this?"

"I played a few video games."

"Where did you get the money?"

"Helped a guy launch his trimaran this afternoon. Then I walked out to the end of the breakwater to look at the *Bewitched*. She's still got some kind of security guard on her. It's funny, her just sitting there dead in the water when we worked so hard to bring her here for the big race."

"Hard work never killed nobody."

"I wouldn't mind staying here if they let us live on board."

"We're going home soon," Harry said. "I take the stand Monday, and after they finish with me, it'll be your turn."

"I got nothing to say against Cully. He's a good guy, like a father to me."

"How come you need two fathers?"

It was an old jealousy that cropped up every now and then like a persistent weed. It could be trampled on, mowed down or even uprooted, but it always returned, nurtured by an unalterable fact: Harry and his wife were very dark while Richie's skin was copper-colored like Cully's. Harry had never voiced his suspicion, but his friends all knew about it. So did Richie, who was pleased at the idea and looked for secret signs from Cully that it was true.

"I don't need two fathers," Richie said. "One is enough."

"Maybe too much, huh?"

"I didn't say that."

"You didn't say it, but I heard it."

Harry laughed. He appreciated his own jokes so much that he didn't care whether other people did or not.

"You want to watch some TV?" Harry said.

Richie shook his head. "Why do they think Cully killed that lady?"

"Money."

"Cully don't need money. He's happy like he is, a ship under him and chicks laying the right moves on him."

"What's that mean?"

"Flinging themselves at him."

"No chicks flang themselves at him that I ever seen. Some old hookers, sure. Every guy gets flang at by some old hookers. You know what a hooker is?"

"Sure."

"Then stay away from them."

Richie grunted. Every conversation with his father seemed to end the same way: Do this or don't do this. It was safer to steer the subject back to Cully, who never cared what people told him to do or not to do. *Me and Cully, we're a lot alike. When they let him go, when we get back to the islands, I'm going to come right out and ask him to tell me the truth: that he's my real father. Maybe him and me will live together just like an ordinary family.*

"If he killed the lady for money," Richie said, "how come he didn't get it?"

"He got some. The rest he hasn't had a chance to sell yet."

"What rest?"

"The jewels in the green case."

"I don't think there was jewels in that case. It didn't feel like it, didn't rattle or jangle."

"How do you know that?"

224

"She let me carry it for her."

"When?"

"Once."

"The stuff must of been all wrapped in cotton. That's it, stuff wrapped in cotton don't rattle." Harry scratched one of his shoulders. It bulged purple-black like an eggplant. "You carried it for her once?"

"Yeah."

"What once?"

"I don't remember. Just a once like any other."

Harry knew he was lying, but something warned him not to try to force or finesse the truth out of him. The truth was often something to stay away from.

"Let's watch TV," Harry said. "You want to watch some TV?"

"I don't care."

"Okay, you pick the program."

"No, you pick it."

Neither of them moved. Then Harry said, "Listen, kid, all I ask is, don't do nothing stupid."

"Like what?"

"You're young. You can make little mistakes when you're young. Don't start making no big ones till you're older."

Richie was leaning forward, his hands on the arms of the chair as if he were preparing to spring up and race away.

"You got something on your conscience, keep it there," Harry said. "Blabbing just spreads it around like manure. I mean, don't tell me nothing, even if I ask."

On Monday morning Defense Counsel Donnelly asked for a postponement of two days for personal reasons. So it was Wednesday before Harry had a chance to wear the new suit he'd purchased at a thrift shop for five dollars, the fifty-cent shirt and the tie and matching handkerchief, twenty-five cents.

The coat was too small, so he kept it unbuttoned, and the pants were too large, so he hitched them up as much as possible with a belt, embossed leather, one dollar.

"You look sharp," Owen told him. "You can get the trousers altered later."

"Why? I don't figure to wear them again."

"Suit yourself. . . . How much does the state owe you for the clothes?"

"Six seventy-five."

Owen paid him the exact amount. "Normally we don't allot money for this sort of thing, but this is a special situation. I want you to look like a respectable, hardworking man."

"I *am* a respectable, hardworking man."

"Certainly, of course you are. But I want the jury to see that for themselves. It's especially important, in view of your race, for you to appear at your best, put your best face forward, as it were."

"I only got one face," Harry said. "You want I should bleach it?"

"I'm simply being realistic, Harry. Civil rights or no civil rights, prejudice still exists."

"No kidding."

"I want you, as I want all my witnesses, to look proper."

Harry wasn't sure what "proper" meant, but he felt there was something wrong with the whole conversation. It aggravated his resentment over the delays and increased his worry and uneasiness about Richie. The boy was too quiet. He spent hours wandering around the waterfront alone and went swimming off the sandspit at the end of the breakwater. The water was too cold for swimming, well below sixty, and Richie returned to the motel, blue-lipped and shivering and mute. Harry said to Owen, "How come there was another delay?"

"Defense counsel had to drive his wife down to a hospital in Long Beach."

"Don't they have hospitals here?"

"Not this particular kind."

"What if there's another delay, and another?"

"You put up with it the same as the rest of us."

"The rest of you aren't stuck in a crummy motel room."

"Blame your friend Cully," Owen said. "He could have saved all of us a lot of trouble."

There was an interval of silence. Harry looked worried. "When I go in the courtroom, where will he be sitting?"

"There's a long table in front of the judge's seat. Cully will be at the far left with his counsel, Donnelly."

Waiting for court to begin, Donnelly was quiet and preoccupied. Gunther sat in his usual place at the railing. He had helped Donnelly take Zan down to the hospital in Long Beach, doing the driving while Donnelly held Zan in his arms in the back seat. The doctor had given Zan a shot, and she was asleep with her head against Donnelly's chest. At first she was light as a bird, and her fragility and helplessness brought tears to his eyes. But as the miles passed, she became heavier and heavier as if molten lead were slowly being injected into her veins, replacing her blood. His arms ached and his tears evaporated in the dry atmosphere of the air conditioner. Then he felt the sting of new tears, this time for himself, for his own helplessness and inability to carry this burden any further. The road was ending almost where it began, in the back seat of a car. Smog, he told Gunther, it was the smog; it always affected his eyes. And Gunther solemnly agreed.

At nine-fifty Cully was brought in by the deputy. In the mornings Cully usually looked bright, even cheerful, but today he was grim-faced, and he sat down in a tentative way as if he weren't sure whether this was his place or not.

Eva Foster smiled at him, and the bailiff nodded, but Cully failed to notice. He said to Donnelly, "I got a note from the kid. It was passed along to me this morning by a guard who often goes fishing off the breakwater."

"That's nice."

"Not nice. Bad. Crazy. The kid's got the crazies."

"Let me see it."

The note was a single sheet of paper folded and refolded into a small rectangle. The message was printed with such intensity that the pen had stabbed the paper in several places.

Dear Cully

I guess I better keep on calling you Cully until you tell me for sure what I know all ready. I thought about this a whole lot and not just the past couple weeks and I know you are my real Dad. You and me can be a real family when we get back. I have some money to start out. The lady gave me a $100 bill so I won't be a drag on you so don't worry about that will you.

Richie

Harry won't mind. He don't like me or you much anyways.

Donnelly refolded the sheet of paper while Cully watched him anxiously.

"Well, what's your advice? What do I do now?"

228

"Nothing."

"But he thinks I'm his father."

"And are you?"

"I told you that night in jail, I'm not. Harry's wife is a slut; she'd go with anyone."

"So she might have gone with you."

"If she did, I was too drunk to remember. It doesn't matter anyway. I'm not going to *be* his father. The hell with living together like a real family him and me or me and anybody else. Jeez, why does everybody think they're entitled to a piece of me just because I'm on trial for murder? Jeez," he said again. "That Foster dame, she wants us to be a real family, too. And you and your god-damn ranch, and my wife and her slob brother. And that crazy Pherson waiting to kill me. Now it's the kid. The whole bloody bunch of you waiting to slice me up like a pie."

"Lower your voice," Donnelly said. He thought of the nursery rhyme: "Four and twenty blackbirds baked in a pie. / And when the pie was opened, the birds began to sing. . . ." This pie had only one blackbird, and there would be no singing.

"I don't want to be anybody's husband, anybody's father, anybody's lover, anybody's target practice. You're sick, you're all sick, coming on to me like cannibals. That's what you are, cannibals. I'd rather go to the gas chamber than be eaten alive by a bunch of cannibals."

"You may not have a choice," Donnelly said. "A lot will depend on Harry."

Harry made a better witness than Owen anticipated. He was solemn and respectful, awed by the grandeur of the courtroom with its vaulted ceiling and crystal chandeliers. To him it was like a church, and God himself in a black robe sat majestically on his throne.

He told of his short acquaintanceship with Mrs. Pherson from the time she came on board the *Bewitched* with Cully. The jury who'd heard it all before in one way or another looked bored until he reached the part where he'd heard a woman screaming in the middle of the night.

Owen asked him if the woman was Mrs. Pherson.

"Must of been," Harry said. "She was the only woman on board."

"What was the nature of her screams?"

"Nature?"

"Was she shouting words you could understand?"

"No. They were just screams."

"How long did they last? A minute? Two minutes?"

"Not that long. Ten seconds, maybe less."

"Did you think of going to investigate?"

"I thought of it."

"But you didn't go?"

"No."

"Why not?"

"I figured if her and Cully was just having a wild time, Cully would be mad if I butted in. Cully has a fierce temper when he's hitting the bottle."

Donnelly made an objection, the judge sustained it and Harry's final sentence was stricken from the record.

Owen continued. "Did you hear Mrs. Pherson's voice again?"

"No."

"Did you think everything was all right?"

"Yes, sir, until—until I went to check on a loose cable."

"What happened at this point?"

"I saw Cully throw something overboard."

"What was this something?"

"Looked like clothes."

"His clothes? Hers?"

"I don't know. I just ducked below before Cully could see me."

"Were you afraid of this man, Cully King?"

"I never been scared of any man," Harry said. "But on a ship the skipper is boss. You don't question him or accuse him, leastways not until you go ashore. Onshore it's just you and him, nobody's boss, no holds are barred."

"What time would you say this occurred?"

"About four in the morning. I saw Cully at the aft rail."

"What enabled you to witness Cully's actions?"

"It was a clear, calm night with a first quarter moon, and we had the running lights on full because we were in a shipping lane and we didn't want to be hit by an oil tanker. I saw him throw something overboard."

"Did he drop this something into the water, or did he dump it out of a container of some kind?"

"I don't remember seeing a container. Everything happened so fast. We were doing ten knots at the time. It's in the log; you and me looked it up together. At ten knots things thrown in the water are left behind real fast, and that includes people, which is not an everyday occurrence. Nobody was ever lost from a boat I was crewing on until this time."

Owen consulted his notes. "Tell me, Mr. Arnold, is it the skipper's job to dispose of the boat's trash?"

"No, sir. On the *Bewitched* that was up to Richie, my son."

"So it would have been unusual for Mr. King to be disposing of trash, especially in the middle of the night, would it not?"

"Very unusual, yes, sir."

"What was Cully King wearing when he threw this stuff overboard?"

"Nothing."

"He was naked?"

"Yes, sir."

"What was the air temperature at four o'clock that morning?"

"It's in the log. I wrote it there myself, forty-five degrees."

"Would a person feel comfortable without clothes in so low a temperature?"

"Objection," Donnelly said without rising or even looking up from his notes. "Question calls for an opinion and—"

"Sustained," the judge said. "But frankly, Mr. Donnelly, the answer is so obvious that an objection hardly seems worthwhile and indeed might even be construed as a waste of the court's time."

Harry, who didn't know whether he was to answer or not, answered anyway. "Maybe an Eskimo."

One of the spectators laughed, and the judge tapped his gavel sharply. "Witness is to refrain from offering any statements that are not responsive to questions. Proceed, Mr. Owen."

"Are you sure he was naked, Mr. Arnold?"

"Yes, sir. Funny thing is, if he'd of been black like me"—his voice had a faint note of reproach as he glanced down at Cully—"if he'd been black like me, maybe I wouldn't of even seen him. But the moon and the running lights caught him square on, and he shone like copper."

This time the response of the audience was a self-conscious titter at the image Harry had evoked, a copper-skinned man standing naked on the deck of a yacht in the moonlight.

The judge was not amused. "You have been asked, Mr. Arnold, not to volunteer any remarks of this nature."

"I was only telling the truth."

"This court is not equipped, timewise or spacewise, to handle all the truths of this world. Please continue, Mr. Owen."

"Let me ask you a hypothetical question, Mr. Arnold," Owen said. "If you were caught naked in a burning building, would you stop to put on your clothes before making an exit?"

"No."

"You'd be in too much of a hurry, would you not?"

"Yes, sir. I'd rather be cold than dead."

"So your motivation would be one of survival?"

"Yes."

"Do you think Cully King's motive was similar? . . . Strike that. Tell me, have you crewed on many yachts, Mr. Arnold?"

"Yes, sir."

"Long trips, short trips?"

"All kinds."

"On any of these occasions, have you seen many people taking a moonlight stroll on deck with the temperature of the air at forty-five degrees?"

"No."

"Any people?"

"No, sir. Nobody, never. Not that I ain't seen some hanky-panky on warm nights in the Caribbean."

This time the gavel came down before the spectators could react. A recess of fifteen minutes was declared.

Only a few spectators remained in the room, along with Eva Foster, Cully and the bailiff, Di Santo.

Di Santo was feeling good. He had convinced his wife that he'd lost five pounds and was promised a steak dinner as a reward. He had managed the weight loss by using a simple trick taught him by one of the other deputies. He moved the scales from a hard surface, the tile floor of the bathroom, to a soft one, the carpeted bedroom. One unexpected result of this deceit was that while convincing his wife he'd lost five pounds, he also convinced himself. His belt felt a little looser, his stomach muscles a little tighter, and the coming steak dinner was beginning to seem like a prize legitimately won.

Eva followed him to the water cooler.

"I'm supposed to drink eight glasses of this stuff a day," he said. "It helps control the appetite. Notice anything different about me?"

"You've lost weight."

"You really noticed, honest to God?"

"No. But you wanted to hear it, so I said it. . . . Zeke, do me a favor, will you? I want to talk to Cully alone."

"Why?"

"He needs cheering up."

"Is that a new duty of the court clerk, to cheer up defendants?"

"This is extracurricular."

"If I didn't know better, I'd say you were finally getting some normal ideas about a man. He's a pretty good-looking dude."

"Really? I never noticed."

"Okay, I'll be outside in the hall in case you need me."

"What would I need you for?"

"Look, this isn't a kid arrested for cheating at marbles. He's a killer."

"Why does everyone assume he's guilty just because he was arrested?"

"We got more reason to assume he's guilty than you have to assume he's innocent."

"I'm not assuming, I *know*."

"Tell it to the judge."

Cully had not seen or heard any of this interchange. He was sitting with his head bowed and his shoulders hunched. When Eva took Donnelly's chair beside him, he didn't even turn his head to look at her.

"Mr. King? Cully?"

He said, "I thought Harry was my friend. Now he's sending me to the gas chamber. Sure, I knew he was a little jealous, thinking maybe me and his wife—but we never did, I swear it."

"Mr. Donnelly will straighten things out in his cross-examination.

"I didn't hear her scream. She was in the cabin with me, but I was asleep. I'd have waked up if there was any screaming."

"What did you throw overboard?"

"Old bedclothes I'd been meaning to get rid of. Mr. Belasco insists on a tidy ship."

"Why were you naked?"

"I told you, I was in bed."

"Where was she?"

"I don't know. All I know is when I woke up, she wasn't there."

"But she had been?"

"She had been."

"So all that business about hiring her as a cook was pure bull."

"No. It was true as far as it went."

"But it didn't go far enough."

"No."

"Tell me how far it went."

"Look, it's impossible to explain to a woman like you that sometimes people do things that feel perfectly right and natural at the time but later seem pretty stupid."

"Do they?" She was wearing a plain gold bracelet that looked like a giant wedding band. It had a clasp which she kept opening and closing. The soft clicking noise it made sounded like a light switch going on and off.

"It all depends on your viewpoint," Cully said, "and viewpoints change."

"Mine won't."

A note in her voice made him twitch in his chair as if it had suddenly become uncomfortable.

"Do you want to hear my viewpoint, Cully?"

"I don't think so."

"I'm going to tell you anyway because it wouldn't be fair to either of us if I didn't. This is a terrible place and a terrible time, but I may not get another chance. And I thought it might help you through the trial if you knew that someone loved you, truly loved you and believed in you."

For the first time since she'd sat down beside him he turned and stared at her. "Stop fooling with your bracelet."

"What?"

"The bracelet, don't keep clasping and unclasping it."

"My *bracelet*," she repeated as if it were a foul word. "You're talking about a *bracelet* while I'm trying to tell you of my love. How cruel, how terribly cruel."

"I don't want your love or anyone else's. I'm a sailor; I can't afford an albatross hanging around my neck."

"Albatross." It was another dirty word like bracelet, a dead bird and a piece of junk jewelry. "You can't be serious."

"Wise up, woman."

"I think you're talking and acting like this to put me off. Maybe you're trying to protect me from being hurt in case you're found guilty. Well, it won't work, Cully. Nothing can stop my love. Minds can be changed, but hearts can't. I bet"—she let out her breath and took in another deep one—"I bet you feel the same way about me as I do about you."

"Holy shit," Cully said.

Harry Arnold returned to the stand at eleven-twenty. He looked more at ease this time as if he were no longer awed by the grandeur of the courtroom, the presence of God in a black robe and the twelve apostles in the jury box. This was now an ordinary courtroom with ordinary people.

Owen asked him when the *Bewitched* had arrived at Santa Felicia Harbor.

"The following morning."

"Where did you and Mr. King tie up?"

"End tie, Marina five. Only it wasn't Cully and me; it was Richie and me."

"Did you see Mr. King that morning?"

"Yes."

"Did you exchange words with him?"

"Yes."

"What did he say?"

"That he was going ashore right away because he had to see a dentist about his toothache. I asked him did he want breakfast, and he said no, his tooth was too painful."

"During this conversation was Mr. King doing anything unusual?"

"Yes."

"What was it?"

"He was holding a handkerchief, a folded handker-chief, against his left cheek with his left hand."

"Did you believe his story about the toothache?"

"I did at the time. Cully's a funny guy. He could have a broken arm and not say a word, but a little thing like a cold or a toothache threw him for a loop."

"Objection," Donnelly said. "Witness is offering a character analysis neither requested nor relevant."

"Sustained," the judge said. "Please confine yourself to answering questions, Mr. Arnold."

"Yes, sir. Okay, sir."

Owen tried to conceal his irritation. Useless interruptions like this were part of Donnelly's strategy planned to annoy him. It was the kind of thing one of his sons might do for the same reason and with the same result. He was annoyed.

"After Mr. King went ashore, what did you do, Mr. Arnold?"

"Made breakfast for me and Richie."

"Did you see Mrs. Pherson?"

"No. I figured she was sleeping late and maybe would show up later."

"What did you do after breakfast?"

"Cleaned up the galley. Then Richie and me started going over the boat, making sure everything was in its place, like Mr. Belasco wanted."

"This tidying up of the boat, did it include the captain's quarters?"

"Yes."

"In what condition did you find this area?"

"Perfect."

"Was Mrs. Pherson present?"

"No, sir."

"Was there any sign that she had been present?"

"None at all."

"No lipstick on the pillow, no comb or hairbrush?"

"No."

"Damp towels or toilet articles?"

"No."

"Did you look in the wastebasket?"

"It's part of my job to empty wastebaskets," Harry said. "Only there was nothing to empty."

"Not even a piece of tissue?"

"No, sir."

"Did you look in the laundry hamper?"

"Yes, sir. Nothing in there neither. It kind of surprised me, finding no towels or nothing in there and the bed with fresh sheets. It began to seem like the whole thing never happened, that she never came on board at all. But I knew she had. I remember her blue and white striped coat because one of our spinnakers is blue and white like that, and it caught my eye."

"Did you ever see her again?"

"No, sir. She just vanished into thin air. If it hadn't been for that blue and white coat that looked like our spinnaker, I might of thought she'd never been there at all."

"Would you say, Mr, Arnold, that the cabin was deliberately arranged to make it look as though nobody had been there?"

"Objection," Donnelly said. "Speculation, opinion."

"Sustained."

"Let me rephrase the question," Owen said. "Did the cabin look as though nobody had occupied it?"

"That's how it looked, yes, sir, exactly."

"So would you say somebody must have arranged it that way?"

"Yes."

"Who could that somebody have been?"

"It had to be Cully King. He was the only one there excepting me and Richie."

* * *

Donnelly's cross-examination took the rest of the week. Under intensive questioning Harry was forced to concede that the screams might have come from a radio.

Considerable doubt was also cast on his testimony about seeing the clothes thrown overboard.

Donnelly said, "By clothes, do you mean wearing apparel?"

"Yes."

"What kind of wearing apparel?"

"I don't know."

"Shirt? Coat? Trousers?"

"I couldn't see what kind it was."

"You couldn't see any particular article of clothing?"

"No."

"Then how do you know it was clothing?"

"I saw what I saw."

"If you're positive it was clothing thrown overboard, why can't you name a single article?"

Harry stared down at his own clothing for a minute. "A shirt. I saw a shirt."

"What kind of shirt?"

"I didn't see it that clear."

"What color was it?"

"Counsel is badgering the witness," Owen said. "The scene lasted only a few seconds. Mr. Arnold can't be expected to tell us that he saw a pink sport shirt with a button-down size thirteen white collar."

"Mr. Arnold claims to have seen a shirt," Donnelly said. "I'm attempting to find out how he reached this conclusion."

Harry's eyes shifted anxiously from counsel to counsel, then finally rested on the judge. "I saw clothing. Maybe it wasn't a shirt, but it was clothing. And those screams didn't come from no radio neither. When Cully brings a woman on board, it's not so as they can listen to the radio."

Laughter spread across the courtroom. Donnelly could have objected and the judge would certainly have ordered Harry's remarks stricken from the record and from the jurors' minds. But Donnelly knew that the jurors would not, could not forget, so he decided to take advantage of the situation.

"Are you implying, Mr. Arnold, that the alleged screaming might have indicated, shall we say, sexual excitement?"

"Wouldn't surprise me."

"Then your answer is yes?"

"More like maybe."

Donnelly waited for the spectators' amusement to subside before taking another tack.

"You testified, Mr. Arnold, that you talked with Cully King after the *Bewitched* tied up?"

"Yes."

"And he stated that he was going ashore so he could get treatment for a toothache?"

"Yes."

"And he was holding a handkerchief against his left cheek with his left hand?"

"Yes."

"And you didn't notice him carrying anything in his right hand?"

"I didn't notice."

"The jewel case in question is rather a large object, is it not?"

"Yes."

"You saw it, did you not?"

"When she came on board, yes."

"Is it possible that he could have been carrying an object of that size without your observing it?"

"Not likely."

"Not even possible, is it, Mr. Arnold?"

There was no answer.

"At this time, Your Honor, I would like to offer in evidence a tape recording."

The tape was brought in by Eva, and the machine to play it on was carried by the bailiff and placed in the middle of the counsel's table.

"I'm going to ask you to listen to this, Mr. Arnold, and see if you recognize the sound."

The machine was turned on. The sound was that of a 671 GMC diesel engine powering at ten knots. It had been made by Gunther on a local yacht under the supervision of two deputy sheriffs.

A low-pitched, vibrating hum filled the courtroom.

"Do you recognize that sound, Mr. Arnold?"

"It's a diesel. Six cylinders, maybe eight."

"Is the sound similar to that made by the engine of the *Bewitched*?"

"Yes, sir."

"What kind of engine does the *Bewitched* carry?"

"Six-seventy-one GMC. That's six cylinders."

Donnelly switched off the tape for a moment. "It has not been established where you were on the boat when you heard the alleged screaming."

"I was in the engine room with my son, Richie. He liked to fool around with engines, you know, like any kid messing under the hood of a car."

"Will you please step down here for a moment and adjust the volume of this recording so the jury can hear fairly accurately what you heard?"

Harry turned up the volume, and the vibrating hum increased. A juror in the back row put her hands over her ears.

Donnelly switched it off and resumed questioning. "Tell me, Mr. Arnold, is there anything special about the way the *Bewitched*'s engine room was designed?"

"Everything on the *Bewitched* is special."

"I'm referring specifically to anything that was done to muffle the engine sound."

"The engine room is well insulated."

"So that people on deck couldn't hear the full noise of the engine?"

"Yes, sir."

"Could it also mean that people in the engine room could not hear the full deck noises?"

Harry didn't answer.

"Did you hear me, Mr. Arnold? Insulation works both ways, does it not?"

"I saw what I saw," Harry said. "And I heard what I heard. My son Richie was with me. Just ask him."

"I will, when I get the chance."

The chance didn't come until the following Wednesday. On the first two days of the week court was in recess to allow the judge time to preside at a special psychiatric hearing in the northern part of the county.

On Wednesday morning Richie made his first appearance in court. He'd had his hair cut very short at his father's insistence, and he was wearing a long-sleeved sweater his father had bought him to replace the tight muscle shirt he usually wore. He looked uncomfortable and sullen, and he spoke in such a low voice that the court reporter had to ask him several times to repeat his answers.

He said he was fifteen, that he'd dropped out of school to take this cruise on the *Bewitched* because he wanted to and because his father said it would be a valuable experience helping to take a ship through the Canal and up the West Coast.

Most of the time he was speaking he kept his eyes downcast. It was only when he was asked about the night Mrs. Pherson disappeared that he looked directly at Cully, almost as if he were asking permission to answer. Cully turned his head away.

Owen said, "Do you understand the meaning of the oath you took a few minutes ago, Richie?"

"I got to tell the truth."

"And if you don't tell the truth, what is it called?"

"Lying."

The audience was as quick to laughter as a church congregation. The sound of laughter in court irritated Owen. He always felt that somehow it was directed against him.

"Of course, it's lying," he said brusquely. "The legal term is perjury, and it is a punishable offense. Now, you wouldn't want to commit a serious offense like perjury, would you?"

Owen knew from the boy's expression that he had taken the wrong approach. It might have worked on his own boys, but this wasn't a boy. He was a man doing a man's job with a man's responsibility. He wasn't a teenager messing around under the hood of his car; he was in the engine room of a million-dollar yacht.

"I was only trying to point out," Owen added, "the serious nature of being a witness for the people."

"I'm not a witness for the people. There were no people; there was just me and Harry."

"Are you referring to the very early-morning hours,

say, halfway between midnight and dawn?"

"Yes."

"Were you in the engine room with your father?"

"Yes."

"Tell us exactly what happened?"

"I thought the engine was making a funny little thumping sound every once in a while, so I called Harry in, and we were both listening for it. And Harry said, 'Hey, did you hear that?' And I said, 'I didn't hear any thumping sound,' and he said no, he meant screams, a lady screaming. I said I didn't hear nothing, and he said, 'You crazy kids are all getting deaf from listening to such loud music.' Then I heard it."

"You heard a woman screaming?"

"Yes, I think so. I think I heard it."

"Did your father say anything about going to investigate?"

"He wanted to go, but he was afraid Cully would be mad if he and the lady were, you know, just having, you know, fun or something like that."

"What happened after that?"

"Harry said the engine sounded perfect to him, and he told me to hit the sack. So I did."

"You went to sleep immediately?"

"Yes."

"I have no more questions."

Donnelly's cross-examination was short, and he did not repeat Owen's error in patronizing the boy.

"You told the court that you think you heard screams. Is that right?"

"Yes."

"Did you hear them prior to your father calling your attention to them?"

"No."

"Are you a little deaf, Richie?"

"No."

"Do you listen to loud music?"

"Sure, like everybody else. Only it didn't make me deaf."

"Is it possible, Richie, that you told your father you heard the screams in order to convince him you were not deaf from listening to loud music?"

Owen rose to object, but before the judge could rule on it, Donnelly said he would withdraw the question.

"While you were listening to the engine, did your father bring another noise to your attention and ask if you heard it?"

"Yes."

"What was your response?"

"At first I said no, and he said all us kids were crazy to let ourselves get deaf from listening to rock music."

"Did you resent this?"

"It wasn't true."

"Did you want to prove to your father that it wasn't true?"

"He's always on my back about it."

"Is that why you agreed with him, to get him off your back about the deafness issue?"

For a full minute Richie sat mute, his eyes fixed on Cully again with a mixture of bewilderment and appeal. Donnelly had the impression that the boy's answer would depend on Cully's reaction. There was none, no recognition, no acknowledgment, no attempt to influence the testimony.

"Did you hear the question, Richie?"

"Yes."

"And what is your answer?"

"I heard the lady screaming," Richie said.

"You weren't sure of that before. Why are you sure now?"

"I don't know. I just am. The lady was screaming."

"If a man says one thing one minute and another the next minute, is it fair to assume he simply doesn't know? You have said, 'I think so.' You have said, 'I don't know.' You have said, 'Maybe.' Now you say you're sure. Doesn't that mean you're sure for right this minute, not necessarily next minute?"

Owen got to his feet. "Counsel is harassing the witness."

"Witness is harassing counsel," Donnelly said wryly. "I have no more questions."

At lunchtime Judge Hazeltine drove down to the waterfront. He parked the old car along the curb of the boulevard to avoid the fifty-cent-an-hour fee charged for parking in one of the lots closer to the marina. This was a matter of principle, not thrift. He considered the fee discriminatory as well as economically unsound. The revenue which was supposed to have been used for harbor improvements had simply vanished into thin air and water thick with oil and debris, the sea's flotsam and the seamen's jetsam.

The judge took off his coat and tie and rolled up his sleeves. He put on a pair of tar-stained sneakers and a Giants' baseball cap and clipped sunshades on top of his regular glasses. He transferred his lunch, consisting of a bologna sandwich and a hard boiled egg, from the glove compartment of his car to a side pocket of his trousers, the egg especially making an interesting bulge in his silhouette.

Thus disguised, he started walking toward the breakwater, past the yacht club, where he recognized a bail bondsman and an attorney having drinks on the terrace.

He passed the row of concrete benches along the seawall where a varied group of people were eating their sandwiches and hamburgers and fish-and-chips.

The tide was receding, leaving the walkway wet and slippery. At the end of the breakwater he sat on one of the huge boulders that formed the base of the lighthouse marking the entrance to the harbor. The foghorn was silent. The revolving warning light was turned on but scarcely visible in the bright sun. It was a typical autumn day, clear and crisp, cool in the shade, warm in the sun.

An old man fishing from the adjoining rock eyed the judge's baseball cap with disapproval. "Know what I'd do if I was managing the Giants? I'd turn them all into hot dog vendors."

"An unusual suggestion."

"Should of been done before. Ten chances to one they'd have botched that, too, probably couldn't even put a wienie in a roll without dropping it."

The old man spoke with the bitterness of a disappointed lover. The judge, figuring there wasn't much to say to a disappointed lover, peeled his hard-boiled egg and ate it with the bologna from inside the sandwich. The bread he fed to the gulls, throwing small pieces into the air. Each piece was caught with speed and grace, only serving to deepen the old man's gloom.

"Them Giants oughta come out here and take lessons."

"A good deal depends on the throw, don't you think? I have," he added modestly, "rather a decent throwing arm."

"Nah. They can catch anything."

"They can't hit."

"Probably could if they had a way of holding a bat."

The judge leaned back against the rock and thought about this. It was a pleasant fantasy, the gulls holding tiny bats under their wings and the air filled with one continual baseball game.

Refreshed by food and fantasy, he started the trip back to his car. He was in the act of unlocking the trunk when his attention was drawn to a woman approaching him from the fifty-cent-an hour parking lot. He didn't recognize her until she was a few yards away.

In the courtroom she took on some of its regal atmosphere, and her manner intimidated deputies, attorneys and even the judge himself on occasion. Here, against this busy background of Monterey seiners and Boston whalers, of joggers and skateboarders and bicyclists, she looked out of place, almost unreal.

"I followed you," Eva said.

"Dear me." The judge looked somewhat baffled. "What on earth for?"

"To talk to you."

"You're perfectly free to come to my chambers anytime and discuss court procedures."

"This isn't a court procedure. It's me, *my* procedures."

"I notice you've been acting a bit odd lately. I thought perhaps it was the full moon."

"You don't really believe in that full moon stuff, do you?"

"There's a full moon once a month. I pretty well have to believe in it."

"I meant, all those stories about animals getting restless and people behaving irrationally."

The judge contemplated his answer while he finished changing his clothes. "I had a coonhound once, used to bay at the full moon. It wasn't of much significance however, since he also bayed at the new moon, fire sirens, garbage trucks, passing trains and automobile horns. He even bayed at my wife, until one day she bayed back at him. It was an interesting confrontation, but I believe my wife won. She had a way with animals."

The judge closed the lid of the trunk with a bang. He recalled his last personal conversation with Miss Foster regarding bras, and lack thereof, and decided to stick to the relatively safe subject of coonhounds as long as possible. "Have you ever had a coonhound, Miss Foster?"

"I don't think so."

"If you had, you'd be sure of it, by the neighbors' complaints, if nothing else. It's an unusual breed. I don't believe mine ever saw a coon. Perhaps that's why he made so much racket, out of sheer frustration. What do you do when you're frustrated, Miss Foster?"

"I don't bay," Eva said grimly.

"Pity. I'd rather like to hear that sound again. Primeval. I have made a small personal study of primeval sounds. Among birds, for instance, I have found the loon's call to be the wildest, not in this area, where they are winterlings and haven't much to say for themselves, but farther north on their breeding grounds. Their call is one of utmost abandon, ecstasy, madness. Human beings have translated these sounds into words, but I must say they're a poor substitute for the real thing."

As the judge warmed to his subject, his audience was rather obviously cooling. With a sigh he unlocked the passenger side of his car, and Eva got in. He took his place behind the wheel, unclipped the sunshades from his glasses and returned them to his pocket. He thought of steering the conversation in a more positive direction by complimenting her on her appearance. In fact, she looked quite chic in a black and white print silk dress with a black jacket and a bright red scarf at the neck. But before he could think of the right words, she began to weep quietly.

"I wish you wouldn't do that, Miss Foster," he said.

She continued weeping. He sat and waited, wondering about this whole business of tears. Like words, they were a creation of man and a substitute for the real thing. This was fortunate under the circumstances. The prospect of Miss Foster wailing and keening—and possibly attracting a few loons as well—was mind-boggling. Miss Foster would undoubtedly wail and keen just as efficiently as she did everything else.

Finally she stopped crying, wiped her eyes, blew her nose, got out of the car to dispose of the used tissue in a trash container and returned to the car. The judge watched this sequence of events with interest. Grief or no grief, Miss Foster never forgot her training.

"I've fallen in love," she said finally. "It doesn't make any sense whatever. There are a hundred reasons why I shouldn't have. I could even see it coming, and I didn't duck or turn and run. I just stood there and let it happen. Now I wish I were dead."

At this point the judge would have opted for some wailing and keening, but it was too late. He sighed, reflecting that he did a great deal of sighing lately. Perhaps there were more reasons for it as the years passed. Sighing was, he believed, simply the act of taking in more oxygen to help the brain cope with an unusual or difficult set of circumstances.

"My life has always been so orderly," Eva said. "Look at the mess it's in now. I'm in love with a man on trial for murder, a black man with kids and a common-law wife. And that isn't the worst of it. He doesn't love me back. I think I could make him love me back if I had the chance. Am I going to get that chance?"

"Are you asking me to predict what the jurors' verdict will be? Nobody on earth can do that. No mind reader, no computer programmed with every detail of every juror's life from day one can give a readout on what a verdict will be."

"Can't you please give me your opinion on how strong the case is against him?"

"That would be highly irregular."

"I know."

"And you're asking me to do it anyway?"

"Yes."

The judge removed his glasses, wiped them with a handkerchief and put them back on his nose. The images seen through them were no clearer: the rear of the car in front of him; his own hands on the steering wheel, misshapen with age; and Miss Foster's face, pale and strained. In the distance there were all the masts of pleasure boats like a leafless forest.

"The evidence against him is purely circumstantial, of course," he said almost as if he were talking to himself. "He took a woman on board the *Bewitched* with him, and that woman was later found dead in the water, tangled in a bed of kelp. An autopsy clearly revealed grooves on her throat, which the prosecution contends were left by thumbs during the act of strangulation. When the *Bewitched* docked, the defendant went ashore and pawned the diamond studs the dead woman customarily wore in her earlobes. He lied to the pawnbroker, as he had to Harry Arnold, about having a toothache and needing the pawn money to pay a dentist. His teeth, according to a deposition given by the jail dentist, are in almost perfect condition. The prosecution contends that what he needed the money for was to pay his living expenses while he holed up in some motel until the scratches on his cheek healed. The question that immediately arises is: Why would a man be so anxious to hide some scratches on his face?

The obvious answer, indeed, the only one I can come up with, is that those scratches implicated him in a crime."

"Not necessarily murder," Eva said.

"True. There is no incontrovertible evidence that the woman was strangled since the pathologists are not in full agreement in interpreting the grooves on her throat, whether they occurred before or after death. The defendant's tendency to drink too much and lose his temper easily while drunk has been hinted but not actually proved.

"Missing from the prosecution's case is a case of another kind—to wit, the green leather one containing Mrs. Pherson's valuable heirloom jewelry. It was in her possession when she came on board, but no trace of it or its contents has shown up. Sometime after the woman's body was found, a fisherman retrieved her coat from the sea. It proved a significant find because it was still buttoned. Mrs. Pherson, the testimony has shown, always hung her clothes carefully on hangers, buttoned or zippered to retain their shape. She could not have been wearing the coat when she went overboard. Wave action can tear a coat off a body, but there is no way it can rebutton it. Common sense tells us it was thrown overboard, and since Harry Arnold claims to have seen the defendant toss some clothing into the water, it's possible or even likely the coat was disposed of in that manner by Cully King. Still, it's not evidence of murder.

"The possibility of suicide has been suggested but not taken seriously. True, Mrs. Pherson had been despondent after the death of her mother, with whom she'd been planning a trip to Hawaii. That this was the destination of the *Bewitched* may have been a contributing factor in Mrs. Pherson's decision to accompany Cully King. We'll never know. We can't read a dead mind. Mrs. Pherson's actions resembled those of a woman bent not on suicide but on having a hell of a good time getting away from the structured life she led with a rather puritanical husband. You may recall the chambermaid hearing her talk to herself in her room before leaving the hotel as well as her conversation with Mr. Elfinstone at the hotel desk. It was the happy, excited talk of a woman who, in her own words, was going to do something she'd never done before and would never do again.

"There is still another addition to the list of questions that haven't been answered and actions that haven't been explained. Cully King cleaned and tidied the cabin so no signs remained that it had been occupied. Why? Having sex with a woman was not a crime he had to hide but something for a man like Cully to boast about. After all, this was no ordinary dock hooker. Mrs. Pherson had class and money. But he didn't boast of his conquest. Instead, he removed every single trace of her presence as if he were erasing her very existence. Why?"

"We'll find out when he takes the stand."

"Donnelly will never put him on the stand. He can't afford to. Cully King would tie himself in knots trying to answer all the questions and explain all his actions. I hope I'm right about this. I'd like to be out of here by Christmas. And I mean Christmas this year, not next year."

He stared at his hands on the steering wheel, the knuckles swollen as if he'd hit someone with his fist.

"I feel time is passing like a train," he said. "And everybody in the courtroom is being left behind, that all our lives have come to a stop at the station. Eventually another train will come along, and we'll get on it and resume our lives."

"Perhaps there won't be another train," Eva said.

"There always is."

"Not for me. I've been waiting a long time for this one."

"This one isn't a train for you, Foster; it's a carousel. Jump off before you get hurt."

"I'm already hurt."

"Then don't make it worse. I'll do my part by arranging a leave of absence for you or a transfer to another courtroom."

"No, thanks. I must stay where I am."

"Why?"

"In case he needs me."

The judge's sigh this time was the longest and deepest yet. "Isn't there anyone you can discuss this with, a family member, a minister, someone who is older and wiser?"

"I don't want to discuss it with anybody."

"Well, dammit, you must have wanted to discuss it with me or you wouldn't have followed me all the way down here. Dammit, I can't afford to lose a good clerk in a morass of mush. You've got to talk to someone about the situation."

"I've already talked to the only one who counts. You want to know what he said?" She tugged at the red scarf around her neck to loosen it. "He said, 'Holy shit.' "

The judge's face was caught in a grimace between a smile and a frown. "Are you sure you understood him correctly?"

"I'm sure."

"Well, at least you were left without any doubt."

"I was left without any anything. But don't feel sorry for me. I'm going to fight. If he's found innocent, I'm going to fight for him. And if he's found guilty, I'm going to fight alongside him all the way to the Supreme Court."

"*Holy shit,*" the judge said under his breath.

Before the first witness of the afternoon session was called, District Attorney Owen addressed the bench.

"Your Honor, I would like the following information included in the transcript. Lieutenant Sommerville, who will now be taking the stand, was supposed to be my first witness. A postponement was necessary because Lieutenant Sommerville is in charge of the locally based Coast Guard cutter *Priscilla*, which was scheduled to go on a two-week training cruise. Because of the length of time required to pick this jury, his appearance conflicted with the training cruise schedule. So I am calling him now instead of as originally planned."

Lieutenant Sommerville was in uniform, a ruddy-faced, serious-looking man in his early thirties. He stated that his permanent residence was in Los Alamitos. He had been in the Coast Guard for twelve years, ever since he graduated from the University of California at San Diego with a degree in marine biology. He was in command of the Coast Guard cutter *Priscilla* when a member of the crew spotted the body of a woman entangled in a kelp bed. Two crewmen were sent in a rubber raft to retrieve the body and bring it on board the *Priscilla*.

The body was tested for vital signs to determine the fact of death. Death had apparently occurred some hours before. Since the body had been found within the three-mile limit, jurisdiction belonged to the sheriff's department, which sent a patrol boat to take the body to the police morgue.

Sommerville identified the pictures offered previously in evidence by the prosecution as being those of the dead woman taken on board the *Priscilla*.

"How much time elapsed before the woman's body was transferred from the *Priscilla* to the sheriff's patrol boat?"

"Roughly about an hour and a half."

"During that period did you form an opinion as to the cause of death?"

"That's not my job. Anyway, I covered her with a blanket as soon as I determined that she was dead. Then I called the sheriff's office and told them we had a floater."

"Is that police jargon for a body found in the water?"

"Yes."

"After the body was transferred to the patrol boat, what did you do?"

"I asked the deputy to be sure and return the blanket."

The audience laughed, and the lieutenant added hastily, "That may seem like a trivial thing to you, but I'm held accountable for every single item on board my ship, and it is my duty to see that items removed are brought back."

"Was it?"

"No."

"I have no more questions. Thank you, Lieutenant."

The judge looked at Donnelly. "Are you ready to cross-examine, Mr. Donnelly?"

"Yes, Your Honor."

Donnelly replaced Owen at the lectern. "Lieutenant Sommerville, you stated that you had a degree in marine biology?"

"Yes, sir."

"Would you tell us what you meant when you referred to a bed of kelp?"

"It is called by biologists a forest of kelp. We see only the top of this forest on the water surface. The stalks, or stipes, go all the way down to sea bottom, where they are anchored by holdfasts which keep the plant in place."

"Are there several kinds of kelp found in this area?"

"Yes, sir."

"Referring to the bed or forest where Mrs. Pherson's body was found, can you identify the species?"

"It's one of the larger varieties, *Macrocystis*. Boatmen

hate the stuff since it can foul up propellers, anchors, keels, but it's an important part of the food chain."

Donnelly went over and spoke to the bailiff, who then left the courtroom and returned with Bill Gunther. Gunther was carrying a large plastic bag and a folding table.

He wore a dirty gray warm-up suit, wet at the seat, wrists and ankles. He was in his bare feet and looked cold and disgruntled. He had filed a protest over the assignment: "I can't think of a single reason why I should row out to the kelp beds when I could pick up a hunk of the stuff from the beach."

"I can," Donnelly told him. "I'm ordering you to."

"I hate the water. What if I drown?"

"I'll send flowers."

Gunther set up the table in the area between the witness stand and the jury box. He emptied the contents of the plastic bag on the tabletop, and the unmistakable odor of the sea drifted across the room. The kelp was a long single strand, light brown and slimy-looking.

"Would you step down here a minute, Lieutenant, and identify this seaweed which my assistant has just gathered?"

"I can tell from here it's *Macrocystis*."

"Commonly found around here?"

"Yes, sir. At a certain water depth there are dense forests of it parallel to the shoreline."

"You stated that Mrs. Pherson's body was entangled in the kelp. Would you explain this more fully?"

"Wave action had rolled her over and over and her body was—well, there's no better word than tangled."

"Was it wrapped around her whole body?"

"Yes, sir. She had to be extricated by cutting away the kelp that held her."

"And how was this done?"

"With a serrated knife."

"So that when the body was taken aboard the *Priscilla*, it was not in exactly the same condition as when it was first spotted, a good deal of the kelp having been cut away before the body could be moved. Is that correct?"

"Yes, sir. The stuff's strong and rubbery. Kids often use it on the beach as jump ropes."

"You have explained what the holdfasts of the plant are, and the stalk, or stipe. What are these leaflike things?"

"They're called blades."

"And these bulbous protuberances about the size of thumbs, what are they?"

"Hollow, gas-filled chambers known as floats. The name is self-explanatory."

"Would you explain it anyway for the benefit of those of us not so biologically oriented?"

"Kelp, like an ordinary plant that grows on land, needs light for the process of photosynthesis, and floats keep it close to the surface where the light is."

Donnelly addressed the bench. "At this point, Your Honor, I would request that Miss Foster bring in the three pieces of modeling clay I gave her earlier. They will be my next exhibits."

This was done, and the first piece of modeling clay was put on the table beside the fresh kelp.

"This is ordinary modeling clay," Donnelly told the jury, "and I'm going to ask Lieutenant Sommerville to press into it two of the floats of this kelp so that we may study the impressions. Will you do that please, Lieutenant?"

"How hard do you want me to press?"

"Just as hard as you think the kelp was wrapped around Mrs. Pherson's throat."

"I can't be sure of that, but I can make a rough guess."

The impressions were made, and the piece of clay was shown to the district attorney, then passed to the judge and then to each member of the jury. When this procedure was concluded, the lieutenant was asked to press each of his thumbs into the second piece of clay, exerting approximately the same amount of pressure. At Donnelly's request he initialed the impressions with a felt-tipped marking pen. This second piece of clay was also passed to the district attorney, the judge and the jury, and the lieutenant returned to the witness box.

"Would you say, Lieutenant, that the indentations left by the two kelp floats and those left by your thumbs are about the same size?"

"Yes, sir."

"Is there any noticeable difference?"

"Yes, sir."

"What is this difference?"

"My thumbnails left a semicircular impression that is clearly visible."

"In other words, the fleshy tip of each thumb is defined by the indentation of the nail?"

"That's what I perceive, yes, sir."

"At this juncture," Donnelly said, "I would like to ask the court's permission to have my client, Mr. King, be allowed to follow the same procedure with the third piece of clay as the lieutenant did with the second. Do I have Your Honor's permission?"

"This is quite irregular," the judge said. "But at the moment I can think of no valid reason why it shouldn't be allowed."

Cully had not been forewarned of this move, and he registered the surprise Donnelly had hoped he would.

Even the most obtuse juror could see the surprise was genuine and not just part of a ploy arranged by defendant and counsel.

Handed the piece of modeling clay, Cully pressed one thumb and then the other into it and initialed the marks with the same pen used by the lieutenant. Again the clay was passed to the district attorney, the judge and jury and, finally, the man on the stand.

"Lieutenant Sommerville, do these two impressions resemble those made by your own thumbs?"

"Yes, sir."

"There are similar indentations left by thumbnails, are there not?"

"Yes, sir."

"I believe that at this point the jury should have the opportunity to reexamine plaintiff's exhibits through sixteen-P. For this reason I would ask that thirteen-M, fourteen-N and fifteen-O be passed among the jurors and that sixteen be put on the display board."

Exhibit M-13 was a normal-sized photograph of Mrs. Pherson's head and throat as first seen by the pathologist, Dr. Woodbridge. N-14 and O-15 were enlargements of the throat itself, and P-16 was an enlargement of the grooves found on it.

"Lieutenant, I would like you to examine all these photographs carefully. Will you do that?"

"Yes, sir."

"Very carefully now, would you tell us which of the pieces of clay these photographs resemble?"

"I strongly object," the district attorney said. "Human flesh is not clay. To compare the two is absurd."

Donnelly went along with the objection without argument. "Very well, I withdraw the question and would instead ask that the next ten items be lettered as defendant's exhibits. I've forgotten what letter we're at now, but I'm sure Miss Foster knows."

The ten exhibits were books on homicide investigation and forensic pathology. All of them contained bookmarks, and a few had several. Viewing the formidable pile of books, the judge declared a twenty-minute recess.

During the recess Oliver Owen called his wife from the pay phone in the main corridor. It was something he often did when he was frustrated and annoyed. He would never have admitted it to anyone, least of all to Vee herself, but the sound of her voice was soothing and made him feel that even if she disagreed with him verbally, she was completely on his side.

Vee was at her desk in the small alcove of the kitchen, paying the more urgent bills and setting aside the others. There was never enough money to pay all of them at once.

"Is that you, Vee?"

"I think so. There's no one else here."

"I wanted to tell you I'll probably be late for dinner."

"That's all right. We're having beef stew and French bread. Both can be heated up in a jiffy."

"How are the boys?"

"They were fine at breakfast. I assume they're still fine since I haven't heard anything to the contrary. . . . What's wrong, Oliver?"

"That creep Donnelly is trying to pull a fast one. What intelligent person would believe that that woman fell overboard into a bed of kelp and was strangled to death by one of the strands? But we're not dealing with intelligent persons; we're dealing with jurors."

"I hope you're in a place where you can't be overheard."

"Of course I am. Do you take me for a fool?"

"It's easy to get a bit careless. To be on the safe side, you could lower your voice slightly."

He lowered his voice. "Have you ever heard of anyone being strangled to death by *kelp*?"

"How did she get into the kelp?"

"Donnelly implies that she fell overboard, and while unconscious but still technically alive, she became entangled in the kelp."

"That's dumb. Boats stay away from the kelp beds, especially big boats like the *Bewitched*."

"What did you say?"

She repeated it word for word.

"Why, Vee," Oliver said in a surprised voice. "Why, Vee, what an amazing piece of reasoning. You're right, you're absolutely right."

"Once in a while us morons get lucky and come up with something intelligent almost like real people."

"You mustn't put yourself down, Vee."

"Oh, I won't. I always have someone to do it for me."

"I mean it. Sometimes you're very intelligent."

"Hurray for me."

"Of course, the boat didn't go anywhere near the kelp. In order to get into the stuff, she'd have had to swim for it. If it was just a matter of wave and current action, it would probably take hours. In water that cold a person might be able to live a short time but definitely not hours. Even staying alive a short time is highly unlikely. Vee, you might help me win this case yet."

"Why is winning it so important to you, Oliver?"

"You know why. It will help me get reelected."

"Yes, but why is it so important to you to be reelected? God knows it can't be the salary. You could do much better in private practice."

"I want to be somebody my sons will look up to and want to emulate. I can't be just an ordinary lawyer. You know what most people think of lawyers. But district attorney, that's a position of authority, a position that demands respect. It gives the boys something to aim at, shoot for."

"You're forgetting that this is an iconoclastic generation, Oliver."

"What's 'iconoclastic'?"

"What I really mean to say is that teenagers nowadays are likely to consider the position of district attorney something to shoot down, not at."

"That doesn't apply to my sons. They respect authority."

Vee thought of the epoxy glue episode and the Latin graffiti in the bathroom, but she said smoothly, "I'm sure your sons would have just as much respect for you if you were an ordinary lawyer."

"Do you really think that?"

"I'm sure of it." There was the faint metallic taste of irony in Vee's mouth, but she swallowed it quickly. After all, the epoxy and graffiti stages would soon pass and Thatcher would be able to memorize all twenty-six amendments and everyone would live happily ever after. *And I'll be the Queen of Rumania.*

"Oliver, before you hang up, I want to tell you that the boys and I will always love you no matter how things turn out."

There was a silence. Then: "I'm sorry. My mind was wandering. What did you say?"

"Nothing. Go look for your mind."

"I have to hang up now. Thanks for calling."

"I didn't call you. You called me."

But the line was dead. Slowly and sadly she replaced

the phone on the desk. She couldn't help loving Oliver, but she reserved the right to think he was often a damn fool.

It was a long afternoon. Court didn't adjourn until nearly six o'clock. The interval between recess and adjournment was taken up by the process of showing to the jurors each of the marked photographs in the ten books Donnelly had offered in evidence. All of the photographs were of female strangulation victims taken in autopsy rooms throughout the country: a prostitute in Omaha, Nebraska; two young sisters from Brownsville, Texas; a housewife from Visalia, California, and another from Bend, Oregon; a Chicago nurse; an Atlanta waitress; a Los Angeles meter maid; a Miami drug dealer; a dental hygienist from Albuquerque; an English tourist visiting Philadelphia; and a New Orleans real estate agent. Photographs of each of these victims were projected on a large screen brought in by the bailiff. The enlarged picture of the grooves on Mrs. Pherson's throat remained on the display board beside the screen. Each photograph flashed on the screen for comparison, showed one noticeable difference from Mrs. Pherson's photograph. The grooves left by the fleshy tips of thumbs were defined by indentations of thumbnails in every victim except Mrs. Pherson.

As each picture was shown, Donnelly used a rubber-tipped pointer to draw this difference to the jurors' attention. Then once again the pieces of modeling clay were passed around among the jurors, and Donnelly's message came across loud and clear: According to the physical evidence available, Lieutenant Sommerville or Cully King might have strangled all the other victims, but neither of them could have strangled Mrs. Pherson because no thumbnail indentations were left on her throat.

Owen's objections were feeble and overruled. By this time he was really worried, knowing better than anyone in the courtroom except the judge that Donnelly didn't have to prove Mrs. Pherson was strangled by kelp, he had only to show reasonable doubt that she was strangled by Cully King. That such doubt had been cast was evident not only on the face of each juror but on that of Lieutenant Sommerville.

When court was finally adjourned for the day, Sommerville waited in the corridor to speak with Owen.

"I thought you said it was a sure thing he was guilty, Mr. Owen."

"It's a sure thing."

"That's not the way it looks right now. I'd hate to have a part in convicting an innocent man."

"You have nothing to worry about," Owen said sourly. "As far as evidence is concerned, you might as well have been a defense witness, not mine."

"I did the best I could."

"Thanks. Meanwhile, don't forget that Donnelly picked those books and those pictures. There must be hundreds of others. And I'm going to find them."

"I hope you don't call me back to the stand." Sommerville took off his cap and wiped his forehead with his hand. "I hate looking at pictures like that."

"Nobody enjoys it," Owen said. "But we owe it to Madeline Pherson, a human being."

In the courtroom only four people remained, Cully King and Donnelly and the bailiff standing at the door talking to the deputy who'd come to take Cully back to the jail.

"You did great," Cully told Donnelly. "That was real convincing. Now I know why you told me to stop biting my nails."

"I told you what?"

"To stop biting my nails. You remember that night when you came to the jail—"

"I don't recall the episode."

"Sure you do. You came in late. I distinctly remember."

"Whatever you distinctly remember, you will now distinctly forget."

"Sure. Okay. Consider it forgotten."

"Communication between lawyer and client is privileged—that is, strictly private. But it sometimes leaks out, occasionally through the lawyer but more often through the client after a few drinks or a little softening up of one kind or another. There is nothing wrong in what I said to you or what you did in response, but it might possibly be misinterpreted as an attempt to obstruct justice. A chatty guy like you might open up to a nice, friendly cellmate who likes to listen. But that cellmate could be a police informant. So what did I tell you to do on the night I came to the jail?"

"Nothing."

"Good. That settles that."

"Not quite," Cully said. "Where'd you get the idea that I was a chatty guy?"

"You and Miss Foster seem to find a lot to talk about."

"I got nothing to say to her."

"Your lips moved. I assume when a person's lips move, he is talking. Is that a fair assumption?"

"I hate sarcastic know-it-all bastards like you."

Cully pushed back his chair, got up and walked quickly to the door. Donnelly heard him exchanging greetings with the deputy about being late and missing the jail bus.

"So you ride in style, Cully boy," the deputy said. "Courtesy of the sheriff, you got a limo all to yourself."

"Do I get to drive?"

"Sure, if you have a key."

Cully laughed, and the two of them walked out together.

Donnelly sat alone at the counsel's table for a long time, his head in his hands.

The bailiff's voice sounded hollow in the empty room. "Mr. Donnelly, don't you want to go home?"

"I'm . . . not in any hurry."

"Well, I have to lock up now. The main doors are already bolted. When you leave, you'll have to use the sheriff's entrance."

"All right. Thanks."

To avoid the evening rush on the freeway, Donnelly drove home through the city streets. He loved these streets and knew them well. As a new arrival he used to walk around downtown during lunch hours like a tourist, and after twenty-five years he still felt like a tourist, privileged to visit a city whose main street went all the way down to the sea. In each of the other directions there were mountains, changing color every hour, every season, from green and gray to pink and violet and sometimes, in the winter, white. On overcast days the mountains disappeared entirely, and the city became a stage setting without a backdrop, and the most imposing part of the setting was the courthouse. Its pure white tower was a symbol of truth and justice, and its massive clock chimed the hours and their message: *Son, observe the time and fly from evil.*

When he reached home at seven-thirty, Mrs. Killeen was the only person in the house. She met him as he came in the side door from the garage.

Her greeting was characteristic. "I suppose you'll be wanting dinner."

"It occurred to me."

"I go off duty in half an hour. Why don't you send out for some pizza?"

"I don't like pizza."

"Everybody likes pizza."

"I don't."

Mrs. Killeen consulted her wristwatch. "I have twenty-three minutes left according to my contract. I suppose I could throw something together in the microwave. How about a baked potato and some lamb chops?"

"Fine. I'll eat in the den."

"And remember, don't give my dog any of the bones. They make her upchuck."

"I think I can remember that," Donnelly said. "Did the hospital call about my wife?"

"No. All's quiet on the western front." Mrs. Killeen turned to leave, then changed her mind. "You probably never tasted pizza."

"I have tasted pizza, and I don't like it."

"Well, don't blame me if things don't turn out right. It's cook's night out, and her sub called to say she had to go to a funeral. And I said, you pull this stunt on me again, and the funeral you go to will be your own."

"You have a real gift of language, Mrs. Killeen."

He went upstairs, took a shower, put on pajamas and robe and came back down to the den adjoining the dining room. It was 8:03, and true to her word and contract, Mrs. Killeen was off duty, but she had left his dinner tray beside the leather chair in front of the television set.

Beside the plate was a note which proved that even in absentia Mrs. Killeen could have the last word: "We were out of baking potatoes and lamb chops. I had to make do. Pizza would have been better. S.K."

The plate contained mashed potatoes, asparagus and pork chops. The potatoes tasted vaguely like cardboard,

the asparagus had come out of a can and brought some
of the can with it and the pork chops were stringy. But
the coffee was hot and fresh, and so was the French bread.

When he'd finished the meal, he called the hospital in
Long Beach, and after going through the proper chan-
nels, he heard Zan's voice on the line.

"Zan, it's Charles."

"I know. They told me." She sounded tired and irritable
but under control.

"How are you, Zan?"

"What do you care?"

"You don't have to talk to me if you don't want to."

"Yes, I do. They told me, 'Be a good girl and talk to
your husband.' If I'd said, 'what husband?' they'd accuse
me of having amnesia or being irrational and some ear-
nest young doctor would come along and ask me, 'Do
you recall being married, Mrs. Donnelly?' You know what
my real answer would be? 'I recall going to a wedding
dressed up like a bride, but no, I don't recall being
married.'"

"Are your wrists healing?"

"What do you care?"

"I didn't want you to die. Dying wouldn't solve anything."

"Living isn't solving much either," she said. "Look, why
don't you just leave me alone for a long time and I'll leave
you alone? I'm going to get over what's bothering me, I'll
get over it. But you'll never get over what's bothering
you. You're stuck with it, Charles. Do you hear me, Charles?
Are you listening? You're *stuck* with it for the rest of your
life."

He didn't answer. There was nothing to say. He put
the telephone back on the table as if it had become too
heavy to hold. Even from a distance of three feet her
voice still came across sharp and clear: "When I'm better,

I'm coming home. It's my home, it belonged to my parents, and I don't want you there when I return. You'll have to get out. Do you hear me, Charles? Get the hell out of my house."

He looked around the room. There was nothing in it, nothing in any other part of the house, that he couldn't walk away from without a backward glance. It was as if he'd never lived there at all.

He thought of the poem written by a young client of his in part payment for legal services, a poet who had committed the unpoetic act of embezzling from his employer. Donnelly couldn't understand the poem at the time, but he remembered it now:

> Who took away the stars?
> What happened to the moon?
> Why have all the flowers gone
> So soon?
> Will I ever love again?
> Will more trees and flowers grow
> And the stars and moon appear?
> I'm tired. Tell me no.

VI

The
DEFENDANT

*H*arry had watched the six o'clock news in the tiny lobby of the motel. An hour later he turned it off and said to the young black behind the counter, "Don't nothing good ever happen in this world?"

The young man dragged his eyes away from the racing form he was studying. "You don't like what's happening in the world, you jump off."

"Where?"

"The edge."

"The world ain't got an edge."

"Then it looks like you're stuck here like the rest of us."

The thought of this made Harry hungry. He walked two blocks up the main street to a take-out stand and bought a bucket of fried chicken. Then, at a discount bakery outlet where day-old goods were sold at half price, he picked up a bag of sourdough rolls and a box of doughnuts.

When he returned to the motel room, Richie was still sleeping on the bed. The long-sleeved sweater he'd worn during his morning testimony had been flung across the back of a chair, and he had on the muscle shirt that was his uniform ever since arriving in California. He looked very young and innocent in his sleep, and Harry thought this was one of the good things that happened in this world, his boy, Richie.

Harry shook him gently by the shoulders. "Richie, wake up. Come and get some supper."

Richie's eyes opened, but there was no other movement.

"Hey, son, come on and eat."

"I'm not hungry."

"I never heard you say you weren't hungry before. Look, fried chicken, doughnuts, sourdoughs, good stuff."

"I don't want any," Richie said. "I had a couple of beers this afternoon."

"Wait a minute. You're not old enough to drink beer."

"I look old enough."

"The hell you do. You look like a fifteen-year-old kid. In this state you don't do no legal drinking till you're twenty-one. That's six more years. You show me the guy that sold you the stuff and I'll have him arrested."

Richie merely stared up at the ceiling with the sullen expression on his face that seemed as much a part of the teenage uniform as the muscle shirt and shrunken jeans.

Harry knew there was no use talking to him, so he sat down and ate three pieces of chicken and a roll, and then he ate three more pieces of chicken and another roll and four doughnuts.

Finally Richie said, "You going to eat it *all?*"

"Why not? There's no one around to share it with."

"I wouldn't mind tasting a piece."

"Help yourself."

Richie ate standing at the window, watching the boulevard traffic and the marina lights softened by mist. He felt sick, not from the beer—he'd bought only one can and hadn't finished that—but from fear and indecision.

Every now and then a cramp would seize his stomach like an iron hand.

"How come you don't talk to me no more?" Harry said.

"I talk. I'm talking now."

"Not like in the old days. You used to wait dockside for me to come in after a job. You'd start jabbering away, telling me everything in your head."

"I was just a kid then."

"You're still a kid or you'd have more sense than to wear those pants tight enough to strangle your balls. They're going to shrivel up like a couple of walnuts. You always had good balls. You got that from me."

"Everybody wears shrink-to-fits."

"Everybody around *here*." Harry emphasized the word as if it referred to a place where people lay around in the sun and committed immoral acts and never held a job. "I shouldn't have brought you here."

"You didn't bring me. Cully did."

"It was my idea. I thought you needed the experience. Little did I know what kind of experience you'd get. But I should have suspected. A friend of mine told me about it, how the crazies all went west and when they couldn't go any farther, they had to stop and that was California."

"Yeah, yeah, yeah."

"What did you say?"

"I was agreeing with you."

"No, you weren't. You were smart talking. No son should smart talk his father."

The iron hand squeezed Richie's stomach again. "Leave me alone."

"What's the matter with you these days? You act like you're losing your best friend."

Richie went into the bathroom and closed the door.

Harry ate the rest of the chicken, the rolls and all the doughnuts except two, which he put away for breakfast. He heard the toilet flush and water running in the basin for a long time. When Richie came back, his eyes were red as if they'd been stung by soap.

"I'm going for a walk," he said.

"Wait a minute and I'll go with you."

"No."

"I got a better idea. Why don't we stay home and watch TV? There's a good movie on, real funny, I seen it before. It's a million laughs."

"I don't feel like laughing."

Harry made one more attempt. "You're barefoot. How come you forgot your shoes?"

"I don't need any."

"What if you step on a piece of glass and get blood poisoning?"

"So I croak, so what?"

"That ain't a sensible attitude."

"Lay off me, will you?"

"Okay, go your own way. But be back by ten."

"Why?"

"Because I say so."

"That don't make it a federal law."

"No. It's just an old family custom: The father gives the orders, and the kids obey them."

"Why are you always harping on this family stuff?"

"Some sons," Harry said grimly, "have to be reminded."

"I'm reminded."

"Ten o'clock."

"Okay, okay."

He walked to the door, his movements slow and hesitant, almost as if he wanted to be stopped. But Harry said nothing more to stop him, and the boy went out. He didn't know if he'd be back by ten or twelve or ever.

Donnelly woke up to the sound of chimes. He often received telephone calls at odd hours of the night so he'd had the chimes installed to replace the shrill bell. The difference in sound made little difference in his reaction. He still woke with a sudden surge of adrenaline and a stopping of the heart.

It was Gunther.

"Charlie, you want to guess where I am?"

"No."

"I'll tell you anyway. I'm at the county jail."

"I suppose you'll also tell me how you got there."

"If you insist. I was out with this chick, and we weren't having such a great time. What with one thing and another. So to liven things up, I turned on the police calls and I heard this dispatcher talking about a BIP at the harbor on a boat named the *Bewitched*. BIP, that's what the cops around here call burglary in progress. See, the people who listen in on police calls figured out long ago what the various code numbers mean, so the local cops switched to letters."

"How clever."

"So I sent the chick home in a cab—you'll find the bill on my expense account—and drove down to the *Bewitched*. And guess what."

"Guessing games at two-thirty A.M. are not nice, Billy boy."

"All right, I'll tell you. The burglar, as in BIP, was the kid Richie Arnold. He got past the guard by swimming out to the *Bewitched* and climbing up the port side. Funny thing, I thought they were crazy to keep a guard on that boat all this time but apparently not. The guard heard a noise, went to investigate and came up with our boy Richie."

"What was he doing?"

"By the time I got there he was sitting in the back of a patrol car, wrapped in a blanket. The cops weren't saying a word, so I followed them out here."

"Has he been booked?"

"No. There's some shenanigans over him being a juvenile as well as a material witness. But the kid's asked for a lawyer. Kids these days watch so much TV that even a first grader picked up for playing hooky will demand a lawyer."

"Did they get him one?"

"That's what I'm doing," Gunther said. "He asked for you."

"Why?"

"Because you're Cully King's lawyer."

"Didn't anyone explain to him that I can't work both sides of the street?"

"Nobody's explaining anything to anybody. But I can tell you there's a lot of excitement in the air, good or bad I don't know, and I don't think they do either."

"What was the boy doing on the *Bewitched*?"

"Stealing."

"Stealing what?"

"Nobody seems to know that either. As far as I could see, it was something wrapped in a dirty piece of canvas, a sail bag maybe. Whatever is in that bag must be plenty important because they've called the DA and even the judge. I think you'd better get down here, too."

"All right."

"You want me to wait or can I go home?"

"Stick around."

"I need some sleep."

"Some scientists believe that people can be trained to

do without sleep entirely. Look on this as a golden opportunity to start practicing."

When Donnelly arrived at the jail, he didn't waste time asking questions that wouldn't be answered. He simply requested a meeting with his client, giving no explanation or apology for the timing.

Even at three o'clock in the morning the jail grapevine was in full operation. When Cully was escorted into the consulting room, his eyes were wide and wary.

He said, "What's happening?"

"I thought you might tell me."

"I heard some kid had been picked up for stealing from a boat down at the harbor. No names were mentioned, but I kind of guessed the boat was the *Bewitched* and maybe the kid was Richie Arnold. What did he steal?"

"What did you hear?"

"That it was just an old canvas bag."

"Containing?"

"Someone said it hadn't been opened yet. They're waiting for the DA and the judge."

"Do you know what was in that bag, Cully?"

"I heard it was a sail bag. So it probably contained sails."

"Does it seem reasonable to you that a kid with as much sense as Richie would swim out to the *Bewitched* and take a chance on being arrested in order to steal a sail bag?"

"That doesn't seem reasonable, no."

"What does?"

Cully turned away with an exaggerated shrug that gave Donnelly as much of an answer as any words.

"You've known Richie for a long time," Donnelly said, "and I've known him for only a short time, but we're both aware he'd need a powerful motive to pull a dumb stunt like that. Do you have any idea what that motive could be?"

"How c-could I?"

The slight stammer in his voice confirmed Donnelly's suspicion that Cully was scared and unpredictable. It would be necessary to prevent the district attorney from questioning him in private about anything, even the weather. Donnelly had long since discovered that the smartest crook in the world could trip over the most basic fact: One word led to another.

"What's next?" Cully said.

"Next, Mr. Owen or one of his henchmen will try to pump you for information whether you have it or not. If you answer some questions and not others, the balk will be fed into a computer. If you don't answer any questions at all, they won't have anything to feed the computer. Whether he asks, 'How are you?' or, 'Did you kill Madeline Pherson?' your reply will be the same: 'I respectfully refuse to answer on advice of counsel.' Understand?"

"Yes."

"So how are you? Do you like living in Santa Felicia?"

"I respectfully refuse to answer on advice of counsel."

"Any complaints about the way you've been treated in jail?"

"I respectfully refuse to answer on advice of counsel."

"Did you know that Richie Arnold has told the police everything? Why don't you come clean and make it easier on yourself?"

"I respectfully refuse to answer on advice of counsel."

The regular night guard came to the cell door, accompanied by a young deputy who looked new and nervous. His voice even cracked a little like an adolescent boy's:

"Mr. O'Donnell?"

"Donnelly."

"Sorry, sir. Mr. O'Donnelly, His Honor Judge Hazeltine has been notified of your presence in this holding facility and has indicated a desire to see you in the hearing room at your earliest convenience."

The guard laughed and said, "That's police academy talk meaning 'Move it.' Cute, isn't it?"

The hearing room was a small area of the jail set aside for special psychiatric or juvenile hearings that weren't suitable for open court. The air-conditioning had been shut off for the night in the interests of economy, and the place smelled of people under stress and of something more identifiable: mildew. It was coming from a canvas bag placed on the table that occupied center stage. Beside the bag was a green leather case stained with oil and brine and a gray-green mold. Only the double steel lock was unmarked by the passage of time and tides.

There were a dozen or so straight-backed wooden chairs occupied by District Attorney Owen and his chief investigator, Leo Bernstein, Judge Hazeltine and Gunther. With the arrival of Donnelly the judge rose and took his place behind the desk. In spite of the hour, he was bright-eyed and lively as if the unusual turn of events had piqued his interest. His voice was sharp.

"This unorthodox meeting has been called in order to be fair to both prosecution and defense. The green leather case on the desk in front of me has been given a great deal of attention during the course of the trial. Therefore, it seemed important to me to preserve it as found instead of trying to break the lock or otherwise forcibly open it. No skilled locksmith is available at this hour, so I am suggesting that we postpone the opening of the case until court convenes tomorrow morning. Is this agreeable to both counsel?"

Donnelly shook his head. "Under the discovery rule I have a right to see all evidence against my client before it is produced in court."

"The discovery rule does not apply since the case has not been offered in evidence by the prosecution. Indeed, nobody knows at this time whether the contents will favor prosecution or defense. Have you any questions?"

"Yes, sir," Donnelly said. "Where was the case found?"

"On the person of Richie Arnold."

"Where did he find it?"

"Obviously somewhere on the boat."

"Impossible," Owen said. "My men searched every inch of that boat from stem to stern."

"Apparently they missed a few inches between," the judge said. "Now, what's happened tonight, or rather this morning, leaves us in something of a dilemma. I was immediately informed of the development because of its legal implications. Here we have a juvenile caught stealing an object from a boat. Since juveniles are not allowed out on bail, they are either held in juvenile hall or released to their families, depending on the seriousness of the crime. Under ordinary circumstances Richie would be with his father right now. But the circumstances are not ordinary. First, he is a witness in a murder trial, and second, the motive for that murder might be sitting on the desk in front of me. So we're not faced with a kid caught stealing hubcaps but a prosecution witness stealing material evidence and thus obstructing justice."

"That would depend," Donnelly said, "on whether or not he knew what he was stealing."

"He must have known or he wouldn't have stolen it."

"How could he? He was not in the courtroom to hear the testimony of previous witnesses or subsequent witnesses. His father, who preceded him on the stand, was

284

admonished like all other witnesses not to discuss the case or his testimony with anyone else."

"It was in the newspapers and on television and radio."

"Has he stated that he was aware of the contents of this case?"

"No," the judge said. "In fact, he hasn't stated anything except that he wants a lawyer and a hamburger. The hamburger part's easy; the lawyer part isn't. He wants you, Mr. Donnelly. I don't know exactly what this means. Perhaps you have a theory?"

"No. However, it occurs to me that as a stranger in town he simply doesn't know the name of any other lawyer."

It was glib and plausible. The judge didn't buy it, but he had nothing to offer in its place. His knowledge of Richie was too sketchy to enable him to estimate the degree of the boy's sophistication. How many times had he been around the block and what had he picked up along the way?

He addressed the district attorney. "Has Richie Arnold ever been arrested for stealing?"

"I'm unaware of any kind of juvenile record on him."

"Are you unaware because he didn't have one or because you didn't seek that information?"

"It hardly seemed necessary. He's merely a secondary witness."

"It seems necessary to me. Has the kid ever been caught stealing, and if so, what? Hubcaps or jewelry? Videotapes or Cadillacs?"

"I guess we'll just have to ask him," Owen said. "Where is he?"

"In an individual holding cell, presumably eating a hamburger."

"Perhaps he could be brought to this room and questioned right here and now. He might be more willing to answer in this more informal atmosphere. I have three sons of my own, and I know how important it is to have the right atmosphere, the right tone."

Nobody in the room was impressed. The Owen boys were becoming well known in courtroom circles.

"Richie Arnold has clearly indicated his unwillingness to provide any answers," the judge said. "Questioning him here, informal atmosphere and tone notwithstanding, would be an infringement on his rights. I suggest we all go home and finish this night in a more conventional manner. We'll meet in court in the morning. Is this agreeable to you, gentlemen? Mr. Owen? Mr. Donnelly? Mr. Gunther, you spoke?"

Gunther sat up straight in his chair, and one of the loose wooden rungs squeaked, making an oddly human sound of protest.

"Mr. Gunther, do you wish to make a statement against my proposal?"

"Oh, no, sir. I find it very agreeable, very, very agreeable."

"That's a few too many 'verys.' Three, to be precise. A person may agree or disagree. Variations cannot properly be expressed by a modifying adverb like 'very.' "

"Sorry, sir."

"I'll see you tomorrow, gentlemen."

Donnelly waited for Judge Hazeltine in the parking lot. The judge came toward his car, whistling. It was an odd sound at that time and place, like a bird singing at night.

"May I have a word with you, Your Honor?"

"Go ahead."

"If a public defender has to be appointed for Richie, it might mean considerable delay until one of the PD men is available. They work on a pretty tight schedule. I am offering to pay for an attorney for Richie—anonymously, of course—solely for the purpose of expediting matters and getting this whole thing over with."

"Is that another of your do-gooder deeds, Mr. Donnelly?"

"The good is for me, nobody else. I want to leave town as soon as possible."

The judge's eyebrows made an inquiry, but he didn't say anything.

"It's not a sudden decision. I'm planning to live on my ranch in Wyoming." In response to another wiggle of the judge's eyebrows, he added, "I expect my retirement to be permanent. If an appeal is necessary in this case, it can be handled by the appeal firm of Esterhaus and Lowry."

"Is your wife going with you?"

"No."

"I'm sorry."

"She's not and I'm not. There's no one else to consider."

The judge leaned his back against the hood of his car, his arms crossed. "You know, Donnelly, I've been hearing rumors about you for years. I never took them seriously."

"Maybe you should have," Donnelly said. "Good night. Why not?"

"Because I figured you as the kind of person who had enough guts to come out of the closet years ago."

"You were wrong," Donnelly said.

In spite of an almost sleepless night, Judge Hazeltine was in good spirits and opened the day's session exactly on time, ten o'clock.

He addressed the jury.

"Ladies and gentlemen, we have an extraordinary situation on our hands which must be dealt with in an extraordinary manner. Mrs. Pherson's green case has been found but remains locked. Since neither prosecution nor defense is willing to accept it as evidence until its contents are revealed, I am therefore taking it upon myself to have it unlocked in the presence of everyone in the courtroom.

"Mr. Lorenzen, the locksmith I've called in, has nothing to do with the trial and is not a witness, will not be sworn. As a nonwitness Mr. Lorenzen is not obliged to answer any questions. His job is to open the case as quickly as possible and go back to his own work. Bailiff, will you bring Mr. Lorenzen in, please?"

The bailiff escorted into the well a small, alert man in his forties carrying a worn black satchel. He nodded at the judge, whom he knew from the judge's habit of locking himself out of his car.

"Your job," the judge told Lorenzen, "is to unlock the green case on the small table between the bench and the jury box. Give the case a perfunctory examination, and make comments if you like, but don't ask questions."

"It appears to be a jewel case, or a makeup case, with a covering of fine old leather. It has obviously been exposed to some dirty water containing oil among other things. In contrast with the leather covering the lock is new. It's made of stainless steel and is considerably sturdier than the small locks usually found on jewel cases, pieces of luggage and the like. Even a novice burglar could open this in a couple of minutes."

"And a nonnovice locksmith?"

"Seven seconds ought to do it. It's one of those locks that are installed to reassure the owner more than for real protection."

From his satchel he took a long, thin instrument, which he inserted in the lock.

"Five seconds," Lorenzen said. "Shall I open the lid?"

"No, I prefer to do it myself. You're free to go. Thank you for coming, Mr. Lorenzen."

The judge waited for Lorenzen to leave the courtroom before he lifted the lid of the case. Then he stepped back to give Owen and Donnelly their chance to see the contents.

Owen looked and turned pale. "Why, it's just dirt," he said. "Just plain dirt."

"It's not dirt," Donnelly said. "It's ashes."

"What do you mean, ashes? Like from a fireplace? My God, you can't mean it's a *person*?"

"I think so. I could be more positive if the bench and the prosecution doesn't object to my feeling the ashes with my hand."

No one objected so Donnelly put his hand in the ashes, using his fingers as a kind of sieve. He found a small shard of bone and a tooth, a molar badly discolored but still identifiable. He gave both these items to the judge, who in turn passed them down to Owen.

Donnelly said, "This is or was a human being."

The Judge returned to the bench, tapped his gavel and declared a ten-minute recess while the counselors met in his chambers.

In chambers the judge sat in the swivel chair behind his desk. He looked at the one-eyed owl on top of the bookcase. Then he turned his gaze on Owen.

"Your case has just been blown out of the water, Mr. Owen."

"I don't believe it."

"Do you believe that a man would murder a woman for a box of ashes?"

"He didn't know they were ashes. He thought they were jewels."

"What would lead him to that conclusion?"

"She told him."

"That's not in character for a woman like Mrs. Pherson."

"Mrs. Pherson was doing a lot of things that weren't in character."

It was the judge's decision to recall to the witness stand Dr. Woodbridge to establish whether the ashes belonged to a person. Woodbridge was not available until afternoon. Another delay. The rest of the morning was declared a recess. Donnelly spoke for the first time. "I intend to ask Your Honor for dismissal of all charges against my client."

"Don't waste your breath. I shall deny it."

Dr. Woodbridge was the first witness of the afternoon. He sifted through the ashes, using his fingers as a kind of sieve. He testified that the ashes were those of a small, thin person. In addition to the molar and shard of bone found by Donnelly, he discovered another shard of bone and a lady's wristwatch and gold wedding ring, initialed on the inside, R. M., B. K. It was obvious that neither watch nor wedding ring had been through the cremation process but had been added after the process was finished.

Tylor Pherson was recalled to the stand. Asked to identify the ring and wristwatch, he testified that they both belonged to his wife's mother, Ruth Maddox, who had died at the beginning of spring.

"Where were Mrs. Maddox's ashes usually kept?"

"In a large Chinese vase in my wife's sitting room. I wanted proper interment in the cemetery, but Madeline wouldn't hear of it. I didn't realize until now how deeply her mother's death had affected Madeline. She always put on a good front for the world. She said she hated to spread sorrow."

"Where did Mrs. Pherson usually keep the green leather case?"

"In a floor safe in her main clothes closet."

"Since her death have you had occasion to open that safe?"

"No."

"Would you say it's a fair guess that the jewels are in the safe right now?"

"It seems like a fair guess, yes."

"Do you know the combination of your wife's safe?"

"No. Madeline and I had a good deal of respect for each other's privacy and belongings."

"Who does know the combination?"

"Her attorney."

"Where does he practice his profession?"

"Bakersfield."

"Would he be in his office right now?"

"I believe so. He's not a trial lawyer, so most of the time he spends in his office."

"If you were to phone him during afternoon recess, do you think he'd be willing to go over to your house and open Mrs. Pherson's safe to ascertain the presence or absence of the jewels?"

"Yes."

"Would you do that, Mr. Pherson."

"All right."

Richie Arnold was the last recall witness of the day. He appeared with his father during the recess. The two sat side by side in the front row. Instead of the court clothes his father had bought him for his first appearance, Richie wore his beach outfit, tight jeans and a muscle shirt. He and Harry had been arguing about it ever since the district attorney had called in the morning.

"You look like a bum," Harry said.

"I'm not a bum."

"Well, you look like one. How are people to know the difference, whether you look like one or are one?"

"Jeez."

"And I don't want to hear no blasphemy neither."

A buzzer sounded the end of recess, and the courtroom began to fill up, with first spectators, then jurors, and finally the judge himself.

The judge's eyes surveyed the courtroom over the top of his glasses and came to rest on the two Arnolds in the front row. "Mr. Arnold, I must ask you to wait in the corridor."

"Why? This is my son, he's a minor. I got a right—"

"The only rights people have in this courtroom are these. I give them."

"That don't sound like democracy to me."

"It isn't, and it's not going to be. Every witness is required to stay outside the courtroom both before and after testifying."

"But Richie was remanded to my custody. I'm supposed to stick right beside him night and day so he don't do anything stupid."

"Bailiff, will you please escort Mr. Arnold out into the corridor? . . . Richie, we're ready for you now."

Richie stood up and opened the gate to the well. A black comb was sticking out of the left rear pocket of his jeans. He ran it through his hair before taking his place in the witness box. With the departure of his father he seemed more at ease.

The judge said, "Both counsel for the prosecution and

for the defense have agreed to let you tell your story in your own words, and after it is completed, Mr. Owen will be given a chance to ask questions, and then Mr. Donnelly. It may be unorthodox, but I believe it will save time and truth."

"Where do you want me to begin?"

"From the time you first saw Mrs. Pherson."

"She was coming up the gangplank with Cully. And Harry said, 'Goddle mighty, he's got a floozy with him.' I could see she wasn't a floozy, but I didn't argue with him. All women are floozies to Harry. He's had kind of hard luck with women, not like Cully who just had to snap his fingers and—"

"Stick to your story, young man."

"Yes, sir. Cully introduced the lady to me and Harry as the new cook. I guess it was some kind of joke because she never went near the galley. The two of them went to Cully's quarters. I didn't see her again until the next day. Cully and Harry were in the engine room and I was taking the cover off the mains'l when the lady suddenly came up behind me and asked would I do her a favor for a hundred dollars. Well, I never had a hundred dollars in my life—Harry always takes my pay and puts it in the bank in St. Thomas—so I said, 'Sure, what's the favor?'

"The favor sounded okay, nothing illegal or anything like that. I was just to hide something for her on the boat where no one else would find it. She handed the green leather case to me, the one on the table over there and gave me five twenty-dollar bills. I asked her whether it mattered if it got sort of wet, and she said no. Right away I thought of the bilge because nobody goes down there unless they have to. So I wrapped the green case in an old sail bag and hid it underneath the iron pigs in the bilge."

"Would you explain to the court what iron pigs are?"

"Pigs are pieces of iron used as ballast when and where ballast will make the boat run smoother. Mr. Belasco keeps a whole pile of them in the bilge. I hid the sail bag with the case in it underneath the pigs. I expected Mrs. Pherson would ask for the case back at the end of the trip. But I never saw her again."

He hadn't told Harry this story. Nor did he tell the police when they were searching the boat. He didn't know what was in the green case, and at first he tried not to speculate. But as more and more references to it were made in the newspapers and on TV and by Harry, he became aware that lost or found, it was an important part of the evidence against Cully. If it was found—some guard might be more curious and more careful than the others—its contents might give Cully a stronger motive for murdering the woman. Richie decided to retrieve the case. He almost got away with it.

He looked down at Cully with a mixture of pride and apology. Cully shrugged and turned away. Any student of body English could have translated the exchange: "I did it for you, Cully." "Don't do me any favors, kid."

"Have you finished, Richie?" the judge said.

"I guess so."

"Mr. Owen, do you have any questions to ask the boy?"

"Yes, Your Honor. . . . Richie, you were aware, were you not, that the police were searching for the green case?"

"I heard some talk."

"Why didn't you inform them that Mrs. Pherson had given it to you to hide?"

"They never asked me."

"Didn't you consider it your duty to volunteer the information?"

"No."

"Do you consider yourself a good friend of the defendant, Richie?"

"He's the boss."

"Is he also your friend?"

"I'm his friend. I don't know for sure whether he's mine."

"Was it as a result of this friendship, one-sided or not, that you swam out to the *Bewitched* and stole the case?"

"I don't think of it as stealing."

"You were arrested, were you not?"

"Yes."

"So obviously other people think of it as stealing, do they not?"

"I guess."

"Do you realize now how stupid it was to put yourself in jeopardy for the sake of someone who may not even be your friend?"

Richie sat in obstinate silence, his arms crossed on his chest. He would rather be punished like a man than scolded like a child.

It was Donnelly's turn. He was in no hurry. He wanted the scene between Richie and Owen to remain vivid in the minds of the jurors, showing the defendant as a man who inspired loyalty and friendship. He rearranged some papers, made a couple of notes and finally stood up to face Richie.

"Richie, when Mrs. Pherson handed you the green case, did she use the actual word 'hide'?"

"I don't remember exactly, but she said something like I was to put it away where no one else could find it."

"Did you wonder what was in it?"

"I wondered why she paid that much money, a whole hundred bucks, to have it hidden."

"When you found out what the case contained, were you surprised?"

"Everybody was. But it kind of explained the way she was acting, nice and friendly and all that, but not quite normal." Richie turned to look at the judge. "I guess that's all. Did I do okay?"

"You did fine, Richie. You're free to go now."

"You mean, go home like to the islands? I don't want to. I want to wait for Cully. Me and him can go together."

"That is not a matter for this court to decide. Please step down, Richie. Thank you. Considering the circumstances I believe we have been very lenient with you. Do you know what that means?"

"Yeah. What it really means is I got to stay with Harry like he was my father."

"That's enough, Richie. Please step down. Thank you."

"At this point," Donnelly said, "I would like to request a ten-minute recess for the purpose of checking page and line numbers of the transcript referring to certain portions of the testimony of Mr. Pherson and of Mr. Elfinstone and Miss Gomez of San Diego. If the relevant passages are read aloud to the court, it will not be necessary to recall these three witnesses."

"You have ten minutes," the judge said, and tapped his gavel. The gavel was comfortable in his hand, the right weight, the right balance. He had heard a rumor that at his retirement dinner he was going to be presented with a silver-plated gavel to replace the old wooden one. But he was not a man who replaced things. He hadn't married again after his wife died, he hadn't bought another dog and certainly nothing would ever replace the dull, earthy thud of wood on wood. The sound of silver was without memory or meaning.

When court reconvened, copies of the transcript were given to the judge and the district attorney. Standing at the lectern, Donnelly read aloud from his copy.

"Mr. Pherson's testimony begins at page six hundred seventy-three, but the relevant portions begin on pages seven ninety-one, line eight. The questioner at this point is District Attorney Owen."

Q: Are there any close family ties, Mr. Pherson?
A: Madeline had a very deep relationship with her mother.
Q: Does her mother live in Bakersfield?
A: No. She died in March. She and Madeline had been planning a trip to Hawaii when her mother became ill. Madeline took it very hard. That was the reason I wanted her to go on a vacation. I thought the change of scene would be good for her, cheer her up. The irony of that haunts me day and night, the irony that I should be responsible for her death while trying to help her.

"Skip now to page seven-oh-one, line eight, Mr. Owen still the questioner."

Q: So you persuaded her to take a vacation, get a change of scene.
A: Yes. She chose the San Diego area. My secretary made the necessary travel and hotel reservations, and I drove her to the airport. She called me when she arrived. She sounded quite cheerful. It was the last time I heard her voice.

"Skip to next page, line twenty, defense counsel cross-examining."

Q: **Mr. Pherson**, you said your wife sounded cheerful when she called you. Did this surprise you?

A: I was happy about it.

Q: Yes, but were you surprised?

A: I thought it would take longer for her to snap out of her depression and begin to enjoy life again. So the answer is, I was pleasantly surprised.

Q: Did she ever talk of suicide?

A: No, never.

Q: I believe you stated that Mrs. Pherson counseled the terminally ill and their families, did you not?

A: Yes.

Q: Wouldn't the subject of suicide come up naturally in the course of these conversations?

A: When I said she never mentioned suicide, I meant in regard to herself. Such a thing would never have occurred to her.

Q: Even though she was, according to your testimony, in a state of depression after her mother's death?

Donnelly took a sip of water before continuing to read from the transcript. Angelino Gomez, the hotel maid, was the witness, Owen the questioner.

Q: Did you enter the room during Mrs. Pherson's absence?

A: Yes.

Q: Had she unpacked?

A: Yes, sir. Everything was hung up in the closet or put away in drawers. She was a tidy lady. All I had to do was replace a couple of towels she had used.

Q: The clothes that were hanging in the closet, had they been put there carefully?

A: Oh, yes, just like they were for sale in a store, all zipped and buttoned on their hangers to keep their shape.

Q: Just where were you when Mrs. Pherson came back unexpectedly?

A: In the bathroom. I offered to leave and come back later, but she said no, it didn't matter because she was going out right away. So I finished tidying up the bathroom, replacing two towels. I heard her talking to herself in the bedroom. At least I guess it was to herself. There wasn't anybody else there. It was like when you're dressed to go out and before you leave, you look in the mirror and say, "Hey, looking good."

Q: Did she sound happy, Miss Gomez?

A: Oh, yes, real happy, like maybe she'd had a couple of drinks.

Q: Did you listen to what she was saying?

A: I had to listen. I was there. You can't open and close your ears the way you can your eyes.

Q: What did you hear?

A: Something like, "You always wanted to go to Hawaii, and now you get to go." Stuff like that. I didn't think anything of it. A lot of people would like to go to Hawaii, me included. . . .

Q: Then she seemed to be looking forward to the trip, is that right?

A: Sure. Why not?

Mr. Elfinstone's testimony began on page 709, line 13. A couple of pages later were the pertinent parts. Mr. Owen had asked Mr. Elfinstone what Mrs. Pherson said when she came to the desk to retrieve the green leather case which she'd just had put in the safe an hour before.

A: That she intended to do something that she'd never done before in her life and would assuredly never do again. Then she laughed. . . .
Q: Were you puzzled by her remarks?
A: Not frightfully. I usually don't pay much attention to what people say. It's what they do that counts.
Q: And what did she do?
A: Took the elevator up to her suite. A few minutes later she came down again, walked across the lobby and joined a man. . . .
    Now that I come to think of it, I recall asking her what she meant to do. She said she couldn't tell me, it was a secret and, if anyone found out, they might try to stop her. *I* wouldn't, I told her. I believe in people reaching for the brass ring, seizing the day. *Carpe diem.* As I watched her cross the lobby, I thought: *Yes, the little lady is going to seize the day.*
Q: Then as far as you could tell, Mrs. Pherson did not appear to be despondent?
A: My word, no. Happy as a lark. . . .

"Skip to next page, line six," Donnelly said. "Here the cross-examination of defense counsel of Mr. Elfinstone by defense counsel begins."

Q: Mr. Elfinstone, how many years have you been in the hotel business?

A: Over twenty years.

Q: During this time have you had any experience with guests checking in and subsequently committing suicide?

A: Alas, yes. Yes, indeed, though we try to keep such things private. People tend to avoid rooms where a tragedy has taken place.

Q: In your years of experience have you observed that potential suicides exhibit similar behavioral patterns?

A: No.

Q: Some were obviously despondent, were they?

A: Yes.

Q: And some quite cheerful?

A: Yes.

Q: Did others have a calm, pleasant manner?

A: Oh, yes. Lull before the storm, you know.

Q: Are you saying, in other words, that you couldn't pick out a potential suicide on the basis of appearance and behavior?

A: If we could do that we would steer them to an establishment run by our competitors.

Donnelly closed the transcript and prepared to go back to his chair. "It's getting late," the judge said. "If you're thinking of starting to call your witnesses, Mr. Donnelly, you'd better postpone it until the next session."

"I'm not calling any witnesses, Your Honor."

"None?"

"None."

"I hope you've considered this very carefully."

"Yes. The prosecution's witnesses did so well by my

client that it seems best to leave it like that."

"Very well. I'd like to see both counsel at the side bar."

After a brief conference at the side bar it was decided that court would be adjourned until the following Tuesday in order to give both Owen and Donnelly time to prepare their closing arguments.

Owen worked on his closing speech the entire weekend. On Monday he taped it, making corrections, omissions and additions and changing voice inflections for emphasis and drama. He listened to the final version with pride and pleasure and on Monday night played it for Vee and the boys after dinner. There was considerable audience defection. Thatcher went to sleep on the floor, Jonathan had a phone call from a girl, an attack of hiccups sent Chadwick to his room and Vee began making out the week's grocery list.

His Tuesday morning audience was more attentive. Donnelly and the judge took notes, as did all of the jurors except No. 2. Elsie Ball was a licensed vocational nurse doing private duty from eleven at night to seven in the morning. She was never quite awake, and Owen's loud, clear voice fell on her ears soft as snow. It didn't matter anyway: On the very first day of the trial she had made up her mind how she was going to vote and she didn't intend to change it.

"Ladies and gentlemen of the jury, you may recall that in my opening statement I said this is a simple case. I would like to say that again now, this is a simple case.

"In the defendant's chair sits Cully Paul King. The charge against him is murder with special circumstances. There is no graver charge in the lawbooks.

"Mr. King is not the average poolroom black. He's had

many advantages denied them. He is trained to earn a comfortable living at an unusual job, that of professional skipper. So if there are any bleeding hearts on the jury, let common sense stanch the bleeding. Cully King has had it good.

"A simple case. Here it is in a nutshell: The racing yacht, *Bewitched*, left San Diego with four people on board. It arrived in Santa Felicia with three.

"The missing passenger, found later tangled in a kelp bed, was Madeline Ruth Pherson, a forty-year-old married woman from Bakersfield. A woman of high character, she devoted a great deal of her time doing volunteer work with various charities, including Hospice, where she counseled the terminally ill and their families. Why would such a woman walk into a hotel bar and pick up a stranger, a man younger than herself and not even a member of the same race? What deadly twist of fate brought them together, these two people from different parts of the world, different cultures, different races?

"Let us turn now to the scene of the crime, the *Bewitched*. When Mrs. Pherson came aboard, she was wearing a blue and white striped coat. A fishing boat later picked up the coat from the ocean. It was completely buttoned, hem to neck, the same way that Mrs. Pherson's other clothing was hung up in the hotel closet, according to Miss Gomez's testimony. We submit that this coat was taken off a hanger on board the boat and thrown into the water. Remember Harry Arnold's testimony that he had seen Cully King on that fateful night throw some clothing overboard. It was too dark for Harry Arnold to identify the articles of clothing, but he could certainly identify the thrower, Cully Paul King, who was trying to get rid of all evidence that Mrs. Pherson had ever been on the boat. Obviously he did not expect Mrs. Pherson's body to be found. The sea does not easily give up its dead, and Cully King figured on this. The sea would be not only his friend but his accomplice. It was a very limited partnership, and it didn't work. If it had, none of us would be here in this courtroom today.

"What Cully King didn't figure on was that forest of giant kelp, which is not found in his part of the world.

"Let us take a moment now to examine a bit of hocus-pocus presented by Mr. Donnelly. He would have you believe that Mrs. Pherson jumped from the deck of the *Bewitched* into the water to commit suicide. The water's coldness slowed her metabolism, making her able to survive during the time that the tide and the wind waves pushed her into that forest of kelp, and the grooves on her throat were caused not by the thumbs of Cully King but by two of the floats which grow along the stems of the kelp.

"Bear in mind that Mr. Donnelly doesn't have to prove that it happened like this. All he has to do is convince you that it *could* have happened like this. Did he convince you? I hope not. I hate to see a group of intelligent men and women taken in by Mr. Donnelly's crude shenanigans.

"But forget Mr. Donnelly's shenanigans for a moment. Forget the forest of kelp, forget the modeling clay caper, metabolisms and Lazarus syndromes. Remember only this important fact: The *Bewitched* left San Diego with four persons aboard and arrived in Santa Felicia with three. What happened to that fourth person?

"Mr. Donnelly would like you to believe that Mrs. Pherson was planning to commit suicide even before she left home. It would be very nice for Mr. Donnelly and his client if you believed this. But you can't. Your common sense won't let you. Mrs. Pherson does not fit the clinical picture of a woman depressed enough to kill herself. She did not sit around the house moping, unconcerned with others, even unaware they existed. Quite the opposite. She went on a vacation. When she called her husband on the phone to announce her arrival, he said she sounded very cheerful. She talked pleasantly to Mr. Elfinstone and was considerate of the hotel maid, Miss Gomez. She appeared at ease in the company of Cully King. Does this sound to you like the behavior of a woman bent on killing herself? Of course not.

"It might be deemed rather peculiar for her to be carrying around her mother's ashes. But remember, they were very close, these two women, and they'd been planning a trip to Hawaii when the mother became ill.

"Peculiar? Perhaps a bit. Depressed? No."

Owen talked until the judge declared a fifteen-minute recess at eleven o'clock. During recess Owen sprayed his throat, then sucked a cough drop while he went over his notes for the rest of the day. He was aware of the fact that the jurors were getting restive: Papers rattled, swivel chairs squeaked, and the night nurse who occupied the second chair had let out a couple of unmistakable snores. He decided to cut the rest of his speech down to its bare bones.

During recess Eva Foster remained at her table. Cully King rose and stretched, and Eva thought what a beautiful body he had and how gracefully he moved it. When she spoke, Cully had to bend down so he could make out what she was saying.

"I bet you're tired of listening to all this talk, aren't you?"

"I can think of worse things to be doing and worse places to do them."

"You don't sound friendly toward me anymore. Why?"

"You were beginning to get ideas."

"Do you disapprove of women getting ideas?"

"Certain women, certain ideas."

There was a brief silence while he sat down and re-arranged himself in his chair.

"Do you like my dress?" Eva said.

"I hadn't noticed."

"Well, notice now."

He turned and looked. "Yeah. It's a nice dress."

"When I wore it the other day, you said it was a great dress."

"Great, nice, what's the difference?"

"It makes a big difference to me whether you like what I'm wearing or not."

"Stop talking like that. Someone might overhear you and think that you and I are—that we have—"

"—have a commitment. Well, let them think it. It's true. I told my father about you last night, how I felt about you and our life plans."

"I want no part of your life plan, Miss Foster."

"You have no part. You're the whole plan."

"Did you tell your father this?"

"Yes."

"What'd he say?"

"That he hopes you get the death penalty."

"Tell him something for me, will you?"

"All right. What?"

"That I hope so, too."

Owen returned to the lectern at eleven-twenty.

"At this point, ladies and gentlemen, I would like to go over some of the highlights of the testimony given by my witnesses. My first witness was Mr. Belasco. He described in detail his boat, the *Bewitched*, and set for us the scene of the crime.

"Was a crime actually committed here? Mr. Donnelly

will ask you to suspend your common sense and believe there was no crime. You may recall the famous movie scene where Jimmy Durante is asked about the elephant he is leading. 'Elephant,' Durante said. 'What *elephant?*' 'Crime?' Donnelly will say. 'What crime?' To that I can only answer, the crime as big as an elephant.

"The county's chief pathologist, Dr. Woodbridge, described to you how Mrs. Pherson died of asphyxia caused by manual strangulation. He showed you pictures of the grooves left on her throat by the thumbs of Cully King.

"Lieutenant Sommerville of the Coast Guard explained how Mrs. Pherson's body was cut away from the kelp that entangled her.

"Tyler Pherson, the dead woman's husband, delineated his wife's character for you and told you about the close relationship between Mrs. Pherson and her mother.

"The testimony of Angelina Gomez, the hotel maid, is of interest in two ways. It indicates that Mrs. Pherson intended to return to the hotel because she'd left her clothes in the closet. Miss Gomez also provided us with an account of Mrs. Pherson talking to herself about a trip to Hawaii.

"Mr. Elfinstone, the hotel's assistant manager, detailed the rather mischievous remarks of Mrs. Pherson when she reclaimed her green jewel box. Mr. Elfinstone interpreted these remarks as meaning she was going off with a man.

"I've left until last the testimony of Harry Arnold and his son, Richie. It was Harry Arnold who heard a woman scream in the middle of the night and later saw Cully King throwing some clothing overboard.

"Richie Arnold was not a witness to the throwing scene described by his father, but he did hear a woman scream. If he sounded less than positive about hearing the screams,

I would suggest that he was just suffering from nervousness at the idea of testifying against a man who was his friend and his employer. Richie also described his meeting with Mrs. Pherson, who gave him a hundred dollars to hide the green leather jewel case. We don't know why she did this, and we probably never will. But it seems logical to think it had something to do with the amount of alcohol she had drunk at the bar. For a nondrinker like Mrs. Pherson double martinis can be lethal. If Madeline Pherson's judgment had not been impaired by alcohol, she would never have gone on board the *Bewitched* with a man like Cully King.

"Let's take a look at this man, Cully King. First and foremost, he is a murderer, without pity, without remorse, without a spark of humanity that might have saved Madeline Pherson.

"Did he kill her for those diamond stud earrings which he sold to the pawnbroker for five hundred dollars? No. The earrings were only a small part of his motive. The rest was in the jewel box, or what King thought was in the jewel box.

"I wish to repeat now what I said at the beginning of the trial: This is a simple case.

"Most murderers are careless. They leave behind fingerprints or footprints, gum wrappers, matchbooks, cigarette butts. Cully King, both by nature and by training, a meticulous man, erased Mrs. Pherson from the *Bewitched* with ease. What tripped him up was not carelessness but a forest of giant kelp, something he was unfamiliar with in his area of the world. If Mrs. Pherson's body had not been caught in that kelp, this case would probably not have come to trial.

"Conducting a murder trial without a body has been done, but it is rare and rarely successful. The people of

California ought to be very grateful for that kelp. It will prevent a murderer from walking our streets.

"It is unfortunate that Cully King did not take the stand himself. You would have seen him getting tangled up in his own lies as surely as Mrs. Pherson got tangled up in that kelp.

"Ladies and gentlemen of the jury, you do not get a true picture of Cully King by watching him sit here in court day after day, quiet, confident, benign. Benign, yes, he can look benign. But I know what he is. He is a cancer. It is up to you, ladies and gentlemen, to get rid of that cancer before it spreads."

The gray jail bus with its barred and screened windows arrived to take the inmates back for lunch. The small group that had been waiting for the bus stood under the arched entrance to the sheriff's department. All wore handcuffs, and one of them had on leg irons.

Richie Arnold had also been waiting for the bus, sitting on the grass in the shade of a lemon tree. When the bus stopped at the curb, Richie got up and approached the driver.

The driver, in uniform, opened his window. "Back off, kid. This is official business."

"I just want to talk to my father a minute."

"Against the rules."

"I know, but couldn't I talk to him anyway just for a minute?"

"So your father's one of our jolly group. What's your name, kid?"

"Richie Arnold."

"I don't have any Arnolds riding with me at the moment."

"Arnold's the name of my legal father. My real father

is Cully King. I am going to live with him when we get back to the islands. I want to start planning the trip, but first I have to talk to him."

"As far as I'm concerned, you can talk from here to Christmas, but the powers that be wouldn't approve. You want to lose me my job?"

"No."

"Then back off, kid."

Richie backed off as far as he could, which took him as far as the group under the archway. They had lined up in twos and except for their restraints looked like a Scout troop about to leave on a field trip. Cully was hand-cuffed to the young man in leg irons. The young man's face was flushed, and he was sweating profusely.

"I have an evil headache," the young man said to Richie. "Can you help me?"

"Leave him alone," Cully said. "He's just a kid."

"I was just a kid, too, when I refused to let Jesus Christ enter my body and the devil came instead and gave me this evil headache. Help me, boy, help me."

"I don't know how," Richie said.

"Pills. Get me some pills."

"I have no money."

"Little blue pills."

Cully told him to shut up, then turned to Richie. "You get away from here and stay away."

"I just want to talk to you for a minute."

"What about?"

"Our plans."

"We don't have any plans. There's no more connection between you and me than there is between me and this pill popper here."

"Little blue pills," said the young man in leg irons. "You take three or four and the pain disappears and you are floating on a cloud. It's like going to heaven. Only then you have to come down again, and that's where I am now, down."

No one was paying any attention to him. The prisoners had heard it all before, and Richie's eyes were fixed on Cully.

"I thought you and me better start planning our trip back home. All it takes to be a family is two people. We can sign on boats together and everything."

"Stop talking crap."

"Little blue pills."

Two deputies came out the door, and almost immediately the line began to move toward the gray bus. As it pulled away from the curb, someone inside waved. Richie couldn't tell who it was. In case it might be Cully he tried to wave back, but he couldn't lift his arm. It was as heavy as an iron pig.

Donnelly spent the lunch hour polishing his speech. Deprived of food, his stomach was making sounds of protest, which the loudspeaker at the lectern would pick up and broadcast to the entire courtroom. This speech was to be the last time he would ever address a jury, and he didn't want it marred by stomach noises, so he bought two chocolate bars at the vending machine outside the jury room and ate them as he walked back down the hall.

Court convened at 2:03, and Donnelly immediately took his place at the lectern.

"Ladies and gentlemen of the jury, this is not a simple case, as Mr. Owen seems to believe and likes to say. It has been a very difficult one, which is now grinding to a halt. I want to thank you for your attention and your patience. After the judge gives you his instructions, you will go into the deliberating room and decide the fate of a man who is as much a victim as the victim herself. Has he been treated like a victim? Judge for yourself. Denied bail, he has spent many weeks in jail. He has been harassed by the district attorney and his staff; he has been accused by the media and condemned from the pulpits.

"Why? What did he do?

"He went into a bar and ordered a drink. A congenial woman his own age or a little older sat down beside him and started a conversation. She was the instigator right from the beginning.

"Allow me at this point to answer some of the questions and respond to some of the charges against my client, Cully Paul King, by the district attorney. First and foremost, the District Attorney tells us, Cully King is a murderer.

"That he is a thief. Use your common sense to answer this one by yourselves. Why would a man like Cully King, who holds an interesting job with good pay, murder a woman for a pair of diamond earrings, which he pawned for five hundred dollars.

"Another question raised by the prosecution is: How could Cully King hire an expensive attorney like myself? That's the easiest question of all to answer. He didn't hire me. I volunteered my services. I don't like to see people being railroaded into prison because of the color of their skin, country of origin, sexual preference or religion.

"One of the most interesting aspects of this trial has been the way Mr. Owen's witnesses have qualified their answers with 'maybe,' 'perhaps,' 'assume,' 'guess.' Every one of these words has left a dent or a hole in the district attorney's case until it looks like a tin can that's been used for target practice. There is no room in a murder trial for assumptions, guesses, conjectures or maybes. When a man's life is at stake, we must stick to absolutes, whole truths, not half or quarter truths, fact, not fancy.

"When you go into the deliberations room and start looking over your notebooks, I want you to remember one thing in particular: My client and I are not asking you for mercy; we are asking for justice.

"In conclusion, ladies and gentlemen of the jury, I wish to thank you for your attention and to urge you, in reaching a verdict, to put your emotions aside and rely on your good judgment and common sense. Thank you."

Donnelly returned to his chair. Judge Hazeltine declared a short recess before he began his instructions to the jury. Before leaving the room by his private door, he motioned to Donnelly to meet him in chambers.

"Sit down," the judge said when Donnelly entered.

Donnelly sat down. "Anything wrong?"

"I think you're going to get that son of a bitch off. That's wrong."

"Why?"

"Because he's guilty."

"He's not guilty until the jury says he is."

"Don't give me that legal bull. He choked her. He's known for having an ugly temper when he's drunk. This was no murder for profit. She said or did something that enraged him, and he attacked her, grabbed her by the throat—"

"No."

"No what?"

"He didn't attack her."

"I suppose *she* attacked *him*."

"It's possible."

"And he killed her in self-defense."

"Maybe."

"In a fit of passionate rage."

"More or less."

"More more or more less?"

Donnelly's only response was a shrug.

The judge looked up at the one-eyed owl on the book-shelf. It seemed to be winking at him, an oddly lascivious wink as if it knew all about men and women attacking each other in fits of passion and rage.

Donnelly went immediately back to the courtroom though there were still six minutes left of the recess.

Cully was waiting for him, his face smooth as glass, anxiety showing only in his voice, which rose in pitch and quavered slightly like a nervous old man's.

"What did he want?"

"To talk."

"About me?"

"Some."

"What'd he say?"

"You wouldn't understand. It was legal talk."

"I don't have to understand legal talk to know he doesn't like me. . . . Does he?"

"I don't know, I never asked him."

"Watch the way he looks at me. Hate. I see hate."

"A verdict is seldom affected by a judge's personal feelings."

"Seldom," Cully repeated. "That means it sometimes is."

"Sometimes."

"How about a lot more than sometimes?"

"It happens. I haven't counted the times." Donnelly had heard judicial instructions so biased one way or another that they amounted to ordering the jury exactly what to do. "Forget it. This is the judge's last case. He won't want to be overturned in appellate court. His instructions will be nice and neutral. And you'll be a free man."

"Will I?"

"I'm sure of it."

"A free man," Cully repeated. "That means I'll be able

314

to go anywhere and do anything I want to."

"Nobody's that free, Cully."

"Why not?"

"There are debts to be paid."

"I can always get money for to pay my debts."

"Suppose this is a big one, like a hundred thousand dollars for saving your life."

"I can pay my debts," Cully said. "One way or another."

"That sounds vaguely like a threat to me."

"I didn't hear any threat."

"Maybe you weren't listening. I was. It didn't surprise me. The word's been around the courtroom since the preliminary hearing that you have a vicious temper when you're drunk. So I'm taking certain precautions. There'll be no booze at the ranch."

The first half of Judge Hazeltine's instructions was fairly standard, explanation of the charge against the defendant, that of murder with special circumstances and the circumstantial evidence on which it was based. After this came a review of the jurors' duties. He admonished them to ignore public opinion, their own emotions and their feelings about capital punishment. He put special emphasis on the phrases "beyond a reasonable doubt" and "to a moral certainty." If certain evidence seemed unreasonable and was presented by a witness who appeared erratic or confused, that evidence should be ignored if it contradicted reasonable evidence given by a more controlled person with nothing to gain by lying.

A special warning was given against reaching a conclusion too hastily without proper and thorough reexamination of all the evidence.

The second half of the judge's instructions was more personal both in content and in viewpoint. The evaluation of witnesses was of the utmost importance. More credence must be given to a man of wide experience like Dr. Woodbridge than to the writers of medical reports in various publications who were not present to be cross-questioned.

"I refer specifically to reports of drowning victims whose lives were thought to be extinct but who were later brought back to life, their need for oxygen being greatly reduced by the coldness of the water lowering their metabolism. These instances do occur, but they are rare, and the chances of such a thing happening in the case of Mrs. Pherson are minimal. Still, it's possible, and that must play a part in your decision. If this possibility is large enough to cast the shadow of a doubt in certain areas, you have to take that into consideration when you're casting your ballot.

"Other doubts may cast their shadows. The grooves left on Mrs. Pherson's throat, were they made by a man's thumbs or were they made by the floats on a piece of giant kelp? Unlikely? Yes. Impossible? No. The absence of thumbnail indentations along with these grooves is puzzling, but it must be remembered that not all thumbnails are the same length, and some may be too short to leave marks.

"Two witnesses who might be regarded as controversial are Harry Arnold and his son, Richie. The boy was indecisive, and the father's claim that he'd seen Cully King throw some clothing overboard must be regarded with some suspicion since Mr. Arnold's feelings about the defendant are obviously mixed. Also, he could not identify any particular item of clothing with certainty.

"One of the most important questions you must ask yourselves is: Did Cully King have a reason to kill Madeline Pherson? A sane man—and we have no evidence that Mr. King is anything but sane—does not kill without a motive. No motive has been proved. It should be noted, however, that because we do not know of a motive one does not exist. This is a big question, however, and must be considered carefully.

"Now, the first thing you'll do when you begin your deliberations is to open your notebooks. Information contained in these notebooks may be freely exchanged among yourselves. When more precise details are required, you may ask the bailiff to bring you back into this room so the parts of the transcript you want will be read aloud to you. Copies of the transcript itself are not allowed in the deliberation room.

"In your notebooks you may have jotted down an impression, an observation, an opinion that will not only refresh your memory but also dredge up the feelings you had at the time on whether or not a witness was reliable or if you had doubts about his or her testimony.

"Before you even begin to discuss the guilt or innocence of the defendant, you must answer the all-important question: Was a murder committed? Some factors point to suicide. If Mrs. Pherson did not exhibit the usual signs of despondency, she certainly departed from her ordinary behavior in a manner that indicated some degree of emotional disturbance. Was it severe enough to precipitate suicide?

"Could her death possibly have been an accident? The ship's log indicates a calm sea that night, so a sudden lurch of the vessel didn't knock her overboard. Nor was it likely she'd been strolling around the deck stark naked in such cold weather.

"The ultimate question you must ask yourself, and the answer you must live with, is one of reasonable doubt. Is there reasonable doubt that Mrs. Pherson was the victim of murder at the hands of Cully King? Reasonable doubt is the deciding factor in most cases based on circumstantial evidence.

"The law states that before reaching a verdict in a criminal case, the jury must be convinced beyond a reasonable doubt and to a moral certainty. 'Beyond a reasonable doubt' is self explanatory, but the latter phrase has caused much disagreement, being one of the few instances where the law is imprecise. I have received a note from one of the jurors requesting a definition of 'moral certainty.' A previous officer of the court defined it as a gut feeling. I'm not sure I can do better than that, although putting too much reliance on moral certainty alone would not serve the interests of justice.

"You will be in the charge of the bailiff from now until the end of your deliberations. I wish you luck."

As soon as the judge left the courtroom by his private door, Eva Foster walked quickly out of the main door and down the corridor to meet him in chambers. He was hanging up his robe when she entered.

"That was," she said, "I mean, your instructions were, very good."

"Maybe your feelings are somewhat colored, if you'll pardon the expression."

"I don't quite under—oh, I see. 'Colored' is the word they used to indicate blacks many years ago."

"Not very many. I'm about your father's age, am I not?"

"Roughly."

"I met your father at the carol sing last Christmas. By the way, could we do without the cards this year?"

"It won't be my decision. I don't expect to be here."

"Still going after this guy tooth and nail, are you?"

"If you want to put it that way, yes."

"Preacher, church, father giving away the bride, the whole bit?"

"No preacher, no church, certainly no father giving away the bride. Maybe no bride, for that matter." She went over to the window and stood looking down at the traffic. Though the window was closed and locked, she took a long, slow breath as if there were air coming in, clean and fresh from the sea. "I don't care if he marries me or not. Just as long as we're together I'll be content."

"Sure of that?"

"Yes. I've thought about it a lot."

"You haven't thought about it, Foster. You've *dreamed*."

"My plans are made. We'll buy a small house; I have enough money for a down payment. We won't have any children, but I'll get a dog, maybe two dogs to keep each other company and to keep me company when Cully's at sea."

"There's a difference between a dreamer and a planner, Foster. A planner would take into consideration the possibility that Cully might not be available to fit into any plans."

"He'll be acquitted, I'm sure of it. Your speech made it clear that you expected the jury to return a verdict of innocent."

"Juries don't do what's expected of them; they do what they damn well want to."

"Cully should have been given a chance to take the stand so the jury could watch him react, listen to him talk. They could have seen for themselves what a good man he is."

"He's a liar," the judge said. "He'd have tripped over his tongue every time he opened his mouth. Donnelly did well to keep him off the stand."

"Why, you sound"—she turned from the window—"you sound as if you think he's guilty."

"I think the prosecution did not prove its case and the verdict will reflect that fact."

"But what do you really think inside your heart?"

"I think you're a headstrong young woman who will continue to believe what she wants to believe about this man. The more he's accused, the more you'll defend him."

"I'm a reasonable person. If you had real proof of Cully's guilt, I would believe it."

"If I had real proof, I'd have presented it to the jury in one way or another, and they would have believed it." The Judge's voice was somber. "I have one piece of advice for you which I believe you're still realistic enough to take. Don't be in any hurry to send in your resignation. At least wait until the guy indicates willingness to go along with you and the little house and the two dogs."

"You sound cold and mean."

"As long as you're wallowing around in this emotional swamp everyone who criticizes him will seem to you cold and mean when, in fact, they're trying to be kind."

"Is this your idea of kind?"

"Yes. I'd like to prevent you from being found drowned in the sea or in an alley with your throat cut or tossed out of a car with a bullet in your brain."

"You can't really believe Cully is capable of such things."

"Sure I can."

"You really are cold and mean."

"And sensible," the judge added. "Very, very sensible."

The first ballot was taken on the third day of deliberations and the final one in the late afternoon of the fifth day. An hour's time was allowed for the parties involved

to reach the courthouse and be present for the reading
of the verdict.

Some of the court watchers who'd been coming every
day awaiting the jury's decision were in line outside the
locked door of the courtroom within minutes of the announcement that the jury was coming in. To avoid the
crowd that was already forming, the court personnel entered through a side door, as did both counselors and their
investigators and Cully himself, this time not in the custody of his usual deputy but of four new ones. They all
were pleasant-looking young men, but their presence emphasized the grimness of the occasion. Then the judge
came in, and the jury, and finally the main door was opened
to the public. The court watchers rushed in for front-row
seats, followed by the reporters, the woman artist who'd
done the sketch of Cully, assorted lawyers and secretaries
who were interested in the trial and witnesses like Harry
Arnold and Richie, who had not been allowed in except
while they were standing along the rear wall. The bailiff
pushed the rest of the crowd back into the corridor.

Cully sat motionless except for his eyes. He glanced at
the jury. They all were watching him, and this was, Donnelly had told him, a good sign. Jurors who had voted
against the defendant seldom looked at him when it was
time for the verdict to be read.

So they're going to let me go, he thought. *And the people
out there will be waiting for me, waiting to lock me up in their
lives, and I'll never be a free man, never.*

The sights and sounds and smells of people filled the
room.

Judge Hazeltine tapped his gavel. "Order in the court.
The jurors having reached a decision, their verdict will
now be read by the foreman."

"We, the jury, find the defendant, Cully Paul King, not guilty of the charges against him. That of murder with special circumstances."

The room exploded with new sounds, but Cully sat in silence. He felt Donnelly's hand on his arm, he saw Eva smiling, and Richie smiling and Harry waving at him, but he did nothing, said nothing, until the judge rose to leave and the jury began filing out. Then Cully got to his feet and started shouting.

"Wait! Listen to me. You're wrong, you're all wrong. I killed her. Change your verdict. Don't let *them* get at me. I want to be free of *them*. Come back. Wait, listen to me. Come back!"

Nobody came back.

"The trial's finished," Donnelly said. "Nothing you do can start it over again."

"I want to be free. Don't let *them* get me. Come back!"

The judge closed the door behind him, and the last of the jurors departed.

Cully pulled away from Donnelly's restraining hand. "Leave me alone."

"Sit down and shut up, you crazy bastard," Donnelly said.

"Don't touch me."

"All right, all right. Sit here quietly until you get hold of yourself. I'll be waiting at the end of the hall near the stairs."

The room emptied almost as quickly as it had filled, and Cully was left alone with the bailiff at the door getting ready to lock the place up until the next murder or the next robbery or embezzlement or assault. There would always be something to fill it again.

"Aren't you going to go out and celebrate?" the bailiff said.

"No."

"I know a young woman who'd be very happy to celebrate with you. I mean, I think she's ready, real ready."

"No."

"Okay, I'll leave you alone for a few minutes to collect your thoughts. You've had a big day, a big week; in fact, I guess it's been a big six months."

"Yes."

The bailiff went out into the corridor. Tyler Pherson was sitting on the bench where he'd sat all through the trial, wearing the same black suit and glasses, the same expression.

"Not much use waiting around here," the bailiff said. "The trial's over."

"Not yet."

"Sure it is. Everybody's gone home."

"The defendant hasn't come out here yet."

"He will in a minute. It's late. Pretty soon the whole place will be locked up. I bet my wife's putting dinner on the stove right now."

"I won't keep you from your dinner more than a minute or two," Tyler said. "I just want to go in and congratulate Mr. King."

"That's mighty decent of you, considering."

"I have considered everything."

Tyler walked into the courtroom for the last time. The gun in his pocket felt smooth as silk and warm from his flesh.

3985